Winner of the 2013
Dundee International Book Prize

"A mesmerising tale of secrets and lies rising from the past to strangle the present."
- Val McDermid

"The Rosary Garden is as good as it gets: a debut shot through with the real, horrifying cruelty of true crime and a heart-race ending."
- Denise Mina

"In the Rosary Garden is a moving, intelligent and courageous book - both a family story and a genuine thriller."
-AL Kennedy

"In The Rosary Garden, Nicola White's superb, pitch-perfect debut, is a compulsive, page-turning crime novel, a haunting slab of Irish family gothic and a moving study of a young woman coming of age in a society deeply unsympathetic to women. Nicola White writes beautifully, with wit, verve, a gift for scene-setting and a compassionate eye for the foibles of her characters. In Detective Inspector Swan, she has given us a most attractive hero, melancholy, wry, charming and determined. I hope we see more of him. I know we will see more from Nicola White. She is the real thing."
- Declan Hughes, author of the Ed Loy novels

IN THE ROSARY GARDEN

+

NICOLA WHITE

"In The Rosary Garden"
978-1908885661
Nicola White
First Published 2013
Published by Cargo Publishing
SC376700
© Nicola White 2013

The excerpt from the Patrick Kavanagh poem "Canal Bank Walk" used by permission of the Patrick Kavanagh estate.

Printed & Bound in Scotland by Bell & Bain
Cover design by Craig Lamont.
www.cargopublishing.com

Also available as:

Kindle Ebook
EPUB Ebook

To my parents, Seán and Mary,
who fed me books

ONE

It was good to be early. A step ahead. He cruised the car to a gentle stop on the canal side of the street, killed the lights. There was a little humpback bridge at the end of the road with a lantern on the top of it. Pretty as a postcard. Through the arch of the bridge he could just make out a wall of water falling over a lock gate, a shadowy unspooling that sounded like someone exhaling forever. It was good to watch, took the edge off his nerves.

On the dot of eight, a light came on behind the splayed bones of a fanlight. The door below opened and she appeared — silhouetted, alone. It looked like she had nothing but a small case with her and disappointment flooded him, but then he noticed the crossing of one arm over her chest, the way she leaned back as she came down the stone steps.

She stepped into the fall of a streetlamp and he could see the bulge of her coat more clearly. It was good that she was trying to be discreet, even if the result was ludicrously noticeable. Luckily there was nobody else on the street to see. He scanned the front of the terrace again for movement at windows. Nothing. The trees along the canal were in full leaf, blocking the buildings on the other side from sight.

He rolled down the window.

'Here!'

Her head swivelled in his direction.

Steady. He called her name gently. Better to stay in the car, make her come to him.

Her steps came close and he reached over to open the passenger door. She put the case in the footwell and lowered herself slowly in beside him. He didn't want to look at her, so he fiddled with the keys.

'How're ya?' Her face was coming towards him. He ducked down and started the engine.

'We'll drive round a bit,' he said, 'eh?'

He checked his mirrors, pulled out slowly. He wasn't sure where he was going, but it seemed a good idea to get moving.

'No one saw me leaving,' she said.

He looked in the rear view mirror.

'No one saw me. I did well, didn't I?'

She was such a poultice.

'Sure you did,' he said.

Her hand was still clamped to the front of her coat where the lump was, her lips struggling with something that wouldn't come out. He should have told her to put it in the back.

They were headed in to the city centre now. He didn't want to go too far, didn't want to get lost. Get her to hand it over, drop her at the train station. That's all.

'Tell me again about the family,' she said.

'They're rich, cultured people. Aristocracy, I suppose you'd call them. Big house, ponies. She'll have the life of a princess over there.'

'They won't send her to boarding school?'

'No, they were very against that,' he said and made himself touch her, put his hand flat on her thigh and give a little squeeze. She'd put on the beef.

'What matters is that we get a fresh start,' he said. 'Nobody pulling us this way and that.'

She covered his hand with her own.

They were driving round Stephen's Green. Round

and round. She didn't seem to notice he kept turning right. A set of lights changed to red and he took the chance to retrieve his hand.

'I have a little bed for her in the back.'

She twisted to look. It was only a laundry basket, but he thought it looked the business, padded out with sheets and things.

'I'll pull in up here and you can put her in, eh?'

He could feel her reluctance fluttering beside him.

'We won't let them bully us,' he said, 'will we?'

'No,' she said, 'we won't.'

The word *we* was all that was needed. He applied it sparingly, knowing she'd do what he wanted for the hope it contained. She was too easily swayed. Soft in the head, really. She would have made a terrible mother.

TWO

Fitz and Ali were late. They got to the door of the nuns' parlour in time to hear the dry beat of one pair of clapping hands rise through a babble of voices.

Ali cracked the door open. Reverend Mother Mary Paul was looking in their direction, one sceptical eyebrow raised even as she continued to clap for silence. The feeling of dread was only reflex — Ali had to remind herself that the nun had no hold over them now.

A dozen of their former classmates gathered in an untidy horseshoe along with a few nuns and lay teachers. Some sheets of A1 paper were pinned to the wall behind her. *GOOD LUCK TO OUR BRAINBOXES* was painted across them, each awkward letter wrought in a different style and colour. An art project for reluctant first years, probably. Ali tried to tuck herself out of sight behind a pair of teachers, slumping to lose height.

Fitz had insisted that they dress up for the occasion — their first time at St. Brigid's without uniforms. She had persuaded Ali to backcomb her hair and put on a baggy pinafore dress. With kohl round her eyes, she had looked bohemian in her bedroom mirror. Now she felt like a big demented farmgirl.

Mary Paul cleared her throat.

'Now that we're all here,' she directed a quick nod at Fitz, 'I wanted to express how very, very proud I am of the girls from the class of 1984 who are aiming to move on to university and third level colleges. We hope there will be twelve of you that will be successful in this, and I have to say this is a very proud result for St. Brigid's, and a real testament to the fine quality of teachers that we have here.'

Wrinkled faces creased deeper into smiles; a lukewarm spatter of applause emerged from the girls. Ali looked around and was relieved to see a couple of the other girls had also dressed for effect, one in a leather biker's jacket, another in a rainbow jumper down to her knees.

'I couldn't be prouder of your achievements, which is why you'll heed me when I say that wherever your God-given brains take you — to the highest levels of commerce or the halls of academe or even the furthest reaches of the known world — promise me that you will not deprive yourselves of the real joys of womanhood. The fruits of the material world are very seductive, but they can't replace the simple satisfactions of home and family. Ireland needs intelligent mothers and wives just as much as she needs bankers and doctors. Think about that, and remember you can come back to see us at any time.'

She raised her hands in exhortation: 'Our doors are always open!'

Again the girls clapped dutifully, eyes drifting to the buffet table.

'What the hell is the 'known world' anyway?' Ali said sideways to Fitz, 'Does she think there's still a big undiscovered bit somewhere?'

'Don't be worrying your womanly brain with that.'

'How long do we have to stay?'

'Give it ten minutes, max. I can't look at that food with this hangover.' Fitz made a gagging face. Ali was ravenous.

It took a bit of shuffling, but Ali soon manoeuvered herself into prime position at the table and put three triangular ham sandwiches onto her paper plate. She was edging her way towards the cocktail sausages when a tremulous black shape docked beside her.

'Alison Hogan. Don't you look great?'

Tiny Sister O'Dwyer, not the worst of them. Long past teaching, but still in nominal charge of the gardening club, which Ali had joined in her first year and signed up for ever since, not entirely for horticultural reasons.

The nun's raw-looking fingers were already locked on Ali's sleeve, and she decided to give herself up to the old soul. It was easier than fighting her off, and more bearable company than she might otherwise get landed with. She peeled another paper plate from a stack and urged the nun to accept a finger of quiche, and steered her to one of the straight-backed chairs that ringed the room.

Ali wolfed down her food while the nun talked about her gratitude for all that Ali had done for the Rosary Garden, stirring the air with her untouched plate.

'There's not many girls would put in the effort, but you and your friend Carmen — what is it you call her — Fuzz?'

'Fitz, sister.'

'Well… you were both great. To be honest, it's become a trouble rather than a pleasure to me lately. You need to be able to get down on your knees in a garden, even more so than in the chapel. The weeds would break your heart.'

'Sure, you'll get some new girls, sister. Some keen young ones, with plenty of bend in them.'

'I suppose. It won't be me that trains them up,

thank the Lord. Sister Bernadette's taking over.'

Sister O'Dwyer jogged her head towards a tall nun who was talking intensely with Fitz. Sister Bernadette was known among the girls as Red Bernie, but Ali had never been sure whether it was because of the ginger hair that peeked out of the band of her short veil or her attachment to social justice. She was always recruiting girls to visit hospices or crochet blankets for Africa.

Mother Mary Paul clapped again, sharp as rifle shot, and announced that there would prayers of thanksgiving in the chapel. Sister Bernadette turned away from Fitz to put her plate down on the table, and Fitz gave a quick glance at Ali, held two fingers up to her lips, blew through them, and pulled an invisible cigarette from her mouth.

'Is she blowing a kiss at you?' asked Sister O'Dwyer, alert to any hints of an unsuitable attachment.

'No, it's something else.'

Fitz was pointing towards the window now and Ali nodded her head.

'What is it?' said the nun.

'Let me help you up, sister.'

It took a while to ease Sister O'Dwyer into the small herd shuffling towards the chapel. Ali stepped back into the emptying parlour, where a couple of younger nuns in big blue aprons were clearing the tables. Fitz had disappeared.

She retrieved her overnight bag from under a chair and slipped back out into the corridor. One side had glass cases full of dull geological specimens and stuffed animals whose fur had been bleached blonde by decades of sunlight slanting through the windows opposite. All these familiar things. She passed the arched alcove that housed a mural of the Assumption, Mary taking off into the wild blue supported by a cushion of cloud and disembodied angel heads. Down the big staircase next, her lone footsteps echoing up through the cold hallways, the empty classrooms, the ranks of desks.

I never have to come back again. She was almost running now, past the cloakrooms to the double doors that led to the grounds. One push and she was out, the sun streaming down.

She thought Fitz would be right there, but she wasn't. She must have gone on to their usual smoking spot, the Rosary Garden. Ali walked on into the grounds. The nets were sagging on the tennis courts, weeds sprouting at the bottom of the chain link fence. Summer holiday shutdown. Passing the junior school windows she could see tiny chairs stacked up on tables.

She turned down the broad path that led to the Rosary Walk, and climbed the four steps up to its gravel surface. Stone slabs, like miniature tombstones, flanked either side at regular intervals, ten on the left, ten on the right. Each slab bore a tile showing a scene from the life of the Virgin. The idea was to say your rosary while you walked, and if you got the pace right, you'd reach a slab at the end of each Hail Mary, completing a ten-prayer decade by the time you'd walked the length. It depended how fast you prayed, of course. Or walked. Before you turned around for the return decade, you could contemplate a life-size statue of the Pieta standing at the path's end, a white-wash-blurred tableau of the dead Christ balanced on his mother's knees. The figure of Mary looked down calmly at the distorted corpse, oblivious to the strain on her thighs.

Halfway along the walk, a path led

away to a small gate in a thick hedge. Ali lifted the latch and entered the shade of the Rosary Garden. She remembered Sister O'Dwyer telling them that the trees around it had been planted to shelter the little formal garden from the winds that blew down across the fields from the Dublin Mountains.

It must have been a long time ago, for nowadays the garden was shaded to the point of gloom and the fields had become housing estates. With the trees in full leaf, it had an almost underwater feel, faint dapples of light moving across ivy-filled beds, the dark gloss of holly bushes. A tiny dwelling stood in one corner, all dimpled windows and painted-on beams. It looked like something from a Grimm fairy tale, but it was just the garden shed.

Ali scanned the garden but couldn't see Fitz. Perhaps she'd got caught up with the chapel crowd after all. A twig snapped somewhere nearby, a blackbird flew from a hedge.

She moved deeper into the garden. Another sound reached her ears, a kind of high whimpering. It was coming from the direction of the shed, and now she noticed that the door was half open.

'Hello?'

'A — li?' The voice that came from inside the shed was Fitz's but sounded weirdly stretched. Ali's skin prickled.

She pushed the door open fully. Fitz was standing in the middle of the floor, her face as pale as milk and her fingers at her mouth. A smear of lipstick was wiped across one cheek. She appeared to be standing in a nest of gardening tools — hoes, rakes and loppers meshed around her ankles. Her eyes were fixed on the floor —

on a wire basket filled with smaller tools. Ali picked up a fallen rake that blocked her way, propped it against the wall. As she turned back she noticed a large mushroom or egg nested among the tools in the basket. She wanted to go to Fitz, to free her from the tangle of handles — but she couldn't tear her eyes from this thing. She stepped closer, wondering at the fuzzy halo around the edge of the egg.

Downy hair on a head.

Ali's vision blurred and wavered. She moved a little to the side and the object resolved itself — couldn't be undone now — as the top of a baby's head. She moved towards Fitz, and the body of the baby appeared, shoulders wrapped in white and the rest hidden by a brown paper bag. The rusting blades of pruning saws and secateurs bristled behind its head, but the baby itself was unmarked, and perfectly still.

'I was looking for matches' said Fitz.

The baby's eyes were closed, the forehead untroubled, but its open mouth was dry and flaking around the lips, and a horrible darkness brimmed inside. She waited for it to move.

'I was looking for matches.'

Ali looked at Fitz.

'For a fag,' said Fitz, insistent.

'C'mon,' said Ali, pulling her out of the jumble of tools and propelling her into the garden.

They were running back to the school in a dream, slow and heavy, and her throat ached with breathing. Sister Bernadette was standing on the path in front of them, appeared from nowhere, and Fitz ran ahead to her, streaming words.

The nun took control — Fitz was to go back to the school and get help, Ali was to come with her, show

16

her the place.

They ran shoulder to shoulder along the Rosary Walk, and plunged into the garden. When they reached the door of the shed, Ali stood aside to let Sister Bernadette go in on her own. There was a gap, a long silence, before Bernadette reappeared at the door, her face distraught, the features pulling themselves apart. She thrust an old china cup at Ali's stomach.

'Get me some water,' she said.

'What?'

'Go on.'

It wasn't until Ali was at the tap that she realised what her errand was. If the nun wanted to baptise the baby, perhaps it was alive. She hurried back, holding the sloshing cup at arm's length in front of her.

Sister Bernadette was waiting outside the shed, the child cradled in her arms. As she shifted her hold to reach for the cup, Ali was sure the baby's head moved.

'Is it all right?'

But the nun just glared at her and bent her head close in to the baby's, mumbling unsteady lines of prayer under her breath. She poured the water in a thin line over the child's face. It didn't flinch. Sudden tears fell from Sister Bernadette's eyes, hitting the baby's still cheek, salt water following fresh. Ali noticed the baby was wrapped in her own paisley print scarf, that her overnight bag was open on the ground.

Bernadette lifted a corner of the scarf to wipe the baby's face.

'That's my scarf,' Ali said.

Sister Bernadette turned hot eyes on her.

'You're a trivial, stupid girl, do you know that?'

She tugged the material in agitation, and the body of the child rolled in response, the cloth falling away to reveal a great purple bloom covering its back and neck.

An acid gush filled Ali's throat even as Bernadette moved to cover the little body, now so obviously lifeless and broken. A crackle of static traveled through the air, a radio rasp. Ali turned to look at the gate, where the silver buttons on several Garda uniforms flashed in the bright sunlight beyond the garden.

THREE

A line of nuns occupied the six plastic chairs in the reception area of Rathmines Garda station. Swan could feel their eyes on his back as he walked up to the front desk and introduced himself.

'Detective Inspector Swan... from HQ.' Some old instinct kept his voice low.

The Garda at the desk nodded and disappeared. Swan tried a casual glance behind, but the nuns were still staring, except for an ancient one on the end, who had bent to her beads.

He had dropped Elizabeth to the train station that morning and the late start led to him working through lunch. When the call came he was the only one in the office.

Swan would have preferred to go straight to the school, have a look about and check that the tech guys were doing their thing, but the Rathmines chief, Munnelly, was anxious to get his station clear of nuns before the papers got a sniff of it. Swan could have said it was Munnelly's fault for bringing them to the station in the first place, but there was no use getting retrospective. You just had to work from where you stood.

The desk Garda came back and pointed Swan to a side corridor where Superintendent Munnelly was waiting. There was often a bit of jockeying when the murder squad was called in to assist the local Gardaí, but Munnelly didn't look put out. A little distracted, if anything. He led Swan to a room for a briefing with the Gardaí who had been first on the scene and a couple of women officers who had been taking statements.

They ran through the facts of the incident quickly, where the child had been found and the apparent cause of death. The two schoolgirls who found it and a nun who had been at the scene were now at the station, and had given initial statements. Yes, they'd been held separately, and yes, their stories tallied — mostly. The nuns in reception were refusing to leave until their sister nun was free to go.

'How do you mean their stories tally mostly?'

'There was some disturbance of the scene, sir.' This was from the youngest looking guard, a lanky fellow with crinkly hair.

'You were there?'

'Yes, sir. The nun moved the infant for purposes of baptism, sir.'

'Why? The child was dead, I thought.'

The Garda shrugged. 'In case it hadn't been before?'

'So she moved it —'

'And poured water on it.'

'And rearranged the shed,' Munnelly added with a sigh. 'We answer to different authorities, eh?'

Swan held his tongue.

He said he would start with the girl who found it first.

'Carmen Fitzgerald.'

'Yes.'

The interview with the Fitzgerald girl didn't take long. She was a nervy little thing and too upset to be fully coherent. She kept going on about matches and cigarettes. He had expected her to be wearing some kind of uniform, but she was in jeans and a blouse, with smeared scarlet lipstick on her mouth, and mascara under her eyes. Not like the schoolgirls of his day.

'What year are you in?'

'I'm not in any year. We graduated in June.'

'Why were you at the school?'

'They had us back for a reception. The ones who were going to college. Can I go home soon?'

Home would be a nice house in Rathgar, or some other leafy address. No wonder she was upset. She was the kind of girl that bad things shouldn't happen to. After the good school, she would take an arts degree at college, maybe spend a year in Florence or Paris, and return to tennis clubs, marriage, children with cod Irish names.

'Off you go. We may have to talk again.' Swan turned to the guard by the door. 'Can we give Miss Fitzgerald a lift to… where is it, pet?'

'Eh… Donnybrook'

Close enough.

As the girl left, Munnelly came in.

'Do you think you could see the nun now?'

Swan pretended to consult his notes before agreeing.

He hadn't been close up with a nun since he was ten and at national school. They hadn't been especially cruel there, though they were quick enough to snap a ruler across small knuckles. Back then he had a dread of them just because they were so alien, towering pillars of blackness. When they patrolled the aisles of desks, the folds of their habits would brush against your bare arm or leg, soft and cold.

This nun was younger than he expected, pale and tall with a touch of the Deborah Kerrs about her. He read her statement aloud and she listened solemnly, absolutely still.

'I have a few questions,' Swan said, putting the page down on the table.

'And I have one for you,' she replied.

'You go first,' said Swan

'The baby. Where is she now?'

'I haven't been to the school yet, but I expect the body is still there while our officers piece things together. Then it'll be brought to our mortuary.'

Sister Bernadette raised her hands to the table, watching her fingers slowly interlace as if they had a life of their own.

'And then?' She addressed her hands.

'Hopefully we find her people and there can be a burial. Why?'

'If there is anything our order can do...'

'Sister — my doctrine is a little rusty — what was the point in baptising a dead child? Surely its soul had already departed.'

The look she gave him had just a hint of pity in it.

'There is always a point in doing what you can.'

'You said in your statement that the child was naked when you took it from the bag?'

'I found something to cover it with — something to hand. I didn't want people — the girl was with me — to see it.'

He was tempted to press her harder about handling the child, but there was little point at this stage. Find the mother, that was the first thing.

Sister Bernadette was adamant she knew of no girl or member of staff being pregnant.

'It can be hard to tell.'

'I'm not a naïve woman,' said Sister Bernadette, 'I see plenty of the world.'

Swan was tempted to let the other girl go home

too, but Munnelly said her recall was particularly good. Swan looked through the pages of statement and conceded. He asked one of the Ban Gardaí to come with him to the interview room this time.

Alison Hogan was drawing some kind of diagram when they entered the room. The sweet diligence of her face was at jarring odds with her bird's nest hairdo. She was dressed like some kind of vampire shepherdess.

She blushed as he introduced himself to her, put a hand over her drawing.

'I was doing a sketch of the shed for the officers,' she explained. 'I'm good at maps.'

Eager to please, despite the hairy get-up. Another nice middle class girl. Good at things.

'May I?'

It was a birds-eye view of the shed, with neat lettering pointing out features — 'door', 'bench', window'. There was a little oval shape in the centre — 'basket'. In the centre of the oval was an X. No word for it.

'Sister Bernie — she shouldn't have moved it, should she?'

'How's that?'

'You're supposed to leave things as you found them — that's what they do on television.'

'Indeed they do.' Swan smiled and laid her statement on the table, turned a couple of pages.

'You say the baby was wrapped in a white cloth. Sister Bernadette and your friend say it was in a paper bag.'

'It was in a big brown paper bag, but there was something white wrapped around it — inside the bag.'

'What kind of cloth was it?'

'Just cloth-cloth,' said Ali. 'You know. Like a sheet or something.'

'How much time passed between you and your friend leaving the shed and you coming back with Sister Bernadette?'

'Not sure. Two minutes. Three?'

'Could there have been someone else in the garden, someone you didn't see?'

The girl's eyes widened.

'I don't know...maybe...'

'I don't want to put anything in your head. No-one you saw?'

'No.'

Swan continued to scan the statement. There was a thin plastic cup of water by the girl.

'Do you mind?'

She shook her head and he took a sip from it. It was stale, with an aftertaste like pencils.

'When do I get my bag back?'

'The bag you say the nun took the scarf from?'

'Yea, it's got a lot of stuff I need.'

'Not for a while. Sorry.'

The girl pursed her lips.

'Do you get on well with the nuns?'

She shrugged. She was going quiet on them.

Swan turned to the woman police officer, a sensible looking sort, with thick black hair pulled back in a knot.

'She's been a great help, hasn't she?'

'Good enough to join the force, I'd say.'

'I'm sure Ms. Hogan has even loftier plans than that. College isn't it?'

'Well...'

'What are you going to study?' said the officer.

'Law.'

Swan and the policewoman shared a smile.

'No offense,' explained Swan, 'some solicitors are a great trouble to us.'

The girl looked upset.

'I'm sorry. You've had a dreadful morning. Why don't we let you get back to your mum and dad?' He went to give her hand a pat, but she flinched from him.

'I don't have a Dad. He died.'

'Oh, I'm sorry.'

'He was a solicitor.'

'Ah.'

'I'll just go and see if there's someone waiting for you,' said the Ban Garda.

Swan walked the girl towards the reception area. She was taller than he had realised.

'We may need to talk to you again, Alison, and in the meantime, I'd be obliged if you kept the details to yourself, eh?'

The girl asked if there was a toilet she could use. Swan flagged down one of the station guards for directions and said he'd meet her at reception. The flock of nuns had departed. Only two people were sitting on the line of orange chairs, an ample woman in an unusual tweed garment and a floppy-haired young man hooped in concentration over a newspaper, folded tight into a square.

'Anyone here to meet Alison?' Swan offered.

'I'm her mother,' the woman said, pressing an anxious hand to her chest. 'Deirdre Hogan. Are you in charge?'

Swan claimed he was.

She rose and came towards him, her layered wrap swirling about her. The garment was held together by a Celtic brooch the size of a saucer. Mother and daughter obviously shared a taste for exotic costume.

'Is it true about Ali finding a baby?' she asked in a low voice.

'Well, she was one of the people there. We just needed a word with her.'

'Is she all right?'

'She's been very calm, actually — very grown up. You should be proud.'

This didn't soothe the woman. She looked round quickly at the young man before taking a step closer to Swan.

'It's not fair…' she said.

'What's not?'

'Once would be bad enough. But twice… it's beyond sense. You see, it's happened before.'

FOUR

Ali woke sweating from a dream. She had been on her knees in the Rosary Garden, trowelling through black clay while Sister O'Dwyer stood over her crying, begging her to come to the chapel, that prayers would start soon. Ali tried to explain that she had to find something, that she'd be along later. She looked down at her trowel and there was half a worm on it — a white worm as big as a finger — writhing, blindly searching for its lost half.

The morning light leaked through her thin curtains. She was telling herself it was just a dream when she remembered what wasn't a dream, and images from the previous day assaulted her.

Ma and Davy had treated her so gently when they collected her from the police station, and later Davy went out and got a bucket of fried chicken and a bottle of white wine for dinner, as if her brush with death called for something — not a celebration, certainly — but an occasion outside everyday rhythms.

After they ate, her mother went to visit a friend in hospital and Ali went to her uncle's room to sit side by side across his bed and watch a spy film on RTE2. They didn't talk much. Davy said he felt stunned by what had happened, so he couldn't imagine how it was for her. They'd shared a half bottle of Southern Comfort until her eyelids drooped and she lost track of who was who in the film. She didn't even remember getting to bed.

She hauled herself out of bed and washed the remains of makeup from her face at the sink in the corner of her bedroom. There was a shower next to the sink, like a plastic phone box parked against the wall, a remnant of the house's former life as a warren of bedsits. Ali used it as a wardrobe, hanging her clothes from the top edge of it, inside and out. She picked up yesterday's dress and hung it over the layers already there. Then she changed her mind and bundled it into one of the boxes of junk under her bed. She didn't feel like seeing it again. When tears started, she sat on the floor and waited for them to pass, like weather.

+

Davy was down in the kitchen reading a newspaper, his fringe almost touching the page. When he noticed her, he made a halfhearted attempt at hiding it.

'Just looking at the jobs,' he said.

Davy had come to stay with them three weeks before. He was trying to find a job in Dublin, saying there were none to be had down in Clare. Each morning he would phone a few companies from the Yellow Pages and asked if they'd anything going.

'Saves the feet,' he'd say.

'But not my bloody phone bill,' Ma complained.

Ali liked having him around. He was the baby of his family, nearer her age than her mother's and had a quick energy to him that altered the dull atmosphere of their house. He pottered around at all hours fixing things, hacking back the garden, surprising them. He hadn't landed as much as an interview for a job.

Davy pressed the paper to the table with his palms. 'I didn't want you upset. I just thought I'd look. There's hardly anything.'

Ali tugged at the paper and he allowed it to

escape. There was a small headline and a paragraph underneath. *Dead Baby Found in Convent.* It was a strange relief to see the words there, the matter-of-factness of it.

'I thought it might be worse,' she said.

Her mother appeared in the doorway. 'That's just the start, apparently.'

She was wearing a loose dragon-print kimono over her nightdress and her dark-dyed hair sat in a careless knot on top of her head, like a cast member of a slovenly *Mikado*.

'Sean O'Loan told me the guards were trying to keep the lid on, but he expects the press will soon be crawling all over it.'

'When did you talk to *him*?' said Ali. 'I thought you were visiting Angela Farrington and her new hip.'

'Well, when I came out of Vincent's I had a while to wait for the bus, so I dropped into Lamb's and he happened to be there.' Ma had assumed her posher voice. She was a lousy liar.

'You told him all about it, didn't you?'

Ma took down the gas lighter and stood silent by the cooker, waiting for its ticktick sparking to ignite the hiss of gas. The blue flames flattened as she put the kettle down and turned back to her daughter.

'Well, I don't know *all about it* do I? You've told us very little. What harm if a friend gets to know something ahead of the pack?'

'The policeman said I wasn't to say anything, and you go straight to a journalist. You could get me into trouble.'

'*You* didn't say anything. I did. It's my affair and I'll take the responsibility.'

'Oh its your *affair*, all right.'

'You're a cheeky little pup…'

'Ah, stop it, now!' said Davy.

Ali felt a stab of shame, just a little one. She wasn't comfortable with the men her mother hung around with. No doubt the media crowd in Lamb's were entertaining, but Ali couldn't get past the fact that all these men had homes and families to return to and dinner waiting in the oven. Her mother was never invited to share that dinner or sit at their tables.

The doorbell rang. They all looked up the hall to where the big panelled door was framed by threads of daylight.

'It won't be for me,' said Davy.

Deirdre Hogan moved, closing the kitchen door as she went. Davy and Ali listened to the muffled exchange on the threshold. The other voice was a man's, and there seemed to be some kind of negotiation going on.

After a minute, her mother re-appeared.

'Love?' she started, and Ali bristled, 'Sean sent a photographer.'

'What?'

'He says they're doing an article, but they've no photos to go with it. All he wants is a quick snap.'

'No way.'

'I'll just have to give him your school photo then.'

'Very funny.'

'It's the only decent one I have.'

Her sixth-year photograph sat framed on her mother's dressing table, under a fine film of talc. In it Ali wore her uniform, a hair-band and a submissive chin-tucked smile. She hated the girl in the photo.

'Hal-oo-oo?' The photographer was walking down the hall.

'You're *unbelievable.*'

Her mother opened the kitchen door. The man had a big canvas bag over one shoulder and a tripod in one hand. He looked around impatiently.

'Is there a cosy corner somewhere we could do this, ma'am?'

Ali stood up, 'I'll just go and change.'

'Change? Change?' said the photographer, 'sure aren't you perfect as you are? You make my job easy. I've snapped all the great and the small, so you're safe with me.'

'How about the garden?' said her mother.

The photographer looked doubtful, then his expression changed.

'A garden was where this thing happened, wasn't it? Just awful — yeah — the garden would do.'

He shot off through the back door and down the steps. Ali got up and checked her reflection in the kitchen mirror. She was wearing an old black jumper and her hair was pulled back in a ponytail. No makeup, no rubbish, just get it over with.

It was lucky that Davy had managed to create something like a patch of lawn by getting down on his knees with a pair of old shears, but a thicket of creepers and shrubs still held sway over most of the garden. On fine nights, she and Davy would sit out on a rug, with candles in jam jars, drinking strange cocktails created from the furthest reaches of her mother's drinks cupboard. Those nights felt like ages ago. Ali clutched the metal rail as she went down the steps, thinking of escape, but moving towards the photographer.

He asked her to stand under the old apple tree and to look back at the house over his shoulder. It was uncomfortable to be examined so intently. The lens was huge, and the clicks kept taking her by surprise. The side of her mouth started to flutter in a nervous spasm.

'Don't smile,' warned the photographer, 'think of… well… something sad.'

Ali let her eyes drift out of focus and allowed the pictures to rise in her mind, the garden, the shed, and with them the feeling that the last twenty-four hours, including this ludicrous photograph, were an elaborate hallucination, a ride over which she had no control.

Something was shifting in her mind, trying to surface, to make itself known.

It flickered into life.

The camera clicked on, but Ali was somewhere else, twelve years in the past.

Because it was so heavy, she held the box across her arms. She hadn't noticed when she lifted it, but now it was clammy against her skin, the cardboard sticky. Ali went down the farmhouse stairs one by one.

The door to the living room was shut and she had no hand free to open it. She was wearing her party shoes for Christmas day, the black patent ones, and she lifted her right foot and pressed a shiny toe to the door. It swung open without a sound. The family were all there. Her cousins on the floor playing with their toys, Davy crouched over something too. Ma looking sad and strange in her tight dress and make up, Uncle Joe bareheaded for once, his hair plastered down, wearing his mass suit.

They didn't see her, not at first. Ma looked up, and the others followed her gaze.

'What have you got there?' Ma asked.

'I found it,' Ali said, 'I found the doll.'

'Turn your head. Chin up, but look at the ground' said the photographer, 'Almost there.'

All of them looking at her. The photographer, now, looking at her. The shame.

'Is that enough?' she said. 'Can that be enough?'

He took the camera from his face, and she headed straight for the house, leaving him to follow in her wake.

Her mother showed him out. Low voices mumbling by the door, a few exaggerated sighs. Ali waited in her bedroom until the coast was clear and went down to the phone.

Their telephone was a black wall-mounted payphone in an alcove under the stairs. They left the money drawer open so that the same well-worn ten pence piece could be circulated around and around.

Ali hooked the coin out of its cranny and put it in the slot. She pressed button A when Fitz answered.

'My Mum's trying to keep me away from the phone,' Fitz said, 'you're lucky you got me.'

'How're you holding up?'

'I don't know. Fuck, Ali, I keep seeing the little face.'

'Yea...'

'Could hardly sleep a wink.'

'Me and Davy got a bit pissed, that helped.'

'You're uncle's cool. I liked him.'

'Did you say anything to the police about where we were on Sunday night?'

'No, they didn't ask. Did you?'

'I only thought of it afterwards. It gives me the creeps...'

'Hey — you won't believe this — a reporter from the Independent phoned this morning, and I had to pretend I wasn't here. I said I was my sister.'

'You didn't talk to them?'

'No way. My Dad says they're vultures. Did they

try you?'

'No calls... but there was a photographer here and my Ma let him in.'

She told Fitz about her mother talking to Sean O'Loan.

'I feel like a right fool.'

She waited a beat for Fitz to contradict her, but Fitz just changed the subject to how horrible the police station had been.

Fitz finished her complaint and a few seconds of silence opened into a chasm. Ali suggested that she could come over, but Fitz said it wouldn't be a good idea, that they were about to have lunch.

'What are you having?' asked Ali, desperate to get back to normal.

She heard Fitz let out an impatient puff of air.

'Salad or something. Its not interesting.'

Ali let her go. The instant that she put the receiver back on the cradle it rang, vibrating through her hand.

'Hello?'

'Hello. Am I speaking to Alison Hogan?' The elongated vowels had a velvety cadence that was somehow familiar.

'Yes, that's me.'

'Great. My name's Mary O'Shea...'

The rest of her sentence was lost, drowned out by the panicky flurry in Ali's head. *Mary O'Shea*. Of course she knew the voice. Everybody knew Mary O'Shea, but the voice should be coming out of a radio, not out of their cracked old phone. Ali tried to catch hold of the flow of words as they poured into her ear, suddenly seizing on the words 'Sean O'Loan'.

'... so Sean said it would be all right for me to give you a little bell and see how things stood with you.'

'Okay…'

'He said you were a very smart girl. Going to do law, he said.'

'I hope so… if I get the results.'

'And he said your mother was a wonderful women, a strong independent spirit was what he said.'

That didn't sound much like her mother, but the outside world judged things differently. Ali looked up to see the independent spirit pass by, still in her kimono, carrying a tray full of mugs and glasses to the kitchen.

'That's nice…' Ali waited for her mother to get out of earshot.

'Look, here's me going on,' said Mary. 'It's hard to have a proper chat on the phone. I know you must be devastated, but I was wondering whether you and I couldn't get together for a little talk. I'd really appreciate it.'

'I don't know…'

'How about coffee at the Shelbourne? Just you and me.'

FIVE

Swan placed the pristine copies of the Press and Herald on the table in front of him. There was nothing on either front page, so he'd just sit for a minute, enjoy his coffee and the dark peace of the Gravediggers on a summer's day. The barman leant his crossed arms on the counter, surveying his own paper spread flat on the wooden surface. A burst of bronchial laughter carried over the top of the wooden screen that separated the small back bar from the front of the pub. He had passed two aul' wans on his way in, drinking glasses of stout side by side, conspiratorial as girls. Here in the back, there was just the whisper of pages turning, the slow tick of the clock and the gurgle of cisterns beyond the brown lacquered toilet doors. All it needed was the thump of a collie's tail on the floor and you could believe you were in some country town.

He should have gone straight back to HQ from the convent, but took a little detour instead. He needed to see what the papers were saying — he needed a think.

Kavanagh, the chief superintendent, had phoned him at home that morning, just after seven, to say he wanted a quick finish to this case, that it had too many 'knobs on'. Crudely put as always, but he understood what Kavanagh meant — this one had knobs, bells and miraculous medals all over it.

A dead baby in a convent — that was slaughter and religion for starters with a background of sexual activity. The fact that it was one of the most affluent schools in the city brought in money and class. Coming hot on the heels of the 'pro-life' referendum where the country had screamed itself into a bitter divide over whether it loved its foetuses more than their mothers, this delicate atrocity was sure to keep the fires aglow. No wonder Kavanagh was jumping around like a bluebottle on a window.

Swan turned to what he had been putting off — checking the evening papers to see what they'd got hold of. The press announcement wasn't scheduled until later, but you never knew. One of those girls could be the daughter of some blow-dried RTE journalist.

He opened the Evening Press and was assaulted by toothy grins on the social diary pages. The high life in Ireland the previous day had consisted of a reception at a stud farm in Naas and the opening of a gallery in the Powerscourt Centre. All the photographs featured good-looking women with big hair and big earrings. It was a world that Swan rarely came into contact with, but it was the world that girls like Alison Hogan grew up to inherit. Easy street.

That thing the mother said about the girl having found another baby at a relative's farm. Buleen, she said the place was. Ali Hogan was just six at the time. He hadn't got much more of the story out of her before the girl appeared and Mummy clammed up. It was grisly luck alright.

If they could spare someone to look into it, though, he'd have some answers ready in case the press or Kavanagh got hold of it. There was that new girl on the team, Gina Considine. She had a lot to prove and looked keen to get the proving behind her. Maybe he'd ask her to check there was nothing there to concern them.

Swan reached for the coffee cup and took a sip. It was cooling now, but the brandy gave a nice gingery kick. If one of the lads happened in to the pub he would look as innocent as a lamb.

As a teenager, Swan had inherited a suitcase full of old paperbacks when his uncle Tony died. They were the first books, apart from schoolbooks, that he could call his own. He propped them up on the mantelpiece in his bedroom with two bricks for bookends and felt himself a man of the world. Half of them were green-spined Penguins by a man called Simenon, and he had spent weeks of one summer lying on his bed reading through them, lost in the pale stone and twisted stair-cases of Paris, mouthing words like *prefecture* and *gendarme* and imagining what an Algerian might look like. Maigret, the morose detective, would pop in to bars throughout his working day for a quick drink, but never got drunk. The French didn't go for swilling bucketloads of Guinness, slopping it over their sleeves and licking the foam from their faces. No, they supped one small crystalline drink, and on they went with their day.

That was Swan's model where drink was concerned. The fact that he signed up with the Gardaí at the end of that summer was coincidence, really. College hadn't been an option. His father wanted him to come and sell furniture with him in the shop in Phibsborough, but the Saturday afternoons Swan had spent there — squeezed between high wooden beds and veneered telephone tables — were like being trapped in a vault. His father standing still among the furniture, so forbearing, whistling through his teeth and dreaming of the pub later, the camaraderie of men and the bottomless pint.

The papers had the story on their second and

third pages, just a four-inch column in one, and a double column with big headline in the Herald. All they said was that the body of a newborn infant had been found in the grounds of St. Brigid's, Milltown. Mother sought. Nothing about the injuries. Good. Nothing too specific about the whereabouts. Good. The Herald filled in some background on St. Brigid's which included the information that the convent housed forty nuns. Just as a matter of record, hint hint. He could see that the nun angle might grow in the coming days.

Was it feasible that a nun might have given birth? It didn't seem likely; it seemed like the stuff of jokes about sexy nuns and randy priests that the tough boys down the lanes would tell. *Candles out before bedtime, sisters.* And it wasn't a possibility that he, a man with two decades of police work under his belt, had had the balls to confront the reverend mother with — not yet.

Mother Mary Paul had greeted him that morning with level eyes, professional to professional, had walked him around the grounds and answered all his practical questions. As she spoke, she kept withdrawing a crumpled hankie from a sleeve, touching it briefly to her impressive nose before tucking it back in to the pendulous folds of her sleeve. It seemed a preventative measure rather than a real mopping operation. Or maybe it was just her way of expressing a kind of regret.

The school grounds were impressive, but depressing — the gloom under the big trees, the holy statues watching over emptiness. They stood together for a while on the raised path they called the Rosary Walk and took in the view. It was a fine bit of land they had still, but beyond an ugly brick wall, new houses pressed in around them, the march of the suburbs.

That was the moment he should turned to her,

and in the voice of a gentle confessor ask her to tell him about the ladies of her community, but he had let it go. Instead, he'd made another appointment to see her in the morning, in her office. He rationalised this as building a steady relationship, but knew he was just putting it off the inevitable, hoping for a lucky break elsewhere.

Beyond those convent walls, dozens of detectives and Gardaí were going door to door along the quiet streets, searching for a woman known to be pregnant but with no baby to show for it, tapping into gossip, nosing out illicit liaisons, sudden weight gain or families where there might be 'issues'. By the time he got back to the office, something might have been shook out of the tree.

The barman stretched his arms above his head and roared out a long yawn. He pointed at Swan's coffee cup and raised an eyebrow.

'Maybe half a cup' said Swan. The barman lifted the coffee flask from its dock and reached up for the brandy bottle with the other.

'Just the hot stuff, Joe' He wasn't going to break the Maigret rule, especially during a wave of self-doubt.

There was something so bleak about the nature of the crime, the pathetic waste of it. What was there to say about a baby? There was no story to a person whose life could be counted in hours. It wasn't like the student nurse coming home alone after a dance or the father of six stabbed in a pub fight. Until they found the baby's people, she floated alone, just an idea of a life.

Nobody had claimed her yet. But things were ticking along, and now he had a new piece of the jigsaw. He looked down at the sealed bag beside him on the bench. What was inside just might be a key.

Swan had parted with Mother Mary Paul outside

the Rosary Garden. A lone Garda sat just inside the gate on a rusty chair, looking eager for a chat, but Swan just nodded briskly and passed into the gloom. A filament of cobweb stretched and broke across his face.

He paused and passed a palm over his cheeks, took in the scene — a few mossy benches, a rockery that looked more like a plum pudding than the side of an alp, beds filled with indistinguishable green plants crawling over each other. *Ground cover* — the phrase came to him from one of his wife's gardening programmes.

The shed in the corner fitted in with the atmosphere of shabby romance, with its little cottagey windows and tiled roof, but green algae crawled up its painted walls and the bottom of the wood slat door had gone soft and gappy. There was always a thin line between romance and rot.

Had the shed been a stopping off point for whoever had the baby? Maybe they went in there to get a spade, but were disturbed by the girls. It would have been difficult to get out of the shed without being noticed.

Two technical bureau personnel were still at work inside, but said he was welcome to join them. The interior was unexpectedly dry, the floor covered with dregs of desiccated peat moss. Chalk marks and smears of fingerprinting dust showed on the floor and walls.

'You taken much out?' asked Swan.

'Not really,' answered on of the men, pulling down his mask. 'A few things that might have been weapons — but look at it.'

The shed was filled to the gunnels with all kinds of metal tools, not to mention hundreds of old pots, boxes, bits of string and netting and a stack of dusty deckchairs. They were going through it all, bit by bit, and so it was that Swan was standing there when the other masked man lifted a deckchair from the stack and opened it to reveal a bundled knot of white concealed in its striped fold. The luck of it warmed him.

A mother of pearl button gleamed on an edge of it, and they could see some brownish staining in the depths of its folds. It could be the white cloth that Ali Hogan said the baby was wrapped in. The technicians slipped it gently into a bag, and agreed he could take it straight back to the labs. It would get there soon enough.

The front section of the pub was growing noisy, the door opening and closing, letting in sweeps of sunshine. Three men in black suits came through and stood together at the bar. Glasnevin graveyard was next door, so funerals were a common part of the custom. He wondered whether the regular intrusion of mourning was one of the reasons he liked it here.

Enough wondering. Swan leaned back to root for coins in his trouser pocket. He picked up the evidence bag, walked over to the phone cupboard at the back and rang the office number. Declan Barrett answered.

'I'm on my way in.' Swan pulled the folding door tighter to damp the background noise. 'Did pathology call yet?'

The baby's body had been moved to the morgue late the previous evening. A tiny thing stranded on an adult-sized slab. No larger than a loaf of bread under the cloth. Full autopsy would take about a week to come in, if he was lucky, but he'd put in an urgent request for a rough estimate of the child's age and time of death.

'Just a tick, boss,' said Barrett, a slight stress of his voice managing as usual to make the word 'boss' sound like a longstanding joke between them rather than his deserved title.

'Here it is — estimated time of death between twenty and sixteen hours before forensics got to the scene at three pm yesterday. Newborn infant, female, approximately two to three days old, cord cut approximately five inches from the body and healing, body washed of vernix, some fibres present. Now, I've looked up the medical dictionary, and the vernix is waxy stuff that coats it when it's born — '

'Barrett, I know what vernix is.'

'So I figure the baby was washed and cared for.'

Einstein.

'Have they checked the wounds? '

'No — the pathologist can't get to it yet. Backlog. I'll call again — harry them a bit.'

'Is Considine about?'

'The girl?'

'She's not a girl, Barrett, she's a guard.'

A pause. Swan could hear a muffled remark and someone laughing.

'She's on the phone. Anything I can help with?'

'No.'

Swan hung up on a wave of irritation. Barrett's keenness needled him out of all proportion.

He shuffled the coins in his hand and thought for a moment. Seeing the child last night, the fullness of its features, made him suspect this wasn't a case of neo-natal panic. There had been an incident last year, a baby left in a carrier bag under a bench by the Royal Canal. He had seen into the bag himself and could never forget the look of the poor scrap — smeared with a mixture of what looked like wax and old blood, its froggy little body squashed into shrouds of newspaper and plastic bag. Suffocated at birth, they said. Hard to tell if the

43

lungs had ever drawn air, the eyes ever registered light.

A bubble of hopelessness rose in him and all at once he was aware of the heat and claustrophobia of the booth. He lifted the receiver once more, put in a coin and dialed his own number.

Just across the square from the Gravediggers, in a terraced redbrick house, a phone rang and rang. He imagined the sound echoing round the hallway, ricocheting off the dark furniture salvaged from his father's shop. He imagined Elizabeth walking downstairs towards the sound, or turning her head among the flowerbeds at the back, rising slowly to her feet. He let it ring until there was no hope of an answer. She hadn't come back yet.

SIX

Ali looked up at a torch-bearing maiden poised on the balustrade of the Shelbourne Hotel, the thin copper drapery emphasizing rather than veiling the statue's voluptuous figure. She remembered staring at these women when she was small, her attention caught by their prominent breasts. Her father had laughed when he saw what she was looking at, and she'd got embarrassed, but he'd swung her hand back and forth, making her body twist, forcing her to smile.

If only she could remember more of him. At least she could still feel that sensation of her own small hand in his large one, the comfort of that.

When he was alive, the two of them would go into to town on a Sunday morning. After mass in Clarendon Street they'd buy Sunday papers from a man with blackened fingers and walk hand in hand to a nice hotel like the Hibernian or sometimes the Shelbourne, and Daddy would read his papers while she drank lemonade through a straw and ate her way through a little dish of salty, bitter-skinned peanuts. Often, an acquaintance of her father would stop by to talk and she would try to look as well behaved as she could.

She hadn't been in the Shelbourne since. The entrance hall was the same, high Georgian mirrors and walls the colour of mint ice cream. And right in the middle of the hall stood Mary O'Shea, surrounded by a gaggle of hotel staff eager with laughter.

'Oh Mary, you're killing us,' said one, clutching his stomach.

'That's the best yet,' said another, holding on to the edge of the reception desk for support.

Even the chandeliers seemed to favour Mary, the light haloing her bobbed golden hair and winking from her shining nails as she waved her hands around.

Ali stood outside the group for a moment, wondering how to make herself known. She thought about walking back out of the place, but just as she started to turn, she heard 'Alison?'

Mary O'Shea walked out of the circle of men to stand in front of her. Ali caught the look of deprivation in their eyes before she herself was caught in the lovely beam of Mary's attention.

'Most people call me Ali'

'So I will too, Ali, I will too.' Mary slipped her hand through the crook of Ali's arm and set off through a sofa-filled lounge. 'It's a bit public here, isn't it? Let's try the bar. Michael?'

Mary didn't even break stride or turn around. One of the reception staff, still pink with merriment, simply drew close behind them, a dog to heel.

'The bar's open, isn't it?'

'We can open it.'

'Good man.'

+

They settled onto a leather bench in a corner of the paneled room. An island bar took up most of the floor, a wooden command centre armed with upturned bottles. It was probably cosy at night, but the steep rays of daylight slanting in from the windows revealed cigarette burns in the carpet and cast the rest of the place into gloom. The air smelt faintly of ashes and stale beer.

'This is fine,' Mary declared.

'Grand,' agreed Ali.

A big, embarrassed-looking lad in a dickie bow appeared behind bar counter and started to switch on lights.

'Can I get you ladies anything?'

'I was just going to have a coffee,' said Mary, 'but it's so hot, I don't know. What do you think Ali, gin and tonics?'

Ali agreed, even though she had hardly ever touched gin, associating it with the juniper tang of her mother's lips when she kissed her on her way out to a party or the pub.

Mary fished about in her handbag. She brought out a tiny tape recorder and a gold compact that she flicked open with one hand and circled in front of her perfectly made up face. She tipped her chin up and rolled her glossy lips back to reveal an even row of small teeth.

'You look great,' Ali said, and Mary threw a smile at her.

'Bless you, but you should see it first thing.' She snapped the compact shut and threw it back in her bag, then turned her full attention on Ali.

'What happened at St. Brigid's is important,' she said, 'Very big. There's going to be a lot of attention paid to this case. Even the British papers will be writing about it —'

The boy appeared with their drinks and put a small dish of peanuts in front of Ali. Tiny ones with their skins still on, lathered in salt. She smiled. Mary caught her expression, misunderstood it.

'No flies on you,' said Mary. *'What does she want from me,* you're asking yourself. Well, I

47

have a question for you.'

Ali met Mary's eyes, facing up to her challenge. This was worse than the police. But exciting too. If someone saw them together. Imagine. She took a sip of her drink. It tasted clean and sour.

'How often do you hear the voice of a girl your age on radio or television?'

Ali shrugged.

'There's a lot talked about young people — your lack of respect, your promiscuous behaviour — but who gets to hear your voice? This case will be chewed over by doctors and bishops and TDs, all men of course, but you were on the spot. The mother could be another schoolgirl. I want to hear what *you* have to say.'

'I don't know I've anything to say. I just happened to be there.'

'Maybe you think you've nothing to say because all your life people have told you that you haven't, told you to listen, not speak.'

'Maybe…' Something stirred inside Ali, some obscure part of her spontaneously inflating. She had a vision of people applauding, rising from their seats. She took a big gulp of gin.

Mary's hand reached for her little recorder, fingered a button on it.

'Do you mind?'

Mary O'Shea was as famous as you could be in Ireland. She had a show on the radio, a Sunday newspaper column and *The Late Late Show* wouldn't go near the subject of women without Mary in the studio. Even Ali's mother, who approved of very few people, loved Mary. She would shout *Go get 'em girl!* at the radio when Mary lured some old reactionary out onto the gangplank of his own absurdity.

'The thing is,' Ali began, 'the policeman... the detective said I wasn't to talk to anyone.'

Mary's brows lifted a centimeter, she widened her smile. The dictaphone went back in the bag.

'Not a problem. The recorder's just handy — I'm desperate at shorthand. I wouldn't print anything against your will, or anything that would harm the case. I am *scrupulous* about that kind of thing. Did I tell you I went to Brigid's myself?'

'The nuns mention it all the time.'

'Probably as some kind of dire warning about condom-waving feminists.'

Ali laughed, 'Just a bit.'

'I hear Mary Paul's in charge now. She was the bane of my youth. She taught me history in second and third year... most of the oppressed or massacred "didn't help themselves", I seem to recall.'

'She doesn't teach now. Too busy imposing the rules.'

'Was she there yesterday?'

'Not in the garden, well... yes, in the garden later. They were all there at the reception, the nuns.'

Ali started to explain why they were at the school, and Mary asked if she could take notes, at least. Ali suddenly couldn't think of the reason why not. When Ali got to the part where she entered the shed and saw the baby, Mary asked, 'When you saw it, what did you feel?'

The gold biro hovered an inch above the page. The brown eyes skewered her.

Ali paused. 'I thought it couldn't be real.' Her face felt hot. 'Fitz was in a state. I wanted to get us away from the shed.'

'And now?'

'Now?'

'How has it left you?'

She could see an image of herself as the photographer had posed her that morning, wistful, misted in sadness. But that wouldn't do for Mary. Mary would want her to be tougher.

'I feel angry.'

Mary stopped writing.

'How d'you mean?'

Ali shrugged, she hardly knew what she meant.

'The way things are... this country.'

'Ah.' Mary sat back against the upholstery and smoothed the material of her skirt over her thighs. 'Did you get Sister O'Dwyer for sex education?' she asked.

'No!'

'That's what we got. She handed out booklets and made us read them in silence — it was all diagrams of fallopian tubes and cell division. She'd sit up at the high desk in front of us — possibly the most innocent nun in Ireland — and she'd say, *Ask me anything*. One brave girl asked how the seed got from the man into the woman and Sister O'Dwyer just pretended she hadn't heard. Told us to turn to the next page.'

Ali laughed.

'And that was very advanced for the sixties,' said Mary. 'What did you get?'

'We got a man. Not just a man of course, a *doctor*. We were twelve or thirteen. He talked to us for a whole day. Most of it was about the Billing's method and secretions and the how to fend off your husband's advances. Because men can't help themselves, he said. It was down to us to hold the barricades.'

'It's no joke, getting pregnant.'

'No. But they always go on about how men want sex, like it's their particular thing, not the women, we just go through with it to be kind. Can't women want it too?'

Mary smiled a slow smile and smoothed her hair.

'It takes a while to get past the programming.'

Ali took another sip from her glass, thought of how nice it would be to be Mary O'Shea.

'You know the referendum?'

Mary sighed as she nodded. She had probably broadcast a hundred discussions on it over the previous two years.

'No one made the men account for their sperm did they?'

'Howd'ya mean?'

'Each little tadpole a potential human soul. No, it was always about the women and the eggs. Those murderous women, those precious eggs.'

'*The most dangerous place in the world is in a women's womb,*' intoned Mary, quoting an archbishop. 'Why do you think the baby died?'

Ali looked away.

'I don't know,' she said.

They fell silent for a moment, Mary looking down at her notebook, Ali stirring the ice melt in her glass with a plastic swizzle stick.

'I had a great friend at school,' said Mary eventually. 'Barbara, her name was. We went to the Gaeltacht together one summer, had a rare time, the boys, the ceilidhs, bonfires on the beach. We ran wild. But when we got back to school, Barbara said her mother had decided she should go to boarding school in the country and that she was leaving St. Brigid's at Christmas. She grew really quiet. I stupidly thought it was because she was so sad to leave me. I wrote to her at the new school, but she didn't answer. It wasn't till years later that I found

51

out the truth of it.'

Ali nodded to show that she understood.

Mary picked up her drink and cupped it in her hands, leaning towards Ali.

'Did that happen to any girls that you know?'

Five minutes before, Ali would have said 'no', but as Mary talked the face of a girl called Eileen Vaughan had risen in her mind. Eileen had been Fitz's best friend. It was only Eileen's sudden departure from school at Easter that left Fitz free to be friends with Ali. There were rumours through the school that Eileen Vaughan had been dabbling in drugs. Fitz wouldn't discuss it. Ali realised now there was a more obvious explanation.

'I think maybe it did. The same as with your friend. A girl left suddenly early this year, no mention of it afterwards, like she'd never been there.'

'When was this?'

'March, I think'

'Hmmm.' Mary counted on her fingers. 'Can you give me her name?'

Ali looked into Mary O'Shea's clear eyes.

'No.'

Mary frowned, disappointed with her.

'Look, Ali. This thing will probably never go to court. They'll find the poor girl who gave birth and send her to psychiatric for a while. It's a tragedy, and a national disgrace, but it's hardly a state secret.'

Ali shrugged. She was thinking of Fitz being angry, not the police.

'Who's the officer in charge? The one who made you promise not to talk to people like me?' Mary made it sound like a game, a matter of poses being struck.

'He's called Detective Swan, I met him in Rathmines Garda station, but he said he worked at the Phoenix Park.'

'Is he a small dark man — neat — reasonably attractive?'

'Well... I don't know about attractive.' Maybe he was to someone of Mary's age. Her own mother thought the oddest men were lovely.

'I know him! He's in the murder squad. I talked to him once at The Gate, at a Wilde play. Not many detectives you can say that of. Maybe dragged along by the wife. A foot taller than him, she was.'

'It's not that I don't want to talk to you, Mary, but he'll know it was me.'

'Sure weren't there others who saw the same thing? All the nuns hanging about?'

'Well, no, not inside the shed...' she was going explain how only three of them had seen the child lying in the basket, when she stopped herself. The gin was making her stupid.

'What do you mean the shed?'

'In the Rosary Garden. It was in the shed. I don't... I told you I can't talk this way.' Her face felt terribly hot.

Mary held her hands up in mock surrender.

'We're on the same side, Ali. Want another drink?' She pointed at Ali's empty glass. Her own was hardly touched.

'I'm fine, thanks.'

Mary dashed off a few more squiggles on her pad.

'Look, I have to meet someone here in five minutes. I could talk all day, but we'll need to finish up. I'll write something for the paper tomorrow. It's nothing to worry about, but I will mention you, and talk about the type of place St Brigid's is. I'd love us to keep in touch — as this thing unfolds.

You've got integrity, and you express yourself well.'

'You won't make it sound like I've been pushing myself forward?'

'Ali. Don't worry. We've nothing to fear from the truth. As somebody must have said sometime.'

Mary opened her bag again and took out a business card. She wrote two numbers on the back and handed it to Ali.

'The top one is my answering service. They can page me wherever. That other one is my home number, so I'd appreciate it if you kept it to yourself.'

Ali smiled at the rectangle of card and slipped it into the back pocket of her jeans. Fitz would be amazed. She was about to stand when Mary stalled her with an outstretched hand.

'Can I ask you one more thing?'

'Okay.'

'Do you think that the baby died of natural causes? Sorry. It's a horrible question. Do you?'

'No.'

'No you don't think so, or no it didn't?'

'I think it didn't.'

They just looked at each other for a minute.

'Oh well, I'm sure they'll make a statement later today... so I'll wait to find out with the rest of the gang.' Mary was putting away the notebook and pen, gathering herself.

'The back of the neck,' Ali said in a small voice, lifting a hand to her own nape, 'was all bruised. And down her back.'

+

She could still feel the squeeze of Mary's hand on

her arm as she stood in the ladies. She shouldn't have told. But Mary had stirred her up with kind words and the notion that she had something say for herself. Just a nudge was all it took.

The ladies toilets were walled and floored in sand-coloured marble. There was a stack of tiny towels by the oval basins. Her face in the mirror was flushed, her eyes strange to her. She filled a basin and washed her face and hands in cool water. She took one of the towels and buried her face in it.

The loops of thread crawled down her skin.

The first one was lying under a towel. A grubby yellow towel. Ali had been looking for her present, the doll called Baby Joy. That's what she asked Santy for because her friend Maura Griffin in Dublin said Baby Joy was just like a real baby, not a stiff girl with nylon hair and clicky eyes. She liked the idea that it would be close to real, like someone new to care for. But there was only one present under the tree for her that morning, a plastic cookery set threaded to a big sheet of cardboard. Her cousins seemed to have loads of stuff. She couldn't make a fuss, not there in her uncle's house, everyone in their good clothes.

Before Christmas, she wondered whether she would get more presents that year because of her Daddy dying. It just came into her mind, but she feared that Santy knew. You shouldn't think that kind of thing.

She sidled up to her mother's chair.

'Does Santy come again if he's forgotten to bring something?'

Ma laughed but it wasn't a kind laugh. It was sharp and drew the attention of the other grownups to her.

'What are they like these days? No, he doesn't.'

Ma had a tiny glass in one hand. A tissue poked out of

the fist of the other. Ali moved away, slipped into the hall and made her way up to the back bedroom.

She hadn't been snooping, not really, although that's what Aunt Una said afterwards, angry with her. It was just that her cousin Roisín had told her about the big wardrobe upstairs. That she had seen presents hidden there. That Santy didn't exist.

The wardrobe was huge, separating two single beds. It had a mirror on its front and she watched herself approach, her moon face looming above the velvet party frock that was painfully tight around her ribs that year, and so short that she could see her bare knees.

As she opened the door, her reflection slipped sideways and away in a shard of light. A smell of mould rose to greet her. She parted the heavy clothes that hung there, looked down among the wire hangers and shoes scattered across the bottom. There was no present. When she stepped back from the wardrobe, she saw there was a shelf above the clothes rail, and could make out some folded blankets there, but no glint or flash of wrapping paper. Still, she felt a high shelf was the very place you would hide something if you wanted to keep it away from children, and it was also the kind of place where a present might get shoved to the back, might get accidentally forgotten in the rush.

She was looking all around the room for something to stand on when she found the box.

It was under the left hand bed, right up against the wall. It was larger than a shoebox. It was the size of a doll box. A box that someone had forgotten to wrap and had forgotten was under the bed. Ali lay flat on the lino and slid under, through a thick layer of dust, to pull the box out to the light. There was a curly pattern on the top and she could read well enough to make out the words 'Baby Joy'.

Her heart beat fast as she lifted the cardboard lid and

saw a crumpled yellow towel covering the doll, its sleeping face just visible through a gap in the folds. She had been right all along, and that sense of rightness was stronger than any scratchings of doubt about the griminess of its wrapping or the odd appearance of the doll.

Baby Joy was supposed to look a little ugly, Maura Griffin said so.

Ali moved the towel. The doll's chest and shoulders were naked, and the colour of the body was strangely mottled, like the skin of her legs when they had been too close to the fire; and though the doll was sleeping, it had a kind of annoyed expression too, as if the dream it was dreaming was something uncomfortable which called for huge concentration. Ali put a hand to the shallow valley on the front of its chest. Cold softness. Not plastic, more like rubber.

She would bring it down and show her Mammy.

+

Ali scrubbed at her face with the towel until it stung, and flung the cloth on top of others discarded in a basket under the counter.

For twelve years she'd put it out of her mind. If she thought of that box at all, it was as some sort of a bad dream. But now it was back with her, as real as what she had seen in the shed.

She should go back and find Mary. Try to limit the damage. Tell her not to mention the bruising, say she might have been mistaken.

There was no one in the back bar, just their two abandoned glasses, conspiratorial on the table. But Mary hadn't gone far — she was in a window seat in the lounge, leaning forward to talk to a man in a grey suit. Ali walked towards her, and the man turned in his seat as he saw Mary's attention shift. Ali knew him. It was her mother's friend Sean O'Loan, a chubby man whose straggly moustache looked like it was trying to crawl inside his mouth.

Sean showed no surprise to see her there. He stood to shake her hand and kiss her cheek with a wet tickle.

'Ali, pet. So sorry for what you've been through.'

He put a hand on her shoulder and squeezed. Ali made a mumble of thanks.

'Fate's very cruel. It was the last thing you needed.'

His pouchy eyes were trying to dig into hers. The hand on her shoulder was a clamp. Sean's attention was beyond plain sympathy.

'The girl probably needs to get home, Sean' said Mary.

Alison took her chance to escape. She had no doubt that they'd been discussing her just before she appeared.

SEVEN

The nun who opened the convent door was dark and nervy. Swan's eyes moved automatically to her belly. Too skinny, he figured. But how could you be sure?

The entrance hall that she led TP Murphy and him into was a double height space with a grand wooden staircase rising up from the centre and dividing into two so that you had a choice of route to the railed gallery that ran around three sides of the upper area. A glass cupola brought light to the gallery, but it had lost most of its brightness by the time it fell to where they stood. The nun pointed at a row of ecclesiastical chairs against the wall. They were the least comfortable looking furniture Swan had ever seen outside of a designer showroom.

'Please, if you wait here,' said the nun, and he sat. TP Murphy eased himself into the next chair with a suppressed groan. The nun was clipping up the stairs now, leaving them to the gloom. Like Pavlov's dogs they were, at the sight of a habit.

Murphy was not Swan's first choice of partner for a case like this, or any case. But he was the only other Murder Squad detective available, since all the rest were up in Dundalk for a double shooting. TP was not only a leadswinger and a slipstreamer, he looked like a right throwback too, with those sideburns and aviator specs, not to mention the wide tie just hiding the gaps between his strained shirt buttons. The best you could say for him was that he didn't take anything too seriously.

Swan stood again, stretched his arms out unnecessarily and strolled about. The walls were crowded with paintings, a variety of saints suffering or beseeching behind layers of amber varnish. Only a few bright details shone out — the flash of an angel's wing, the white of an eye rolled heavenward, the glint of sword. There were also portraits of nuns sitting at their desks with a bible in handy reach or praying on their knees, their plain, redoubtable faces framed by elaborate arrangements of stiff white cloth.

He hated this atmosphere, the varnish and cold tile incarceration of it. Clearing out the attic that spring, he had come across a picture of himself in altar boy's vestments. Ten years old or so. The pious solemnity of his younger face, his small unlined hands pressed together and pointing skywards. Before he knew what he was doing, he'd torn the photograph to confetti.

The first stages of the investigation had turned up nothing. All the babies born in hospitals and registered maternity homes had been accounted for. A few tip offs were being followed up — a travellers' camp by the Dodder, a hippy commune in some old mansion. Most likely the mother was local and had given birth in secret. That was the simplest explanation, and Swan liked to keep things simple until he was forced to complicate them.

A small, precise cough drew their attention upwards. The nun had returned, and was gesturing for them.

They climbed up into the light. She led them down a series of corridors featuring the same orange-coloured wood everywhere, shiny panelling and rails and doors and benches. They finally stopped at the end of a wide corridor lined on one side with glass cases. Another row of straight-backed chairs stood to one side of the door and a small card on the door read *Reverend Mother* in crabbed gothic calligraphy. It was hard not to imagine a line of fretful small girls sitting there, awaiting punishment.

The nun took it upon herself to knock and a voice within called 'Come!'

Swan had been expecting Mother Mary Paul to be alone, so he did not welcome the sight of her sitting shoulder to shoulder behind her desk with a priest. The man was wearing a well-cut black suit and a dog collar. A gold chain with plain cross added to the elegant effect. He had close-cropped hair at the sides and a polished baldness on top. Maybe the nuns had given his pate a rub of the cloth in passing.

'This is Monsignor Kelly,' said Mother Mary Paul. 'The archbishop has been good enough to take a special interest in this tragic event, and has sent the monsignor to assist us. Monsignor Kelly is trained in law.'

The priest offered Swan a thin smile, verifying confidence in his qualifications.

Swan introduced TP, and they sat down on their side of the desk. Swan had hoped for an informal, wide-ranging chat. With God's lawyer present, he doubted if there would be much in the way of that. The monsignor already had a pen in his hand, poised over what looked like a typed list of names.

'I think it would help, detectives, to get us off the ground as it were, if you'd outline the scope of your investigation so far — and perhaps indicate which areas you think we might assist with, and we can take it from there.'

TP looked at Swan and crossed his arms. He was

on his own.

A knock sounded on the door, and the dark nun entered with a tea tray. No one spoke as she settled the tray on the desk, filled four cups and handed them around.

'Thank you, Sister Dreyfus,' said Reverend Mother as the nun exited backwards, the empty tray held to her chest like a shield.

Once the door had closed, Swan looked to the head nun. 'Sister *Dreyfus*?' He had decided to ignore the monsignor.

'It's an unusual name in these parts,' agreed Mother Mary Paul. She dropped her voice, and leaned towards him. 'Family came here in the war. Converted.'

'Yes,' said the monsignor, 'perhaps we could —'

'Tell me, Mother,' said Swan, riding over him, 'why is it that some nuns have Christian names after the 'Sister' and others have family names?'

Mary Paul stroked her veil as he had seen other women smooth their hair.

'Well, it varies from order to order. In the Sisters of the Annunciation, both apply. Nuns like Sister Dreyfus keep their family names while nuns such as myself and Sister Bernadette who you've... em... met, were moved to adopt the names of saints or holy people who had particular meaning for them. I took the name of our founder — Blessed Mary Paul Grammaticus.'

'I never realised that.'

'Most interesting,' said Monsignor Kelly without a shred of sincerity, 'but I'm eager to know, detectives, whether you've identified who the poor child was.'

Swan let TP waffle on a bit about the case, how everything that could be done was being done and so on. He told them the enquiries were concentrating on the community surrounding the convent grounds.

'I wish now that we had put gates across the back lane,' said the nun, 'but we've never been in the habit of locking our doors to the world.'

'That may have to change,' said Monsignor Kelly.

'It's difficult to lock the world out entirely,' said Swan. 'Besides, gates wouldn't necessarily have prevented this from happening, just meant it happened elsewhere. Unless the baby was already in the convent. In that case, our task might be narrower in scope'

The monsignor and the reverend mother stiffened.

'It's a theory I have to consider.'

'That isn't possible.' The nun was adamant.

'How can you be sure? This is a very large establishment, Mother.' Swan suddenly realised how odd, and somehow disloyal, it was to be calling an acquaintance *mother*.

'Out of term time it's a very quiet place. We nuns live together in a community with just a few lay helpers for the grounds. We eat and pray together every day. Not much goes by me.'

'So there's been nothing different?'

'Nothing.'

'I'll bear that in mind when I speak individually to the nuns.'

The monsignor and Mother Mary Paul exchanged a glance.

'Is it necessary at this stage?' asked the monsignor, 'The disruption and anxiety have taken their toll on these women already.' Mother Mary Paul looked annoyed for an instant, but worked her face into an expression of passivity. Not a women that cared to be patronised, even by a monsignor.

'I wouldn't be doing my job if I *didn't* interview the nuns. There is no accusation to be inferred — it's simply procedure.'

Monsignor Kelly sighed, but didn't press the matter further.

'I'll need a list of all the nuns, even if they weren't here on Monday, and also names and telephone numbers of the hired staff that you mentioned.'

Mary Paul jotted some notes.

'We'll need that today, Mother,' said TP, 'and it would benefit us if you could include each woman's age?'

The nun looked up. 'Their age?'

Swan's patience vanished.

'Look, we're not suggesting a strip search,' he said, 'We just need to know the age.'

Swan watched her write 'AGE' and underline it.

'As you can imagine,' said Monsignor Kelly, 'the phones have not stopped ringing here and at the diocesan office since news of this came out. The last thing we want to do is to fan the flames of any salacious publicity. The Archbishop is concerned that the police don't encourage this kind of insinuation by the line of their enquiries.'

And no doubt the Archbishop had many friends in Garda HQ and in the Dáil with whom he was willing to share those concerns.

'There is no insinuation, Monsignor. And for what it's worth, flames get fanned when an investigation can't progress quickly and the papers have to fall back on their imaginings.'

'It's confidentiality that concerns me — things leaking out.'

'Not from my investigations, they don't.'

Sometimes Swan wondered at his own idiot reflexes.

Monsignor Kelly smiled. 'You haven't seen this morning's papers, then.'

Swan looked at TP, who gave him back a miniscule head shake. They had been shut in the case conference, hadn't had the time. But someone would have shown him if there was anything important.

Swan arranged to have the list collected and said they would need to set up interviews with all of the nuns within the week.

'I realise that it's hard for you, for all the sisters, coming into contact with something like this.'

The look she gave him was fierce.

'Don't make the mistake of thinking we sit in our holy tower arranging flowers and sweeping floors. Some of my nuns work with the least fortunate in the city. They see poverty and degradation and death.'

'Point taken.'

Swan rose to his feet, TP followed.

'I just don't want them subject to suggestions of… promiscuity or whatever. It wouldn't be… fair.' She reached up her sleeve for the wad of tissue. He had wondered when it would appear.

Monsignor Kelly shifted one hand over so that it lay in front of the Reverend Mother. A restraint.

'The church will assist in whatever way it can. In fact, the Reverend Mother has thoughtfully drawn up a list of girls she thought might be worth talking to for your purposes.'

The monsignor passed the piece of paper that had been lying on the table to Swan. He sat back down to study it. It was a list of girls' names, divided up into little sections headed 'sixth-year' 'fifth-year' and 'fourth-year'. The second half was divided by year headings 1983, 1982, 1981. There were about thirty names in all.

'It wasn't necessary to go any younger than fourth year, I thought.' Mother Mary Paul had recovered herself. 'The others are girls who left in the last few years.'

Swan just looked at her.

'We thought it would help,' said Monsignor Kelly, 'if you had a list of girls who their teachers suspected may have been in intimate contact with boyfriends and the like.'

'How can they tell?' said Swan.

'You can't, for sure,' said Mary Paul, in a reasonable tone. 'But in every year there are always a few who test the limits, and no doubt test their parents too. They're the risk takers, and sometimes they wind up in trouble.'

'Do you have a reason to believe that any of these girls were pregnant?'

'Just one for certain. Sixth year... Eileen Vaughan.'

Swan found the name on the list.

'She's not the one you're after though.'

'Oh?'

'She left the school in March. I've enquired and she was delivered back in May.' The nun pressed her lips together.

'I'll need her address. And all these others?'

'Suggestions.'

'Thank you, we'll look into it.'

Swan took the list, folded it and put it in his inside pocket. The hypocrisy of them. It wouldn't be right to mention sex to any of the nuns, but here's a bunch of schoolgirls you might want to grill instead. Again he rose to his feet, and this time the nun and priest rose too. TP's hand was on the doorknob when Mother Mary Paul's grave voice said, 'Perhaps a little prayer for the baby?'

They stood with clasped hands and bowed heads while the nun led them in a Hail Mary linked to some longer bit that Swan only half-recognised. Who was the hypocrite now? He mumbled the 'Amen'.

Monsignor Kelly walked them back through the maze of empty corridors, trying to interest TP Murphy in the history of the building. Swan's mind was on the list of girls. Just because their teachers thought them a bit wild didn't make them child murderers. Even if this Eileen Vaughan had been politely disappeared, that just proved the point. Most of these girls would be well taken care of if they slipped up — a trip down the country for a few months or a shorter trip to England in some cases. Swan knew infanticide mainly happened in conditions of ignorance or secrecy. It wasn't the bolshy, confident girls you wanted. It was the quiet, mousy ones with only a vague grasp of the mechanics, or the ones being abused at home, or by a neighbour or friend of the family. Friend of the family. That's how they always referred to some old bastard with his eye on the kids.

Thing was, this time felt different. The other cases he knew were plain tragic, drenched with desperation. But this one: three days of food and care, love perhaps, before someone changed their mind. Maybe the mother was being watched by her own mother, say, and had to wait for her chance to do away with her child. Or was it the reverse — the mother had been content with the child, then someone else had discovered its existence?

Outside, Monsignor Kelly stepped into a shining black Mercedes and drove off with a roar.

'Great car,' said TP Murphy as it swept

out the gate.

'Off to another crime against the faith,' said Swan, 'Do you ever get the feeling there's more than one police force in this town?'

'If it wasn't for the whole celibacy stuff, I'd join theirs.'

'I can't quite see that,' said Swan.

'You'd pass,' said TP, 'you've a whiff of the incense about you, and we've never seen this wife you claim to have.'

Swan glanced back and caught sight of a pale old nun watching their departure from a first floor window.

A maroon Ford was pulled up beside their brown one. DS Barrett was propped against it, reading a paper in a slightly studied way. At the opposite end of the car, Detective Garda Gina Considine stood with her arms crossed, scanning the convent windows.

Barrett folded the paper back on itself and held it up in front of his chest like a sign. 'You should look at this.'

Swan took the paper and TP pressed in beside him to share the reading. The pictures registered first; a portrait of Alison Hogan looking like she'd lost her puppy, a landscape shot of the gate to the Rosary Garden, its metal scrolls thinned with rust in a way that looked suddenly sinister. And at the top of the page the incongruously smiling face of Mary O'Shea rested on a thick stripe of black, below it the headline: Suffer the Little Children: the Tragedy of The Rosary Baby.

Shit.

Less than forty-eight hours since the find and she was interviewing key witnesses. How had they got hold of that daft girl? He skimmed the article: *Under the petrified gaze of a stone pieta — eerie bower — tiny corpse*

— *privileged walls*. It was mostly a colour piece, a lot of breast beating about the truths behind respectable surfaces — nothing substantial. Swan's glance froze on one sentence. *According to witnesses the baby did not die of exposure, but suffered a violent death at the hands of a person or persons unknown.'*

Ali Hogan was quoted extensively, saying although she was shocked by the find, she couldn't find it in herself to condemn. *'This can be a cruel country for girls in trouble.'* The article went on to say that even in a school like this, girls were not immune to mistakes and that St. Brigid's had experienced one schoolgirl pregnancy last year. *Shit and damn.*

This was what the monsignor meant about leaks. Summer was slow news time and this was probably only the start. Give me a nice bank shoot-out any day, thought Swan, where nobody feels they have to talk through the symbolism of it all.

The article took up a whole half page. Superintendent Kavanagh was bound to see it and he would have to endure a session in the great man's office, laced through with anecdotes about the glens of his youth.

Swan shook the paper, folded it clumsily and thrust it back at Barrett.

'Why am I only seeing this now?'

'It's the second edition, boss. Wasn't in the first.'

'And what are you doing here, Considine?'

'Dinner time. No-one's answering my calls. Thought I'd take the chance to have a look at St. Brigid's. If that's okay.'

'She was very insistent,' said Barrett.

'Good you're here. I need you to go down to Clare — check out this baby Ali Hogan's supposed to have found twelve years ago.'

'I could phone the local guards.'

'No. Do it face to face. Find out what happened — if anything happened at all. Be sure, but don't waste time.'

'Yeah,' said Barrett.

'Have you not got back anything more from forensics?'

'We've a blood type on the baby, but no post mortem yet.'

'Jesus. Give me the type.'

Barrett pulled a notepad from his pocket and looked at the last page.

'Blood type A, boss.'

Common as brown hair or blue eyes. He'd hoped for something a little more exotic.

Swan took the list the monsignor gave him from his breast pocket and scanned it quickly. Sure enough, the name *Alison Hogan* appeared in the list under the heading 'Sixth Year'. Risk taking, attention seeking.

'Back to the phones, both of you. None of this is good. You and I should swing by and pay the Hogan girl a visit, Murphy. Screw the lid on.'

EIGHT

A dying note of pipe and fiddle whined from the big monitor hanging in the corner of the greenroom. The screen showed a close-up of Gay Byrne applauding. Pointing off-camera, he said, 'Ladies and Gentlemen, the legendary Chieftains!'

The applause engulfed him like a flurry before he soothed it down with an elegant swoop of his hands and moved on to announce the next item on the programme.

The door of the greenroom opened and the six members of The Chieftains walked in, passing close enough to nod to Ali as they headed to the drinks table, some with instruments still in hand. It was weird, like a photograph in a book suddenly coming to life. Ali clutched the wet neck of her beer bottle and tried to still her nerves.

She would be enjoying it all if she didn't have to go out that door and be in front of the cameras herself. Mary O'Shea was on the other side of the room chatting happily to a small curly-haired woman from the North who Ali had often seen on *The Late Late*. In a corner beyond them, a middle-aged man sat on his own, looking very serious as he flipped through a wedge of papers. He looked familiar too.

The Late Late Show. It would be like walking naked down Grafton Street with a neon arrow over her head. Up on the screen, Gay was talking to two men who had rowed around Ireland in a *currach*. They'd been here just five minutes before, a pair of burly lads debating whether to keep their Aran jumpers on in the stifling heat. Comfort won the argument, and now their pull-overs lay discarded on a greenroom sofa like a couple of empty sheep.

Mary had phoned Ali at home that morning — her newspaper article had gotten a huge response, she said.

'They want both of us, Ali. On *The Late Late*. And you're not to worry, its not about the case — they want to talk about girls and sex education, so I told them you'd be good for that — a real girl, for god's sake. It's a great opportunity.'

Ali had let herself imagine it. A sea of blurry faces, all turned to her. Being scared was no reason not to do it, though. She had been mortified when she had read Mary's article, all those quotes that made her sound firm and opinionated. But Mary was right. Girls her age never did get the chance to speak out. A light would shine on her and she would be tested.

Her mother was mad with pride, and slipped her money for a taxi to the studios. She had already bought three copies of the newspaper with Mary's article in it.

'It's a lovely photograph,' she said, 'despite the circumstances.'

Davy had mastered a wicked impersonation of the newspaper photo and would tilt his head to one side and jut out his lower lip each time Ali passed him in the house. Meanwhile, Fitz was mysteriously unavailable whenever she phoned, and Ali worried that she was angry with her for the reference to Eileen lurking in Mary's column.

Detective Swan had called round with another man on Wednesday afternoon, angry with her too. The men sat in the kitchen, drinking coffee, like they were on a social call between crimes, but then Detective Swan started in on how *personally disappointed* he was. At least her mother had had the grace to take a bit of the blame, passing the buck onto Sean O'Loan, making out that the press had squeezed details out of them against their will. Ali promised there would be no more talk of what she had seen.

Yet here she was, waiting to go on television.

At the RTE studios a skinny-hipped girl collected her from reception and rushed her up two flights of stairs. The girl had big earphones hanging around her neck as if she had recently been unplugged from some important broadcasting machine.

'There —' the girl opened a door on a crowded office. Mary O'Shea was sitting on a desk in the middle, swinging her crossed legs for an audience of two young men in shirtsleeves.

'Ali!' she cried when she spotted her, thrusting both arms out as if a hug was expected. The men turned to look at her, appraising. Ali threaded her way towards them through a maze of desks.

'Look at you! Look at your dress — so sweet.'

'Maybe I should have worn something more— '

'No, no, sweet is fine. Sweet is more than fine. We don't want them thinking you're a hard-nosed old bag like me.' And Mary threw back her head and laughed at the thought. The men joined in.

'I'm worried what to say.'

'Just nerves. By Tuesday you'll be a pro.'

'Tuesday?'

'My radio show. Remember? We'll see how things go tonight, and work up a few topics together beforehand — that thing you said the other day about girls not knowing their sexual desires — that could be dynamite.'

The two men looked at Ali with renewed interest.

Mary put an arm around her and was saying how fine everything was going to be, when there was a shift in the atmosphere.

A slight figure in a blue suit had entered the room, causing all around to change their behaviour, the loud ones fell silent, the diligent ones lifted their heads from their typewriters and called out for attention.

It was Gay. Gaybo. Mr. Byrne. He managed to looked both mild and of consequence and his charisma was unsullied by a ruff of tissues sticking out from his collar to protect it from the fall of peachy powder that covered his face. He had a certain grace, like a dancing master.

Gay made even Mary look like an ordinary Joe. His radio show was bigger, and his TV show was required viewing, as obligatory for most people as mass. *The Late Late Show* had always been there, as long as Ali could remember. You never knew beforehand who would be on — politicians, movie stars, farmers, ventriloquists — and there might just be something remarkable.

Gay waved over in their direction.

'He never talks to guests before the show,' Mary whispered.

Ali watched him on the greenroom monitor, swiveling behind his desk and chatting to the *currach* men, taking polite questions from a beaming audience, laughing often. It would be okay. The beer in her mouth tasted of nothing at all, but something like vinegar was swilling around her stomach.

The girl with the snake hips appeared beside her.

'You're next.'

She gathered up Mary O'Shea and the quiet man from the corner and herded the three of them downstairs to stand together in the darkness at the edge of the bright studio.

'... and we'll be back with you after the break.' Gay's voice came from beyond a tangle of cameras and equipment.

Chatter rose from the audience while Ali's group was guided forward over cables into a lit arena. They were directed to a curved line of chairs facing a seating bank full of people. Microphones pointed at them from the low table in front. A hundred lights pressed down, baking the mascara that the make-up girl had pasted on Ali's lashes to a tight crust.

Someone called for hush and Gay walked towards the audience. Ali looked across to Mary for reassurance, and Mary smiled briefly at her before reapplying her eyes to Gay, who had started to speak.

'... we're not going to go over old ground here, so you can put your badges and banners away. What we have here is a human story, a sad story, a story about some things that maybe don't change, even after all the talk. Tonight we have with us a young woman, Alison Hogan, from Ranelagh here in Dublin. You might know from the papers that Alison was the person who found the child now known as the Rosary Baby. Despite this ordeal, she has gone on to make a public plea for better sex education in schools and for the abolition of illegitimacy as a legal category.'

Ali frowned at his back, not recognising the girl he was describing. He was making it sound like she had held a press conference or something.

'And we're delighted to welcome back journalist and women's rights campaigner Mary O'Shea, who has been collaborating with Ali. We also have with us an expert on sex education in schools and author of the bestselling pamphlets *Life Talks for Boys* and *Life Talks for Girls*, Doctor Donald Beasley…'

The audience were clapping politely now, but Ali wasn't looking at them. She had turned to stare at the man who had been in the greenroom and was now sitting just on the other side of Mary.

How could she not have recognised him? The knitted brow and slightly prissy expression. Doctor Beasley was the man who had spent a day with the second year girls of St. Brigid's explaining the romance of the sperm and the egg. His detailing of private parts and monthly cycles had impressed them at the time because they had never heard anyone speak in that way. She remembered the manic embarrassment of that day and coming away from the hall quietly, carrying strange knowledge like a weight.

Before she had time to collect herself, Gay was upon her.

'Alison, we're not here tonight to talk about the Rosary Baby case. The Gardaí are still looking for the mother, and its all *hush hush* for now.'

Ali nodded, not chancing a word.

'I was just wondering, though, how have you coped with coming across something like that? A thing no one, let alone a young girl, should see?'

Ali turned her face so that he was the only one in her vision. She would pretend that this was a normal conversation.

She opened her mouth and spoke, realising within a sentence that she had to make a choice between thinking and talking. She started with something her mother had said about not being able to understand why someone couldn't have handed the child over alive, and let her mouth flow from there, listening in to what she was saying after she had said it. She railed against the hiddenness of things, she raised the issue of contraception. Gay was running out of sympathetic nods, was starting to look a little alarmed. She found the end of a thought and pulled up to a halt. The last thing she said was, '... we don't seem to want these babies that we go on about loving so much.'

Her heart was hammering but maybe it hadn't been so bad after all. She had spoken for her generation.

The audience were muttering, shifting in their seats.

'Ah now,' said Gay, 'Surely this case is not the normal run of things.'

'I think it happens all the time.' Her words were defiant, but she spoke quietly, not wanting an argument, not wanting anything now but to go home.

'We'll come back to that,' said Gay.

A few hands poked up rigid among the heads and shoulders in front of her — bids put in with Gay for future notice. He didn't pay them any attention, but turned to the other guests.

'Donald, Alison here seems dissatisfied with the way she was taught the facts of life. Now you're the man that devises those classes — do you think there's a need for a new approach?'

'Hello, Alison,' said Dr. Beasley with a creeping smile, as if he remembered her well.

'We only aim to supplement the parents' own teachings, you understand, Gay. The home is still the foundation of sexual morals.' He spoke on about the merits, the responsible science, of his own system. Mary jumped in to question whether it wouldn't be better for a woman to be teaching these things to girls. Ali half-listened, but was also trying to replay her own impassioned speech and see if she had said anything stupid. Her eyes ran over the faces in the audience, some sneaking their eyes diagonally upwards to check the monitors and see if their reactions were being broadcast home.

Mary was getting worked up, plying her outstretched hands as if she was shaking an invisible football. She was angry with Beasley about something, then she turned and pointed to Ali, saying something about St. Brigid's. Ali strained to pay proper attention, but her mind kept skating around, thoughts like beads on glass.

'That's hardly my fault.' Beasley said.

Gay swiveled to look straight at Ali.

'Do *you* blame the doctor, Ali?'

'For what?'

'For what you told me,' Mary interrupted, 'about the girl in your school that got pregnant and went missing...'

'Missing?' asked Gay. There was a silence without air, a vacuumed-out pause waiting for her.

'Not missing,' Ali managed to say. 'She left our year, that's all.'

Mary rode away with it. 'You see, it happens again and again — whisked away — a whole culture of secrecy.'

The audience was simmering, desperate to add their bit. Hands strained towards Gay, patting the air. He finally turned, scanned the rows.

'We can't discuss individual cases, of course — let's go to our audience. Sir!' he said, pointing into the crowd.

A strained-looking man with a side parting stood up.

'I have fourteen children,' he paused, 'and each one is a precious gift from God.'

'Is your wife with you tonight?' Mary called out. A twitch of a smile moved on Gay's lips.

'As it happens, she's at home…' The sound of female laughter drowned out the rest of his words, and Gay pointed at someone else, leaving the man stranded, with no choice but to sit back down. A woman in a yellow tweed jacket stood up and looked at Ali. She had a tight, excited look about her.

'I have a daughter just your age, and do you know, I'm terrified for her. Terrified. There's so much pressure on her to have sex — from the media, from boys, from other girls even. Tell me, as a young one yourself, how do you stand firm?'

Ali was at a loss. She tried to imagine what Mary would say.

'Maybe I don't.' A slight gasp came from the audience, and Gay wheeled around to look at her. 'Maybe it's not just about girls saying no, but about ways of not bringing an unwanted child into the world. Ways that are more effective than what we were taught.'

'Promiscuity is hardly a solution!' shouted Beasley.

The woman with the question raised her voice. 'Well I'm glad my daughter isn't a little slut like you,' she said.

'Ah now! There's no need…' said Gay, but the audience was in uproar again, everyone talking at once, Mary and Dr. Beasley leaning forwards to speak into their microphones. Ali caught sight of the monitor to one side of the stage and her own face was filling it — stricken eyes, flaming cheeks.

+

Swan sat in his mother's front room, disbelieving his eyes and ears. His mother was on her knees at the side of his chair, mopping up the tea he had knocked over when Alison Hogan had appeared on the television screen.

'Leave it!' he said again.

'Don't be at me. It's my rug and I'll save it if I want.'

Her gray head bobbed by his left elbow. He could either argue or listen to what that little rag was saying about the case, and he should know by now that his mother was immune to argument. The innocence of the Hogan girl's face was amazing, given her lust for the spotlight. Two days ago she'd sworn to him that she wouldn't talk to any more journalists and he'd believed her, and now here she was opinioning away about the state of the nation. She was trouble.

Just as well he'd sent Considine down to the country to look into the girl's past, that other baby. With any luck it would turn out to be nothing, bad dreams, imagination.

His mother exhaled an *oof* as she got up and threw the dishtowel over onto the table, where the remains of their dinner still lay.

'I've a lot of time for that Mary O'Shea,' she said, settling back into her chair.

Swan grunted assent. His mother's appreciation was probably of a different flavour to his own. That night he met her briefly at the theatre, he'd fluffed it. Words had failed him. He was still amazed that someone as elegant as Elizabeth had agreed to marry him, but Mary O'Shea, she was in another league entirely.

The screen was filled with Ali Hogan's face, a glisten of tears in her eyes, the whipped look of her. Hard to fake that.

'She's not getting an easy ride, your girl. Did you see that aul' bitch in the audience go for her?'

'No one made her go on,' said Swan, 'I'm not sure the nuns at her school will appreciate it.'

'Pity about them.' Mrs. Swan took up the paper, folded it to the crossword page. 'The spare bed is still made up if you want to stay. Save you going back to an empty house'

'Ach, I shouldn't,' said Swan, but his attention had returned to the screen.

+

Mary was saying how we would do well to listen to young people rather than old men. Doctor Beasley got offended at being referred to as an old man and started tugging at his tie.

'Eh — eh — eh — ' he said, stuttering to find a gap in Mary's tirade. Gay held his hands out, one palm facing the audience, the other towards his guests.

'Please.' Silence fell at once.

Out of the corner of her eye, Ali noticed one of the cameras rolling silently towards her.

'Mary, you said back there that no-one could understand what Alison had been through, and Alison herself said a curious thing. You said you thought things like this happen all the time. Last week wasn't the first time you've seen this kind of tragedy, was it? Is that why it matters so much to you?'

Ali looked at Mary, but Mary was just staring back at her, waiting. She remembered Sean O'Loan talking to Mary at the Shelbourne. Her mother must have told Sean what had happened in Buleen. She wouldn't discuss it with her own daughter, but she had told Sean.

'Is there anything you can tell us about that?' Gay was in touching distance now.

The camera moved a little closer. There was a red light beside the lens, just like a little warning. She thought of all the people beyond that lens, watching her. Aunt Una and the rest them at the farmhouse.

'I was six... I can't really remember.'

But that was a lie. The memories were turning up in force now, pressing their noses against the glass, wanting to be let in.

+

'God help me, I'm a dreadful mother.'

'Jesus,' said Davy, 'He's talking about what happened at the farm. Isn't he?'

Ali's face stretched across the old black and white screen at the foot of Deirdre Hogan's bed.

I was six... I can't really remember. Ali's voice as thin as wire from the little speaker.

Gay moved the discussion back to Mary O'Shea, then rounded it up without going back to Ali. As the cameras drew back for the end shot they could see she was looking at her knees, not up at the cameras like the others.

'She was so excited to go on — I should have stopped her.'

'Well, you didn't.' Davy got up from the little armchair draped in clothes, and leaned over the end of the bed to reach the set. 'Do you want me to turn it off?'

'No, just turn the sound down a bit.'

'You shouldn't have told that policeman,' he said with his face turned from her. He heard her sigh,

'Well it was just so weird, you know, happening again. You remember it, don't you?'

'Not much…'

'Ach, you were practically a child yourself.'

'I was sixteen.'

Davy left his sister to her regrets and went down to the big sparse room he'd been using as his own. He pulled a suitcase from under the single bed. It was an old case that Una had turned up from somewhere in the farmhouse, made out of cardboardy stuff and reinforced with metal corners and clasps, sandy with corrosion. He dragged a pile of his things out of a corner cupboard, started throwing them into the case.

Dublin wasn't far enough, that was the problem. Things hadn't worked out this time, but once he had some money, he could do it properly, go further. A fresh start. He snapped the clasps shut.

The only thing left in the cupboard was that cheap bottle of whiskey, plenty left. He grabbed it and spun the top off with a swipe of his hand. He remembered that Christmas all right, much better than his sister ever could.

+

The farmhouse had been full to bursting. Una's four kids were home from school, and Deirdre and Ali were staying with them since Ciaran's funeral. The only peace he could get was late at night. He'd go down to the kitchen, drink a coffee, listen to the big radio. He could tune in to a foreign station and pretend he was somewhere else — somewhere with pavement cafés, jazz clubs and cobbled streets, not a boghole in the middle of nowhere.

On Christmas Eve, he'd gone downstairs at about two. The light over the range was on as usual. There were presents for the kids on the table, some wrapped, some not. He didn't even notice her at first. He filled the kettle at the tap and stepped over the dog on the way to the range.

'You get up on the sofa, boy, I'll tell no-one.'

But the dog stayed where he was, his eyes fixed on the heap of rugs on the sofa, like he was scared of it, his tail sweeping slowly across the flagstones, gathering crumbs. The heap gave a groan and Davy nearly jumped out of his skin. A glob of water hopped from the kettle spout and hissed on the hotplate.

He was annoyed. He couldn't have his peace with her sleeping there. Why couldn't she go home? She groaned again, deep like a cow lowing, and the dog moved a step closer, keeping his belly to the floor.

She must have heard him, but wouldn't let on, her face turned to the sofa back. When he'd asked her about her condition before, asked her straight, she'd denied it, wearing a big man's jumper to cover it, struggling to bend or rise.

He took the dog by the scruff and led him out to his kennel in the yard. Then he stood by the kitchen window and looked back in at her. She threw the blanket off after a time, and he could see everything; the sweat on her, the strain in her bare legs. It was a cold night and he wasn't dressed for it, but he couldn't go back in. The moon gleamed off the pig shed roofs and frost whitened the upper field.

Eventually she heaved herself off the sofa and squatted beside it, hanging on to the arm, looking down into herself. She was huffing and grunting, the hair plastered to her skull. Somewhere in the middle of it she turned her head and looked at the window, looked right through him.

He remembered the awful streaks of blood on her haunches as something bulged and slithered from them and onto the dirty rug she had put beneath her. She was bent over the mite, arse in the air, pulling at the cord that joined them. He saw a puny arm rise from the rug, trembling with anger was what it looked like, shaking its little knot of fist in the air, and he felt exultant, something bursting in his chest, coming from nothing and filling him full.

NINE

When Ali got to the bus stop outside the RTE studio there was already a group of people gathered there. Several turned to look at her.

'Don't they drop you home in a limo?' said one women.

They were from the audience. Ali looked at her watch and walked away from the bus stop as if she simply didn't have the time to wait. Maybe there really was a limo — she hadn't stayed around to find out. Now she'd have to walk home.

She could hardly believe how her mouth had run away with her. Imagine talking about sex like she knew what she was on about. She had *had* sex. A couple of times, but it wasn't what she thought it would be, it was clumsy and mystifying, not the transformative experience she had been expecting.

Ali turned up Eglington Road, limping in her high heels now, but half way home. A car drove by slowly and came to a halt in front of her, its brake lights glowing. She moved closer to the houses on her left and looked away from the car as she passed it. She heard it start up again but thankfully it just continued off up the road. She remembered the heavy makeup she was still wearing. The heels, no coat — she must look a sight. She stopped and unbuckled the straps of her shoes. Better barefoot than hobbled. She kept her eyes on the pavement ahead for streams of liquid or glints of glass.

Why had her mother never discussed the first baby with her, never tried to explain things, let her believe it was in her head? Her aunt and uncle, they had seen it too, but no one could speak of it. Someone must know who that baby was, where it came from. She recalled how her mother lay in bed all day, upstairs in the farmhouse, crying and crying, the curtains closed.

'You okay?'

Ali was standing at the edge of the pavement, waiting for the lights to change. She might have been standing for some time. A girl was stepping onto the crossing, hand in hand with a sullen man. She craned her neck to look back at Ali.

'Okay?' she asked again, and her boyfriend tugged her onwards, away from involvement.

'Fine...' Ali managed, and trotted across behind them.

She was glad to see the pool of light that fell on the pavement from the all-night shop. Her home was behind the shop. After her father died, Ma sold their little house and bought a property full of sitting tenants and with a shop out front for rent. It was the practical thing to do, she explained. When her mother told her their new house had a shop in its front garden, Ali imagined it as some kind of little striped kiosk in the middle of a green lawn. What her mother should have said was that there was a shop *instead* of a front garden. She walked up the narrow passage at the shop side and into a small yard filled with bread trays and stacks of flattened boxes. The house rose like a cliff in front of her, stone steps leading up to the front door. Above it, her mother's bedroom light shone through the gap in her curtains.

Ali opened and shut the front door quietly. There were no signs of life downstairs, but she could hear the muffled sound of the television above. She went up.

Her mother's room was large, stretching across the front of the house. It functioned as a workroom as well as a bedroom, now that her mother had taken up mending china as another way to make a bit of money. A huge dining table filled one side of the room, covered with broken things — dishes, vases, a large statue of the Child Of Prague, and dozens of ornaments missing vital pieces. Saucers of glue and paint sat along the edge, wooden sticks and brushes bristled from jam jars.

On the other side was her mother's ornate bed, hemmed in by small tables toppling with book, draped chairs and screens, lamps, and in the middle of it all, like a hen on her nest, her hair loose over her shoulders, her mother waited.

Ali sat on the edge of the bed. A film with subtitles was playing on the TV; a beautiful woman in a tight shift dress leant smoking against a wall while a man remonstrated with her. Ali promised herself a cigarette once she'd got this over with.

'You watched it, I presume.'

'Your dress looked nice...' said Ma.

'Jesus, my *dress*?'

Ma looked away, blinked quickly. Ali took a deep breath, tried to keep her voice steady.

'You told Sean O'Loan, didn't you? About what happened in Buleen.'

'I was upset that night. It just came out. I'm sorry. And I should have stopped you going on that.' Her mother pointed at the television.

'You have to tell me about it, Ma.'

'I wasn't even sure you remembered, you never mention it.'

After all these years, they were talking about it. The thing that couldn't be spoken of was out in the world.

'It was your baby wasn't it?

'What — No!

'It would have been my brother or sister.'

Her mother put a quick hand to Ali's shoulder.

'Really, it wasn't. God, things were bad enough, but no, not that. I can't believe you thought that.'

Ali looked back at her.

'Then who?'

Ma hesitated.

'I always presumed it was Joan's — do you remember Joan? Its funny, I never even asked Una about it. It was such an odd time. All I could think of was losing your father — I'd nothing to spare for someone else's troubles.'

Ali cast her mind back to Joan, who cooked the meals at her uncle's farm. Freckle-faced Joan, who was timid in company but so funny when the two of them were alone in that big kitchen, Joan who sang songs about bathtubs and farting, who showed her how to roll out pastry, and let her mark the cross on the brown bread before it went into the range.

Ali stood up and wandered over to the work table. She picked up a little Bambi-like fawn that was lying on its side, four delicate broken legs sticking out rigidly from its white spotted belly.

Her mother reached for the glass on her bedside table. 'She came from an odd family, you know. I'm not sure what went on there. I'd no idea she was expecting. She still comes to the farm sometimes, Una says, looking for her job back — though she's been in and out of hospital mostly. Psychiatric.'

'Because of what happened to her baby?'

'I'm not sure. She was always a bit not there, a bit

wandering. I really did think you'd forgotten.'

Ali balanced the fawn gently on its stumps so that it appeared to be wading lopsided through the polished grain of the tabletop. A little oval base lay nearby with four matchstick hooves protruding from it, tiny blades of grass painted about them.

'Some of these things have been here forever,' said Ali, 'If you can't mend them, you should get rid of them.'

'Hey,' said Ma, 'what's all this about you campaigning for better sex education?'

'That's not what I said.'

'Or more contraception or something.'

'I looked like a right fool.'

'No, love, not at all.'

They lapsed into silence. A raucous burst of Italian came from the TV. Ali lifted her eyes. A young man was being chased through a market but he was laughing as he ran. She wanted to run with him.

'Mary O'Shea wants me to go on her radio show.'

Her mother tilted her head, then quickly shook it. 'I'm not sure that's —'

'I don't *want* to — I'm never going to leave the house again.'

'That's a bit melodramatic.'

Ali picked up the little Bambi figure and laid it on its side once more. She ran her finger down the sharp chalky edge of a broken soup tureen.

'Don't!' said Ma. 'I did buy you that doll, you know.'

'What?'

'The doll you were looking for. Baby Tears or whatever it was called, but I couldn't find it to wrap it for you. I thought I was going mad... well, I was going mad, those days.

'I know.'

'You should go to bed, love. It'll feel better in the morning.'

Ali went over and bent to kiss her mother goodnight. The yeasty smell of the bedclothes rose around her like a comfort.

She didn't go up to her room, but crept downstairs to stand outside Davy's door. No light shone from under it. Ali pressed her ear to the yellowed paint of one panel and listened hard. There was a gently whooshing sound that could have been his breathing, deep in sleep, but might just as well have been the sound of her own blood circulating.

'Davy?' She spoke quietly into the crack of the doorjamb.

'Yea?' The reply came loud and from the right. Ali jumped and turned to see Davy emerging from the dark of the back hall, grinning, a glass in hand.

'You bastard.'

She followed him back to the kitchen, crossed it quickly and turned on the small light over the cooker. On the table stood a bottle with a yellow label — *Queen Anne Whiskey* emblazoned in garish script.

'What are you doing in the dark?'

'Pull up a pew and sample some hard liquor. I'm having a wake.'

Davy was drinking from the glass with the Flintstones drawings on it, one she loved when she was a kid. She fetched a glass for herself — a fancy-looking stemmed one from a petrol station giveaway.

'What are we having a wake for — is it me?'

'You were all right.'

'I don't remember half of what I said. It was a nightmare.'

The whiskey was harsh and smelt of disinfectant. She went to the sink and diluted it.

'I would say… you don't make things easy for yourself.'

Ali groaned and pressed the heel of her hand into her forehead.

Davy smiled and shook his head slowly, 'Cheers.'

She sat across from him, took her packet of ten out of her dress pocket and lit a cigarette. 'So, what are you celebrating?'

'Celebrate is too strong a word,' said Davy, flapping his hand to divert the smoke. 'I've got a job.'

'Brilliant. Where?'

'Buleen. My family needs me, it seems.'

'You're going back already? We're your family too.'

'I can't go on living off your mother.'

'I do.'

Davy laughed and poured himself another drink, pointed the bottle at her. Ali put her hand over the top of her glass.

'Thanks, but it's disgusting.'

'Two ninety-nine. It should be disgusting.' He clinked his glass against hers forcefully, a dull *thunk*. 'Brendan's got this business thing…' Davy spun a hand in the air, looking for words. 'Gaming machines in pubs. He needs a hand. He'll pay.'

She watched his hand come to rest on the table and thought about touching it.

'Can I come with you?'

'Don't know if you're strong enough, those machines are bloody heavy.'

'I'd like to get away from Dublin, Davy, far away from Mary O'Shea.'

'I wouldn't run away from her.' He leered over the rim of his glass.

'Shut up. Will you ask Una if I can come and stay?'

'No need. Sure, she's always asking about you. Our darling niece. You haven't visited them in years.'

She swirled the last of her whiskey and water round the glass.

'I was talking to Ma just now about the time we stayed with you, you know.'

Davy frowned into the depths of his drink.

'Do you remember?'

When he looked up his eyes swam with the effort of focusing. Ali left him at the table, kissing the top of his head as she passed and making him promise to go to bed soon.

She went to the sink in her bedroom, turned on the tap and waited for the water to run hot. It didn't. She shut it off and went to bed with her clothes on.

TEN

The cat would be raging — it was way past his usual breakfast time. Swan shoved his newspaper and packet of rashers under one arm while he struggled with the front door mortice lock. It took him a moment to realise it was already unlocked, that's why he couldn't turn the key. He slipped the Yale into the lock above, clicking the door open easily.

Benny was sitting in the middle of the hall, licking himself, a back paw sticking up over his shoulder like a Nazi salute. He'd obviously had his breakfast and was on to the next task of the day. Beside him was Elizabeth's small blue case. A smell of coffee beckoned from the kitchen.

'Vincent?'

His wife didn't sound worried or annoyed, just calmly checking that it was her husband rather than a key-toting stranger. She was sitting at the breakfast room table, the garden a blaze of greens behind her.

'I stayed at my mother's,' he said. 'She needed the bit of company. When did you get back?'

'Aunt Bridie was driving up early to the sales. She dropped me off half an hour ago.'

'You should've phoned.'

Elizabeth shrugged. Swan placed the paper in front of her, put the bacon in the fridge, and helped himself to coffee from the pot on the table.

'How's Aunt Josie?'

'Oh you know… up and down.' Elizabeth was scanning the front of the paper, didn't look at him as she spoke. 'How are things with you?'

'I guess up and down would cover it,' said Swan.

They never talked much about his work. He preferred it that way, preferred to keep her away from it. She was wearing a pale lilac jumper he couldn't recall having seen before.

Not for the first time he wondered whether there was a secret part to her life. He had absolutely no reason to doubt her. Elizabeth had always been close to her posse of aunts in Kilkenny. As they entered their fragile years, frequent health crises naturally pulled their only young relation back to them. But it was hard to judge the urgency of their calls, why they needed her to stay so often.

'It isn't as though I've much to do here,' Elizabeth had said as she packed. Her voice was apologetic but somewhere in that statement another intention lurked — something pointed.

'That film you wanted to see is on at the Carlton,' she said now, 'the one with the gangsters.'

'I have to go in to work for a while — but I should be free in the evening.'

She took her eyes from the paper and studied him.

'They should give you a proper weekend. You look tired.'

'It's been a busy week.'

The light shifted in her eyes. 'It's not the baby case is it? Oh, Vincent…'

This was why he preferred not to tell her things. Especially this case. Now she was upsetting herself, and it had nothing to do with them. *Oh Vincent…* like he'd brought the corpse home in his briefcase.

'I think we should look at the garden after coffee

— talk about that arch thing you said you wanted.'

Elizabeth produced a patient sigh. 'If you like.'

+

Swan was changing into his work clothes when the doorbell rang. Elizabeth went to answer it and he heard a woman's voice in the hall. By the time he got downstairs Gina Considine was sitting at his table and Elizabeth was asking if she wanted tea or coffee.

Considine was only a bit younger than his wife, but they made such a contrasting pair that he felt like he was looking at women from different eras; Elizabeth subtle and airy in her pale clothes, a vase of garden flowers beside her, Considine with angled cuts in her black hair, shiny leather boots, jacket belted tight against all comers.

They hardly acknowledged his arrival. He could feel the charge of mutual curiosity between them, the way Considine followed his wife with her eyes, the returning glances that Elizabeth kept sneaking over her shoulder as she prepared tea.

The mug that Elizabeth put in front of Considine was sprigged with little pink roses.

'I'll leave you two to talk.' She closed the door behind her.

'Sorry,' said Considine, 'I didn't mean to intrude. Your wife insisted. Barrett said to come and collect you if I had the time.'

'Where's Barrett?'

'Following up leads in Dodder Vale.'

And putting Considine in her place, thought Swan.

'So how was your visit to east Clare?'

'Good. The policeman I met has been there forever. Nice little town, I suppose, the Garda station's the size of this kitchen. He brought me to see a doctor who knows the family and it turns out he was asked to the house on Christmas Day in 1972. He says the baby was stillborn.'

Swan took a seat opposite her. 'The doctor saw it?'

'He said he examined the mother. She wasn't a member of the Devane family — that's their name — she was a girl who cooked and cleaned for them. Joan Dempsey she was called, but I've written it all up for you. It's on your desk'

'How did our girl come to find it?'

'Oh… I didn't ask that. Sorry. Not sure he knew. I think he was called afterwards.'

'Did you talk to the family or the mother?'

'You said not to waste time.'

'So I did. That's fine.'

A stream of piano notes floated down the hall. Schubert, perhaps. He was never certain.

'Is that a record?'

'No, it's Elizabeth. She's a musician.'

'God, that's amazing.' Considine smiled in open admiration and Swan's chest tightened with pride even while he worried she'd tell the others, that they'd find something to ridicule in his wife's talent.

He left Considine to finish her tea, and went to get his jacket from the coat hooks in the hall. He slipped into the front room to kiss the back of his wife's neck. Elizabeth smiled and kept playing.

'I'll try to get back in time for the pictures,' he whispered.

Swan hummed the tune as he folded into the passenger seat of Considine's little hatchback. It was all right that she'd come into the house, seen something of his life. It was fine.

She drove fast through the dawdling weekend traffic, nipping into gaps, her hand always on the gearstick.

'Barrett said you got the post-mortem results yesterday,' she said.

'Mmmm.'

'He didn't have time to tell me about them.'

'No huge surprises. Cause of death was the severing of the spinal cord from a single blow to the nape. The bruising on the back was also caused by trauma from some kind of blunt weapon — a bar or heavy stick. The skin was broken in places. Harbison thinks this might have been after the blow to the neck.'

She was silent for the rest of the journey. Swan knew they were both doing the same thing; playing out scenes of violence in their heads, imaginations reaching into the dark for actions that could fit the consequences.

ELEVEN

Ali watched Davy sleep, his cheek vibrating against the train window, his skin the colour of lard. She ate crisps and drank tea from a plastic beaker, watching hedges and fences scroll by. In an hour or so, she would be at her aunt and uncle's, see her cousins for the first time in years. She had four cousins in Buleen — Roisín, married the year before, Brendan, the eldest, who now worked the farm with his dad, and the twins Michael and Eamonn — those rowdy boys who teased her when she was small and made her cry. She hadn't seen them enough over the years to think of them as friends.

A man passing down the aisle turned his head to stare at her, and she wondered whether he recognised her from the telly. There was no way of telling how conspicuous she had become. She kept her eyes on the window as much as she could. After a time, she shook Davy's arm.

'Hey, we're almost there.'

He stretched and rubbed at his mouth. He frowned at the passing view and executing a wailing yawn that gave her a full view of his gullet.

'My, what a big mouth you have.'

'All the better to regurgitate my innards through,' he said.

'You shouldn't have drunk all that whiskey. Tell me what Una said on the phone. Are you sure it's okay?'

'She said you were more than welcome. She's making up Roisíns old room.'

'Davy?'

'Mmmn?'

'I've only ten pounds with me, and I don't know how long I'm staying. I feel I should give her something.'

'Nonsense, she's your aunt. Buy her some Milk Tray. You might need a bit more for drinking money, though. Maybe Brendan will make me rich and I'll give you a favourable loan.'

'Gee thanks'

Her cousin Brendan was leaning against an iron pillar on the platform at Kinmore. Last time Ali had seen him he was an almost mute adolescent. He still looked grumpy, still wore glasses, but was as tall as a drainpipe and, in his narrow black trousers and wrecked denim shirt, somehow more youthful than he had been as a child. She was immediately conscious of wanting him to think well of her.

He greeted Davy with an open-handed blow to his shoulder.

'Alright?'

Davy just winced.

'Travel sickness,' said Ali.

'Me arse,' said Brendan, 'looks self inflicted to me.' He looped his arms around Ali in an awkward hug.

'Saw you on the telly!'

Ali groaned.

'You're not to mind Mam if she gets at you for some of the things you said. She's old-fashioned.'

'She'll probably have the priest waiting to exorcise you,' Davy said.

Brendan gave a short laugh. 'Not everyone gets called a slut on *The Late Late*. It's quite an honour for us.'

A faded red transit van stood outside the station and Brendan urged them to praise it, even though rust frothed at the door corners. He found space for their bags among a collection of bulky gaming machines in the back. Their fake wood sides made Ali think of coffins.

They sat in a high row behind the windscreen, Ali sandwiched in the middle. They left Kinmore and sped along beside high hedges and overhanging trees heavy with summer's growth and the dust of the road. The Clash sang about Spanish bombs on the tape deck, and Brendan shouted along, thumping the steering wheel. Davy was leaning out the open side window, jaw clenched against nausea.

They turned on to a main road. Here there were no hedges and Ali could see fields stretching out around her, rising and falling in gentle humps. Between two hills the bright silver pan of Lough Dreena appeared briefly.

'Why are we going this way?' asked Davy.

'Just a little side trip, Big D.' Brendan pointed ahead to a large ochre-coloured building. It sat naked on empty ground like a box fallen from the sky. Big red letters made to look like rustic logs spelled out 'Red Rock Saloon' on the gable end.

He pulled the van into the vast car park, executing an unnecessarily tight turn into one of its empty bays. They could feel the machines tip and bang as they bumped to a halt.

'Give us a hand here — I'll run you in gently.'

Davy grunted and climbed out of the van.

Ali followed, standing on the hot tarmac while Brendan hooked a wooden ramp to the back of the van and manoeuvred one of the machines down it on a porter's trolley.

'Get the plug will ye?'

Davy picked up the trailing flex and walked after

Brendan. Ali waited, glad of the stillness and sunshine. A liver-coloured spaniel walked along the side of the road, all on its own. When it spotted Ali, it increased its pace, trotting by and looking over its shoulder as if it didn't want to be associated with the likes of her. Maybe it had seen *The Late Late*. The word *slut* wouldn't leave her ears.

The boys finally appeared again, bickering loudly. Davy had staged some kind of miraculous recovery from his hangover. His colour was better and he was laughing. Brendan carried a cloth bag in his hand, heavy with a clot of coins. When they got back in the van she smelled the beer.

'We had to,' protested Brendan, banging the gearstick into reverse, 'you can't be stand-offish in this business.'

It wasn't long until they came to the grotto on the outskirts of Buleen. Ali craned forward to look at the town. They passed the church first, a big Italian-style basilica the colour of strawberry ice-cream.

'I see God's sticking with pink,' said Ali.

'Man!' said Davy, 'I could sell a machine to Father Philbin to put in a side chapel. That'd bring in the young folk alright.'

'In your arse.'

They drove down the wide village street. Brendan slowed the van and stopped outside a tiny pub with the name Melody over the door.

'Won't Auntie Una be waiting for me?'

'No rush,' said Davy, opening the door.

'It's business,' said Brendan, 'I'm persuading them into a CD jukebox.'

Ali didn't follow them in immediately. Buleen hadn't changed much from her last quick visit, down for granddad's funeral about five years before. It looked a little fancier maybe — the hotel had been freshly white-washed and frothing hanging baskets flanked the door. A blackboard was propped beside it with a list of dishes that made her mouth water — poached salmon, chicken casserole, lasagne. She'd eaten nothing but a packet of crisps since breakfast.

She entered the pub and stood for a moment, letting her eyes adjust to the dimness. Brendan was at a table with two pints and a glass of lager. Davy was up at the counter, talking with Mr. Melody. She went and sat beside Brendan, lifted the lager to her lips.

Brendan put his pint down, adjusted the beer mat under it, cleared his throat.

'Are you alright? After what happened… are you okay in yourself?'

'Yea, thanks. I'd rather forget it, though.'

Brendan nodded, pushed the beermat again.

Davy was shaking hands with the barman, telling him, 'You won't regret it.'

'I don't fucking believe it,' said Brendan under his breath.

Davy joined them, lifted his pint and gave Brendan a toothy grin.

'You jammy bastard,' said Brendan, 'he's going to take the jukebox?'

'Nothing to it — persuasion is my particular gift.' Davy sank his lips into the cream of his pint.

'You couldn't persuade yourself into a job in Dublin,' said Ali, lighting up a fag.

Melody's was not the kind of pub where a jukebox would look at home. Dusty bottles of lime and lemon cordial stood beside a ceramic Johnnie Walker striding out in his top hat and cane, the lino was studded with decades of cigarette burns. Through the door at the back of the bar you could see tea towels and pillowcases hung to dry over a range in the Melody family kitchen.

'I said he could select his own music from a list of thousands of CDs and I'd give him his own free code so he could play it to himself whenever he wanted.'

Brendan struggled to keep his voice down. 'Then he'll tell the regulars and we'll make nothing.'

'He won't, he hates giving anything away.'

Ali looked up at the bit of blue sky visible through the clear panes of glass above the window shutters. Brendan was telling Davy about the record decks he'd got cheap, how he was setting up as a DJ on the side. Mr. Melody polished the bar surface with a cloth. It was so still that her smoke settled in a thin layer just above their heads.

Davy rippled through it as went up to get another round, buoyant with success.

'Business is going to boom, Bren, now that you've me on board,' he said on his return, 'The old Davy Brennan magic touch.'

'Not so magic in all areas, is it?'

Davy gave his nephew a cool look, took a deep swallow of his pint.

'What?' said Ali. '*What?*'

'Didn't he tell you he's been unlucky in love?'

She looked at Davy, but he had turned away. He hadn't mentioned anything about a girlfriend, ever.

When Brendan suggested a third drink, she managed to persuade them against it, insisted she needed to eat something.

The light was already fading when they got

outside. She was wondering where she had left her purse, when Davy thrust it into her hands.

'The food in the hotel looks nice,' she said.

'Dunno,' said Brendan, 'never been in — it's just for tourists.'

They climbed back into the van and Brendan steered a fast U-turn, then turned left over the old bridge and out onto the road that gradually swept them a field's distance from the river. She recognised the little landmarks along the way — the ruined chapel, the cattle mart, the brutal concrete of the handball alley in front of Glinchy's farm. Petrol blue squares of pine plantation patched the hills over towards Ennisbridge.

In moments she would be at the farm, with a bathroom and food and afterwards a bed to lie on. She could make out the white gate posts ahead, but instead of turning up the driveway, Brendan drove past it and pulled into a rough track about a hundred yards beyond.

'You don't want to go to the old folks yet,' said Brendan, 'you want to see Davy's new place first.'

She looked at Davy but he just laughed. They bumped up the track and stopped in front of a new bungalow, identical to thousands of others throughout the country, a low grey shoebox with a brown tile roof and nothing to recommend it beyond the cheapness of the build. This one wasn't quite finished. The breeze-block foundations were left bare, and the ground around was churned mud, baked dry into ruts by the summer heat. A lone oak tree rose from the wasteland, a couple of its lower limbs roughly lopped. Ali suddenly recognised the site as the place where the farm's stables used to stand, home to an ancient carthorse and her cousin Roisín's envied pony, Skipper.

'So where does Skipper live?' said Ali, confused.

'She's long gone', said Davy, and Brendan drew a finger across his throat and grinned.

'Dogfood. Davy and the twins have supplanted her.'

'Are the twins living here?'

'They were here on sufferance!' said Davy, 'And they can get their own lodgings when they come back.'

'Does it have a toilet?' said Ali.

'It did when I left,' said Davy, 'but God knows what those gurriers have done in the meantime.'

It looked like the building process had been abandoned just before the final push. An open ditch ran around the outside walls with pipes laid along the bottom. Near the front door a pillow of solidified cement stood on its end, the plastic bag that once contained it blowing in tattered ribbons around its base. The step up to the porch was knee high.

'Did they not finish the front steps?' asked Davy.

'Nothing to do with me, D,' said Brendan.

'They're supposed to have done work in exchange for rent,' Davy said as they hauled themselves up onto the doorstep. He opened an elaborate front door with patterned glass panes, and held it wide for her, annoyance bringing a dark flush to his face.

Ali thought Davy had come to Dublin to make a new life in the city. It was odd he never mentioned this place. The walls and doors and brass coloured light switches were all pristine, but the floor was a concrete screed, raked like corduroy. In the front room, an old sofa was complemented by a massive low table made from a sheet of chipboard propped on breeze-blocks. The battered television in the corner stood on an empty cable reel.

Davy stopped in the middle of the hall, looking dazed, as if he hardly knew the place.

'Toilet?' said Ali.

'Second door on the right,' said Brendan, bringing up the rear.

She wandered down the corridor, passing a bedroom furnished only with a mattress on the floor and glamorous mirror-fronted wardrobes built in to the walls. The bathroom had a new suite but no toilet seat. The edge of the bath still had paper tape on it. Ali hovered over the cold porcelain to pee and hoped that no one would try the lockless door.

Brendan was in the corridor waiting when she came out.

'Y'alright?'

'Shouldn't I go down to the farm?'

'Don't be fretting.' He went into the bathroom and shut the door.

In the front room Davy was pulling out bottles from a six-pack of beer that must have come from Melody's. He had an unlit cigarette in his hand.

'You don't smoke,' she said.

He looked at it for a moment, wondering, put it behind his ear.

'Sometimes I do, but it's horrible.'

Ali sat beside him on the sofa, retrieved the fag from his ear and lit it herself.

'Where *are* the twins?'

'They got a job in a pea factory in England. Seasonal work. That's why Brendan needs a hand.'

'A pee factory? Is that a joke?'

'Not at all. A pea factory — P-E-A — little green yokes, canning them, eh Brendan?'

Brendan edged around the table to join them

on the sofa.

'Give us a bottle there. D'you want one Ali?'

'I'm okay, thanks.'

'But we only got Smithwicks 'cos you like it.'

Davy put a bottle in her hand and gave another to Brendan.

Ali slumped into the couch and the boys talked over her, Brendan giving wandering updates about the local team and minor village scandals. They weren't going to mention the baby. They weren't going to mention *The Late Late*. It was good to come here, to escape it all.

She let her head fall to the side and come to rest on Davy's shoulder. She turned her face so that her nose was buried into the wool of his grey jumper. He kept his arm still so that she could stay there, even while he thumped the sofa arm with the other hand. She started to drift.

A sharp rapping shocked her awake. Outside the plate glass window a figure stood in a dusk that had gathered from nowhere. He wore a cap and a mackintosh, but she couldn't see his face. The boys exchanged guilty glances. Davy motioned the figure to come inside.

Her Uncle Joe had aged a good deal since she had last seen him, and his open tweed jacket framed an impressive dome of belly. He was wearing an old cap with a greasy-looking brim, and a vexed expression.

'Una had dinner ready an hour ago. Did ye not think to bring her down? Hello, Ali.'

'Sorry Da,' said Brendan, 'lost track of the time.'

Joe looked pointedly at the bottles and the butt-strewn saucer. With a push from Davy, Ali got to her feet and went over to kiss her uncle on the cheek.

'I'm sorry, Uncle Joe. I'll come down with

you now.'

'You coming too?' he asked the boys.

'We'll be down later. Few things to sort out here, about the business, like.'

Joe gave a little snort, and lifted Ali's rucksack lightly onto his shoulder. She followed him out, stepping carefully off the front porch into the darkness.

They followed a path through trees that widened into a dirt drive. She could sense the bulk of the barn looming to her right — darker and heavier than the gloom about. Up the hill on the left, she could make out the roofs of the pig sheds, the dull gleam of iron. They walked around the corner of the barn, and the lights of the farmhouse appeared, the kitchen window spilling a buttery glow into the greyness.

Ali caught her breath. She could see the corner of the big range, the table with its faded oilcloth, the dresser stacked with delft. Nothing had changed; it was like stepping out of the dark and straight into the past. Sensing her pause, Joe stopped too and for a moment they stood wordlessly in the dark, looking on as Aunt Una appeared like a figure on a stage, passing through the lit square with a stack of plates in her hand.

'I'm sorry' were Ali's first words of greeting to her aunt.

She wondered if there ever would be a time when she wasn't feeling sorry or ashamed. Una stood with her back to the range, a thinner, more worn-away version of her own mother. Her face was plain, and her short bobbed hair was pushed firmly behind her ears. It was a lighter colour than Ali recalled, a kind of faded blond. Una came forward to press her dry cheek to her niece's.

'Your dinner's in the range.'

'She was kidnapped,' said Joe.

'Is Davy not with you?'

'He's up in the bungalow with Brendan,' said Ali.

'Talking *business*,' said Joe, taking off his jacket and cap in the scullery, 'like a pair of Nelson Rockefellers.'

Ali sat at the kitchen table, and Una put a big plate of stew in front of her, yellow domes of boiled potatoes rising from a brown pool, dry skin on its top. Una said that she and Joe were going through to watch *Tenko* and Ali could come and sit with them when she had finished.

'You don't mind, do you?'

'Not at all,' said Ali.

'We'll talk properly tomorrow, eh?'

'Sure.'

If discussion could be put off once, it was more likely to be put off again. Ali mashed her potatoes into the stew and started to bolt it down, but by the time she was halfway through she felt stuffed.

She didn't want to seem ungrateful, so she took her plate through the scullery to the back door and surrendered it to the yard cats. Five creatures ran to her — skinny black and white cats with splodges of tabby brown on some. They hissed and swiped at each other as they fought for position around the plate, licking frantically.

She remembered a kitten she fell in love with that December, a little black one with a white front paw. She smuggled it upstairs to sleep in her bed, but woke in the dark to find the kitten curled tightly around her neck, making it hard to breath. She moved the kitten away, but it kept trying to be at her neck. Every time she removed it, the kitten would mew, showing its tiny needle teeth. She grew scared of those teeth next to her

110

neck. She couldn't make it understand. Finally, in exhausted tears, she snuck downstairs and put it out the back door into the freezing night.

There wasn't a speck of stew left on the plate, but two cats still worried away at the glazed surface with rasping tongues. Ali lifted it and stepped back into the kitchen. As she closed the door, she remembered something else. That long-ago night, taking this very same route from yard to kitchen, a groggy voice had called to her from the sofa in the corner. She had nearly jumped out of her skin with fright. But it was only Joan, sleeping under a pile of blankets. Telling her to go back to bed.

Only Joan. Joan's face filled her mind, the paleness under the freckles, the distant look she often wore as if she was hiding inside herself. The cloud of hated curls. Ali remembered taking the chance to pat those curls one morning when Joan was crying over a lamb that hadn't made it through the night. Joan seemed so much older than her then, a woman like Aunt Una, but was probably only the age that Ali was now, only a grown girl.

The old sofa was still there, dressed in a flowered slipcover now. It was strange to realise how well she knew this house. She never gave it a thought in Dublin, but it was here all that time, waiting for her.

TWELVE

When Sister O'Dwyer appeared in the doorway of the convent parlour, Swan and Barrett rose automatically to their feet at the sight of such frailty. The old nun might have been all of five foot if she was able to stand up straight, but gravity or curvature of the spine had bent her towards the ground so that she now cleared no more than four. Barrett stepped out from behind the table and supported the last leg of her journey by placing his hand under the nun's right arm, steadying her. Her other hand clutched the knob of a varnished blackthorn stick that she poked into the carpet in little hops. But Sister O'Dwyer's frailty was only physical, Swan noted. As she took her seat she tipped her face up to look at him eagerly, berry-eyed, apparently delighted to engage with a couple of policemen.

Swan smiled warmly at the woman.

'I'll assume you know why we're here — what happened in the Rosary Garden — but I've been hearing that some girls call it Sister O'Dwyer's Garden.'

'Well, I've been supposedly in charge of the place for thirty years now, so the girls associate it with me. It's only called the Rosary Garden because of the Rosary Walk beside it. It has no religious use of its own. In fact some would say it's quite a pagan place.'

'Why would they say that?'

'You mustn't take me too seriously. All I mean is that the girls who use it don't necessarily have God on their minds. Gossip, sweets and the odd cigarette

112

are their main devotions. Oh, and the occasional bit of forced labour with a rake.'

She gave him a dry smile.

'It's a credit to you.'

'I wouldn't go that far. Even if I had the knowledge, I don't think you could make any decent kind of garden in that particular spot. Too shady, too dry. But gardening's not really the point.'

'It isn't?'

The nun leaned forward, her face aglow, light through parchment. Swan sensed Barrett shift beside him, impatient at this circuitous talk.

'Are you familiar with the term *sanctuary*?' said the nun.

'Of course.'

'It has religious connotations usually, the sepulchre, the place of something precious. But I'm an admirer of St. Francis, detective, and when I think of the word sanctuary, I think of a bird sanctuary. That is what my garden is — in a literal sense because of all the birds in those hedges — but really, it's a *girl* sanctuary!' and she clapped her hands together and wheezed a laugh.

Barrett was doodling on the page in front of him, drawing a man's face, bland, square jawed. *You wish*, thought Swan and gave Barrett's leg a little kick. He should do the woman the courtesy of looking like he was listening.

'That seems a wonderfully liberal approach, sister. Can I ask, when were you last in the garden yourself?'

Her face clouded. 'On Monday, after they found the little thing.'

'And before that?'

The nun looked down at the carpet beside her chair, as if the answer might be in its pattern.

'Sometime in spring. I seem to remember crocuses.'

'But you run the gardening club.'

She looked up at him and frowned. 'Perhaps you're trying to flatter me. As you can see, I don't get about like I did. My supervision has been at a distance for some time, but someone else will be running the club soon.'

'Another nun?'

Barrett was jiggling his leg now, sending vibrations up Swan's chair.

'Yes, Sister Bernadette, a wonderful young woman. She'll pull it back into shape, I know.'

'She seems very cool-headed, all right,' said Swan.

'She's far more than that — Bernadette is worth ten of me to our little community. She knows nursing, she did a course in social work, she leads all of our city initiatives... such energy.'

'Sister — I need to ask you something directly. If your girls thought of the garden as their sanctuary — is it so unlikely that one of them might bring their baby there?'

'I don't think any of them were in that kind of trouble. And none of them would murder a child.'

'How can you know for sure? You weren't around much.'

'I know it in my heart.'

You could go so far questioning these nuns, it seemed, then something closed down.

'Could the child have been born to anyone in the convent?'

He expected immediate rebuttal, but Sister O'Dwyer appeared to think it over, as if running through an album of people in her mind.

'We would have known.'

'So what do you think happened? Indulge me. I can see you're a woman with a decent imagination.'

Sister O'Dwyer smiled slightly at her clasped hands and strained her face up to meet his eye once more.

'Do you know cats, detective?' she said.

'I have one who abuses my hospitality, yes.' He thought of Benny, curled tight as a snail on Elizabeth's side of the bed, even when it was empty of her.

'Well you'll know how they sneak away to a dark place when they're sick or giving birth. My garden is a place like that. I think it was a local girl or woman who sought it out by instinct.'

'Is the shed ever locked?'

'No. Though Bernadette says we must do that, from now on.'

'Sounds like Sister Bernadette might be a bit stricter than you.'

'I don't like expecting the worst. Not that Bernadette does, that's not what I'm saying. She's out in the world more than I am. It's a different perspective.'

'We'll be talking to Sister Bernadette later,' said Barrett.

'Oh, I thought she'd be at St. Jude's, it's a Saturday today, isn't it?'

Barrett drew himself up in his chair, moved a sleeve over his doodle. 'We stipulated that all the nuns be here today to talk to us, sister, I believe Sister Bernadette has agreed to that demand.'

Sister O'Dwyer raised her eyebrows and gave one slow nod of her head to Barrett, acknowledging or perhaps mocking his great power.

'What's St. Jude's?' asked Swan. He should be

winding this up, they had more nuns to see.

'It was where I trained as a novice, detective, before the order moved out here to the suburbs. A lovely house by the canal, on Percy Place. It was once the home of a famous writer — now was it Gogarty or Synge... ? Are you fond of reading?'

'Enormously. What is the house used for now?'

'Oh...' the nun looked confused for a moment, losing focus, 'I believe it's a... *community project*.' She said the phrase triumphantly as if she had retrieved it against the odds. But the light drained from her suddenly and she looked even smaller than when she came in. Swan tried to calculate her age as Barrett went through the rigmarole of giving her a card and asking her to get in touch if anything etcetera. More than eighty, certainly. Possibly in her nineties. She asked Barrett to ring a bell beside the fireplace. Within moments, the young Sister Dreyfus appeared to help Sister O'Dwyer out of her chair and guide her to wherever she spent her daytime hours. Swan hoped it was somewhere comfortable, light-filled.

Swan asked Sister Dreyfus to send Sister Bernadette to them.

As they waited, Swan sneaked a look at the day's Independent. The public hand-wringing went on. The Rosary Baby was being dragged into expositions on the family, the decline of religion, the promiscuity and ignorance of the young. There was no editorial that couldn't be spiced up with an innocent dying for society's many sins. Only the banal or brutal truth would put an end to it. Kavanagh was pressing him for results, but all the technical personnel and most of the Murder Squad had been diverted to work on an armed robbery at a creamery outside Dundalk where a woman office worker and an off-duty Garda had been shot dead. What kind of cheapjack set up was it when the country could only deal with one murder at a time?

'Shall I get us a coffee, boss?' asked Barrett.

'Yea, see if you can whistle up a cup.'

Barrett was gone only a minute when the parlour door opened and Sister Bernadette walked in. She wore a veil that reached just past her shoulders and what looked like a black pinafore over a longish black dress. She reminded Swan somehow of that picture of Alice in Wonderland after she had drunk the bottle that made her grow. She was so long and pale and had an odd way of stretching the back of her neck up when she looked at you.

'Please sit down sister. I know we talked at the station, but now we're building a fuller picture of events.'

'I see.'

'And you'll have had time to gather your thoughts.'

Sister Bernadette walked over to the table, pulled the chair back and sat in front of him. The action was compliant, the face wasn't. It was the face of someone willing to endure something unpleasant for God's sake.

'My colleague has gone to fetch coffee. We'll have to wait for him to get back.'

She acknowledged his statement with only a bat of her pale lashes. There was no question that she was a striking woman, even in that get-up and with the veil covering her hair. Red hair it was, he could see peeks of it at her temples. But she wasn't freckled at all. She had this amazing pale skin, like a lily, he thought, before catching himself. She's a nun, *jaysus*, man. But he kept looking — the violet shadows under her eyes intrigued him. Had they been there on Monday?

Sister Bernadette kept her face turned from him, to all appearances fascinated by the view out the window. He remembered a film he'd seen at the IFT, something arty Elizabeth had dragged him to. Arty? Debauched more like, with Vanessa Redgrave as a nun and Oliver Reed as a priest — I ask you — and all of them rutting away, rolling their eyes. But that was all made-up stuff, wasn't it? He once attended a raid on an illegal sauna near the quays where they found two nuns' habits among the French maid and nurse outfits that the girls wore. What a country.

This silence was becoming uncomfortable.

'We're grateful you could spare the time for us. Sister O'Dwyer said you usually spend weekends at St. Jude's, was it?'

The pale hazel eyes flicked to his instantly, then away. He had only been making conversation, but had somehow hit a nerve.

'What sort of place is that, now?'

'It's one of our projects. Community work.'

Her voice was stiff and two pink spots were emerging through the paleness of her cheeks. She had that kind of complexion. Volatile.

'That's interesting. What do you do there exactly?'

'Oh. I couldn't... I do some admin, help with maintenance, boring stuff. We have many different projects around Dublin — we help run a nursery in Sherriff Street, you know.'

He loved this. He wasn't sure what she was trying to hide, but he was going to have it.

'I hear a famous writer once lived there — in the Percy Place house.' She met his eye, offering nothing. 'This famous writer, do you think he'd happy about his home being turned into a... a...' He circled his hand at her lightly, cueing her to supply the missing word.

The door banged open and Barrett appeared with a tray, looking flustered. Swan lifted his hand from the table to signal him to wait, but Barrett barged across the carpet, his tray dripping at one corner. The nun was immediately out of her chair, ushering him over to a side table, helping to mop the spill with a lacy cloth.

Swan kept his seat as the two of them fussed about. When Sister Bernadette finally handed him a cup and saucer, he said 'thank you' with a deliberate evenness to convey that he had lost none of his focus during Barrett's comedy entrance.

When Barrett sat down, Swan resumed.

'Sister Bernadette here has been telling me about some of her community work. You have to excuse my ignorance of these things, sister, but who is it that you're serving at St. Jude's — is it, like, an old folks home?'

'No'

'What is it?'

'Its... a drop-in centre.'

'For women?'

She nodded, looked down at her lap. She had a rope of wooden rosary beads attached to her belt, and was spinning one of the beads between forefinger and thumb.

'Is it for battered women, domestic stuff?'

She raised her head, something firmer in the set of her jaw.

'Not really. It's for the working women in the area.'

His mother, who was into any left-wing cause, had told him about radical nuns. He'd seen a few on CND marches, their faces painted white as skulls, but he hadn't yet come across the ones that she claimed were working with street prostitutes along the canal, giving them food and check ups and running the risk of the church's wrath by — it was rumoured — ensuring they used condoms.

That would account for her discomfort.

'I think you probably do a great deal of good out there. It's a dangerous scene now with the drugs.'

'Fair play to you, sister,' said Barrett.

She received their regard passively for a minute, running the beads through her hands, and dropped them abruptly.

'I thought you had further questions about the child,' she said.

Swan drew out a sheaf of papers from his folder.

'A few things that came up from your statement… can you confirm that when you came upon it, the child was naked inside a paper bag?'

'Is that what I said?'

'It is.'

'Well, then…'

'Not a white cloth?'

'… I don't recall one.' She sounded less certain than in her statement.

'We found a piece of white clothing in the shed, sister, and one of the other witnesses said the baby was wrapped in white when she saw it.'

'Are you asking me to change my statement for neatness sake?'

'It's a curious anomaly, that's all.'

'I can't swear I noticed the exact nature of the wrappings, it was the child I was thinking of — the possibility that something could be done.'

If Ali Hogan was telling the truth, someone had

removed the blouse and tried to hide it in the sling of the deckchair. Both girls said they hadn't touched the baby, so either Sister Bernadette was that person, or someone else was on the scene.

'You were walking in the grounds for some time — I think you said ten minutes — before the girls found you. Thinking back now, did you see anyone else about during that time? Or anyone in the garden?'

'You asked me that before.'

Swan was getting irritated with the ice queen act.

'Yes or no?'

She gave him a look of forced patience. 'No. I saw no one in the grounds.'

They went over a few more details, but Sister Bernadette would give them nothing useful or new.

As he waited for Barrett to bring in the next nun, Swan looked out of the parlour window at the mountains rising hazy beyond the empty hockey pitches, beyond the avenue of horse chestnuts that curved up from the main road. For all their talk of community projects, these rich acres were lying unused, while inner city kids played in the summer traffic. Withholding. That's what they were good at. Even if one of these holy women had seen something, he was not convinced they would tell it to him.

THIRTEEN

The bell jingled, a cue to kneel; Ali never went to mass in Dublin. On either side of her, Aunt Una and Uncle Joe pulled themselves forward onto the padded kneeler. She wondered whether to stay sitting, to separate herself from the rigmarole. There were people kneeling close behind her — she could feel someone's breath on her neck. She moved forward onto her knees and Una gave a tiny, satisfied hum as she drew level.

She had been woken early by her aunt, with a mug of tea and a slice of fruit bread, flicking the curtains open and saying that it would be a good thing if Ali came with her to ten o'clock mass. People could get a good look at her, Una said, and having seen her, wouldn't be bothering the family with nosy questions. Ali still felt guilty about being late for dinner. Una said they'd be leaving in fifteen minutes.

A clinking of coins at the end of the aisle announced the collection. A couple of gaunt men supervised the safe passage of baskets through the congregation. Una brought her handbag to her knee and pulled out a pre-folded note. Ali passed the wicker bowl across her lap, a weighty nest of money. The organist filled the hiatus with a swirling noise that suggested a tune might emerge by and by. Against this wash of sound individual noises rose to the curved roof — someone at the back suppressing a chesty cough, a toddler whining, the occasional jackpot jangle as the collectors poured the takings into a large wooden box being trolleyed up the centre aisle.

Afterwards, the congregation milled around in the bright morning, a busy crush between railings and church front. Car engines revved and the road was filled with a sudden traffic jam. Up the street, some people were heading into pubs for an après-mass pint. A striking man with thick white hair and glasses moved in front of her and held out a hand for her to shake. Was it her imagination, or was the crowd thicker around them than in other parts of the churchyard?

'You remember Doctor Nolan,' said Una as Ali surrendered her hand. She remembered him, but his hair had been dark back then. He asked politely after her mother and her own prospects. A picture of him from long ago bloomed in her head — Doctor Nolan standing in the doorway of the living room, holding a gift wrapped in shining red paper. It must have been Christmas Day.

Doctor Nolan turned to talk to her aunt. A finger tapped hard on her shoulder.

Ali looked round to find a large florid-faced man smiling at her.

'I saw ye on *The Late Late*,' he said, as if claiming kinship. 'I thought ye were great.'

'Thanks very much.'

'And that Mary O'Shea, she's great too, though I wouldn't want to be married to her.' He laughed, and two other young men who had drifted over to flank him joined in. Ali was distracted by a glint on the big man's lapel. A familiar gold badge — two golden beans each topped by five pinhead dots — the footprints of a foetus, the tiny soles of the endangered womb dweller. It was a badge to signal that its wearer was a dedicated pro-lifer, a man unashamed to defend theoretical babies.

'Would you like to come for a drink with us some-time?' His companions exchanged a delighted glance.

'Go on with you, Cathal,' said Uncle Joe, appearing beside her.

'No harm, Mr Devane.' The three men sloped off in the direction of Melody's.

A small woman with a headscarf scooted forward and pressed something into Ali's hand and muttered that she would pray for her.

'Thank you,' said Ali to her departing back. 'Do you think we can go back to the car now, Uncle Joe?'

'We're waiting for Roisín.'

'We are?'

She opened her hand to see what the woman had given her. It was a medal, light as a feather, the metal thin and chalky, a jellied pool of blue glaze on the front holding a scene of the adoration at Lourdes. Or that's what she presumed it was — the medal was so small and crudely made that the figures looked like stalag-mites in a cave. Ali slipped it into the back pocket of her jeans, her fingers brushing against Mary O'Shea's business card.

'Who's the woman in the headscarf?' asked Ali.

'She's a religious nut. Don't mind her.' It seemed that in Uncle Joe's mind there was a subtle but impermeable barrier between the nuts and the very devout. 'Maeve Dempsey' he added.

'Anything to Joan Dempsey?'

'You've a good memory. Her mother.'

There had been a passing likeness between them, the slightness and quickness of Joan turned to a kind of bony agitation in the mother.

'And is Joan about?' she tried to make the question casual, just a polite addition to what went before.

Joe glanced past her, cupped his hands to his mouth and shouted, 'Roisín!'

Over by the railings, two young women were talking, small children churning around their legs. One turned at the sound of Joe's voice. Her cousin was still beautiful, Ali thought, lean like a tennis player, her fair hair now cut into a little crop, sensible, brisk. Roisín ran over to give Ali a hug.

'God its been years! I'll bring her over to mine, Dad, and have her back to you later.' Ali had no choice in the matter, it seemed. Like the evening before, she felt like a parcel passed from hand to hand.

Roisín talked non-stop on the way to her car, pointing out sights that Ali already knew, asserting her old bossiness. Her cousin had four years head start on her, a gap that presumed Ali would always be trailing behind in sophistication and experience. That was the deal between them. Recently, Roisín had upped the stakes by marrying a handsome GAA captain, Colman Carroll, and soon after, baby Emer arrived.

Ali always thought Roisín wasn't bothered about what anyone thought of her, but as they drove, she kept going on about how it was a mobile home — not a caravan — that they were living in, and how comfortable and convenient it was.

The caravan site that Colman managed was half a mile outside the village, where the river ran into Lough Dreena. Roisín turned down a narrow *boreen* between high hedges. Half way along they pulled in to the side to let another car pass. A fuchsia bush crushed against the window beside Ali, deep pink bells with violet lips starfished against the glass.

The road crossed a metal bridge and carried on over the brow of an open field where, all at once, the white oblongs of caravans came into view, clustered like giant cattle under the lakeshore trees. The nearest caravan was larger than the rest and was surrounded by a knee-high wooden fence. A rotary washing line trembled beside it in the breeze.

As Roisín stopped the car, the caravan door swung open, and a well-built man with a bush of sandy hair came down the steps towards them, his face clenched.

'Rowsh! I told you I had to get to the grounds by eleven. Out.'

'Colman. Darlin'. This is my cousin Ali.'

He spared Ali a quick once-over while snatching the car keys from Roisín's hand.

'You the famous one?'

'I wouldn't say that.'

'Well, you're famous here,' he said and reversed the car off in a wide curve.

'Don't mind him,' said Roisín, 'Bear with a sore head. Where's he left the child?'

In the middle of the tiny living room was a playpen that reminded Ali of a lobster pot. Sitting in the middle of it, a tiny Buddha among soft toys, was Emer. The baby's mouth dropped open in awe at the sight of a stranger. Then a wriggle of delight convulsed her and she lifted her chubby arms in celebration. Roisín plucked the baby up into the air, spun her around once, and brought her to rest on her hip, babbling loving nonsense all the while.

Roisín took her on a brief tour. Ali nodded at the two bedrooms, feigned amazement at the plumbed-in bathroom with its tiny pink bath. She said that it was a lot better than Davy's house and Roisín laughed.

'They're no better than apes, those boys.'

'I didn't even know Davy had a house.'

'Well — I'm not surprised he didn't say...'

'Why?'

'He thought he was going to be setting up a little home, didn't he, but nothing came of it, of course.'

'A little home with who?' she managed to keep her voice conversational.

'You wouldn't know her. Girl called Valerie. She only moved here a couple of years ago.'

'Oh.' Ali walked away to look at a picture of a football team over the decorative mantelpiece. He hadn't told her anything about it, but it was serious enough that he built a house.

'I'll make us coffee. You go to Ali, Emer.' Roisín handed her the baby and went to busy herself in the kitchen area.

Ali held the baby at arm's length for a moment, unsure of herself. The baby looked unsure of her too. Her brow started to pucker, and Ali brought her into her chest for a cuddle. Emer capitulated, slipping one plump fist into the opening of Ali's blouse to come to rest stickily against her collarbone, just above her heart. Then she laid her cheek on the curve of Ali's shoulder, stuffing her thumb in her mouth and sucking on it re-flectively. Ali walked away into the front area of the caravan where a wide window brought in the view of the lake.

The baby was limp in her arms, accepting. Ali hummed a made-up tune and stroked the baby's hot back, her palm tickled by the intricate pattern of her little cardigan. The fingers under Ali's shirt flexed and curled in time with the thumbsucking. Emer's hair was pale and fine, growing here and there in curls on her shell pink scalp. With a jolt, Ali realised what it was she was holding — this was what was lost, this.

Her stomach gave an awful lurch. She wanted to sit down, but all her concentration was needed for holding on to the baby.

She must have made some kind of sound, because Roisín was hurrying towards her.

'Are you okay?'

Ali nodded, but it felt like the child could turn liquid and slip through her arms. She looked down. Emer had rolled her gaze to look up at her. It was a look from a hundred years ago or a thousand miles off. Roisín was by her side now, the baby was being taken from her grip.

'I'm sorry,' said Roisín, 'I didn't think.'

Ali was going to protest that it was fine, fine, but no words would come out. She went to sit on the sofa, while Roisín put Emer into her playpen.

Roisín brought the coffee to her. Ali didn't want to talk about what had just happened, so she asked her cousin normal, boring questions, about her job, about the wedding, about Colman. But Roisín was incapable of finishing a whole sentence without her eyes sliding over to Emer, her conversation fragmented with little bursts of baby talk directed at the lobster pot.

'An odd woman came up to me after mass today,' said Ali, 'gave me a medal. Your Dad said it was Joan's mother — Joan Dempsey's.'

'Oh yea? Seemed like they were all gawping at you.'

'I didn't see Joan there.'

'Well, you wouldn't,' Roisín said, 'She's in the hospital — that mental place in Kinmore — Damascus House, you know, that big building on the road into town.'

'That's awful. I remember her really well. From the time we stayed you.'

Emer started to whinge, bored with her incarceration.

'Yea, well, the less said the better,' said Roisín. 'My mother's got a real thing against her, so don't start reminiscing to her.'

Roisín got up and lifted Emer into her arms just as a woman passed outside the window.

'Shite,' said Roisín. A knock came on the glass door. She put the baby on her hip and went to open it.

'Peggy!' she said, like she was surprised.

At first glance, Ali had the impression that the woman who entered was middle-aged, but soon she realised it was just the heavy set of her body and her old-fashioned coat — a blue mac down past her knees, not right for the day. Her broad face was young, with full downturned lips and her thick auburn hair waved backwards from her face, as if she were standing in a breeze. Ali wouldn't have recognised her if she passed her on a Dublin street, but now, with the prompt of a name and this place, she knew her, could see the trace of the girl she had been.

'You remember Peggy, Doctor Nolan's daughter? This is my cousin Ali.'

'Yeah, hiya,' said Peggy, unsmiling.

Roisín's behaviour with her was careful, kind. She coaxed the ugly coat from her and got her sitting on the sofa. Ali offered to make more coffee.

'You haven't seen the baby for a while, Peggy, hasn't she grown?'

'Uh huh.'

Ali prepared the coffee as slowly as she could,

leaving the two of them to talk. By the time she brought the mugs over, Peggy was haltingly talking about a shopping trip to Limerick. Her eyes were on Emer though, as were Roisín's. Conversation sputtered between them, then converged on the baby. Emer wriggled on the carpet and they sipped from their mugs and watched, calling out praise for every fat handclap or tumble. Ali could feel the energy draining from her.

She got to her feet and walked into the kitchen area, rinsed her mug under the tap.

'Ro — I've got to get back up to town,' she called over her shoulder.

'If I had the car, I'd drive you,' offered Roisín, taking the opportunity to get up and move about. 'But this one needs her nap anyway. Peggy, would you mind walking Ali up to the town for me?'

Ali started to say there was no need, but Roisín gave her such a fierce look she shut up. She already had Peggy's coat out of the slim cabinet that served as a cloakroom.

'Oh Ali, I've got that thing for you. In the bedroom, I forgot.'

'What thing?'

'The thing I told you about.' Her eyes were insistent.

When they got to the bedroom, Roisín hissed.

'There is no thing, ya eejit. I needed to say something.'

'What?' Ali was sure they could be heard.

'Since you're here on your own, you should pal round with Peggy a bit. She's lonely. You could cheer her up.'

'I doubt it.'

Roisín pushed her towards the door. Peggy

was already outside the little fence, staring back at the caravan. There was something unnervingly still about her, like a post or a stone.

Ali and Peggy walked up the field in silence until they reached the bridge.

'I remember you,' Peggy said, 'you wouldn't let me play with you.'

'When?'

'It was a Christmas. You had a cookery set — was it? — and you wouldn't speak to anyone or let them join you.'

It was hard to tell whether Peggy was annoyed, or just teasing.

'Sorry, I don't remember that. I do remember the fancy coat you had on, though. Pale green, with a black velvet collar. You matched your big sister. I was jealous of those coats.'

Peggy stopped and smiled. 'Brown velvet collars,' she corrected, 'and velvet buttons too.' She looked down at her raincoat. 'Wish I had it still. This thing's horrible — my mother bought it for me.'

'Take it off. It's too hot for a coat.'

Peggy looked up at the blue sky for verification. 'You'll be thinking I've some kind of mad coat fixation.' But she unbuttoned the white plastic buttons, removed the coat and draped it over her arm.

Ali could see the end of the *boreen* ahead. They would be back in town soon, she could make her excuses and get away.

'Where's your sister now?' Ali said.

'Dublin.'

'Does she like it?'

'Suppose so.'

Ali hardly remembered Peggy's sister beyond

the fancy coat. It made her wonder what her life would have been like if her mother had decided to stay on in Buleen. Would she have had the gumption to escape to Dublin, or turned out strange and morose like Peggy. She might even have gone mad like Joan.

'Sorry,' said Peggy suddenly. 'I'm not myself these days.'

'Could be the sun,' said Ali lamely.

Peggy managed a smile, 'Could be.'

'What do you do yourself?'

'Nothing much. I do reception at my Dad's surgery some days and my mother is finding out about teacher training college for me.'

Ali couldn't find anything to say about teacher training and they walked on in silence.

They reached the junction with the main road. Ali could see the shops of Buleen to the right, and a familiar figure leaning against the phone box.

'How's your Uncle Davy?' asked Peggy.

Ali looked up towards the phone box again. Davy had vanished.

'He's good,' said Ali, 'we came down yesterday in the train.'

'I'm going this way,' said Peggy, pointing at the road out of the village.

'Okay. See you then, Peggy.' She watched her walk away. Funny how people turned out. When you were a child, other kids were all of the same tribe. Then they grew up and became really hard to talk to.

She started up the main street. Just past the phone box, Davy jumped out at her from a laneway.

'Boo!'

'Are you really older than me?' said Ali. He drooped an arm over her shoulder and carried on up the street with her.

'What were you doing with Peggy Nolan?'

'I met her down in Roisín's.'

'Roisín's too soft. How's about a little libation for the Sabbath?' He drew out some crumpled notes and a cluster of change from his pocket.

'Just one. I don't want it to turn out like yesterday.'

Cathal, the man with the baby feet badge, was sitting on Melody's windowsill with another guy, watching the world go by. The friend was tall, fierce-looking and fair as a Viking. Davy took his arm off her shoulder and walked ahead into the pub

'Are you needing company, Ali?' Cathal wheedled.

She flicked them the V sign.

'Ooo-ooo,' they chorused, the mocking note swooping after her as she stepped into the dark.

FOURTEEN

Detective Superintendent Francis Kavanagh was big in every direction. He looked like the kind of man who should be out in the open air, striding the hills of Kerry with a sheep across his shoulders or a maiden in his arms. Even his hair was vigorous; a sprinkling of grey giving vital sparks to his straw-coloured crop. Yet Swan had never known Kavanagh to take exercise or leave the confines of a building or car unnecessarily. And his rosy complexion was probably due more to a combination of bluster and drink than the wind coming in from the Blaskets.

When Swan walked into Kavanagh's office on Monday morning he found his boss sitting behind the desk in a vest, revealing gouts of chest hair, shoulder freckles and the outline of nipples under thin ribbed cotton. It was all Swan could do not to raise his palms in front of his eyes.

'Do you want to me to come back later?'

'Get that prissy look off your puss, Swan. I spilled coffee down my shirt. Could happen to anyone. I asked Considine if she could wash it out, and the look she gave me would freeze a waterfall in spate. Your man Barrett steps in, thank god, says he knows a laundry and he'll have it back by noon. I've a lunch at the Castle today, the Dutch Prime Minister... or is it Belgian?'

Kavanagh looked around his desk for the invitation card, distracted by the possibility of a diplomatic *faux pas*. The current Garda Commissioner wasn't much of a man for canapés and glad-handing, so it fell to his deputies to represent the force on ambassadorial occasions. It was a task the fitted Kavanagh well, with his man-of-the-people bonhomie.

He waved a stiff card at Swan. 'Belgian! — Brussels, mussels, pissing statues. Right. Let's get on with it.'

'Well, our enquiries are continuing on two fronts. We're looking closely at the people on the spot — the religious community, their staff, former and current pupils —'

'The nuns — have you won their trust?'

'It's been slow enough. They're very resistant to any suggestion that anyone in their community might be implicated. Problem is, they think they're above the law, or answering to a different law, and I can't have that.'

'You *can't have that*? Careful, Vincent, a little softness doesn't go amiss — you don't want to get into one of your intellectual struggles about what is Caesar's and what is God's, eh? Let's just concentrate on finding the mother. Whatever way you can.'

There was a knock on the door and Barrett swooped in with a pale blue shirt on a hanger, draped in a gloss of polythene.

'Good man,' said Kavanagh, rising from his desk to grab the shirt. He tore off the plastic cover, threw the hanger in the corner and started to battle with the buttons. Barrett stood holding out the superintendent's jacket by its shoulders, waiting to help him on with it like some shop assistant.

Swan continued with his report.

'We checked out the pupil who left the school earlier this year. Eileen Vaughan.'

'She's back with her parents in Terenure,' offered Barrett.

'Want to tell the chief what you found?'

Barrett beamed for an instant, then the super turned towards him and lifted the jacket from his hands, giving him a suspicious look. With a flick of his hand he directed Barrett back to the public side of his desk. Barrett took his place standing beside Swan and recited, in a flattened voice,

'The girl was delivered of an infant six weeks ago in a refuge in Arklow...' He stopped to dig out his notebook.

'You're not in court, Barrett, just talk,' said Swan.

Barrett kept flipping through pages, so Swan took up the tale, sensing that Kavanagh's growing agitation wasn't just to do with buttoning his cuffs.

'We talked with the mother and girl yesterday. The baby went to adoptive parents, we checked it out with the agency that handled it.'

Swan had given his Sunday morning to visiting the girl at her home. The smell of frying lingered in their kitchen, making his stomach mourn for his usual Sunday morning ritual of scrambled eggs, black pudding and an onion roll from the Bretzel. The mother had refused to let them speak to Eileen alone, and kept chipping in her opinions. The girl herself seemed monosyllabic with misery, a baggy grey sweatshirt pulled over her still-heavy stomach, her lank hair curtaining a face that wore a look of protracted shock.

'And the baby?'

'Yes. The agency gave us the details of the adoptive family and Barrett went for a visit yesterday.'

'He's been keeping you busy.'

Barrett shrugged modestly.

'No problem, chief. Big house out in Sutton. The husband is a banker, the wife was too. They're all thrilled to bits. I'd say the little chap is very lucky.'

'So what's your second line?' Kavanagh addressed Swan.

'Pardon?'

'You said you had a second line of enquiry — come on.'

'It's very possible that the mother would go to her doctor for some medical attention afterwards. TP Murphy's leading a small team talking to all doctor's surgeries in the area, all Dublin hospitals too.'

Kavanagh was buttoning his jacket now. Looking around for his cap. Swan quickly told him they had identified a couple of families known to the social work department, one where a daughter already had an illegitimate daughter living in the home, the other where there had been two suicide attempts in the family in the past six months. Neither admitted to a baby having been in their midst.

'Murphy can tell you more. I thought he would be here.'

'Ah yes. Meant to say — I've sent Murphy to assist with the Dundalk shooting, there's a lot of pressure on that one and the usual cross-border shenanigans.'

Swan's first feeling was one of relief. He never could hit it off with TP and now he could co-ordinate things as he liked. But if they didn't find the woman, if things didn't work out, it would be entirely his responsibility.

He carried on as confidently as he could.

'Forensics have identified two types of fibre found on the baby's body. There are carpet fibres, blue, woollen twist, good quality, and there are also white polyester fibres which Dr. Flynn has identified as a type used in a looped stretch cloth, consistent with coming from a babygro or other towelling item. She's working on finding matches to specific manufacturers, but in the meantime, it does point to the baby being kept in a domestic situation for some of the time that it lived.'

'So what's your theory?'

'Something different from the usual panicked cover-up. Girl delivers baby at home, possibly with help. Things go normally for a day or two, baby fed and clothed, then either a change of heart, or its existence is discovered by someone hostile to the child.'

'You think it's not the mother.'

'Most likely it is, but the extent of the violence isn't typical.'

A knock at the door announced that the Superintendent's car was ready. He ushered them out alongside him.

'So you'll have something for me soon?' The boss liked to demand unfounded reassurance.

'We're still waiting on more technical reports, if there's anything you can do to hurry them—'

'All right, but I don't want to see another witness on national television, Vincent, especially not that same witness again. What is she at?'

'She's young. She won't be doing it again.'

'You make sure of it. What was this about her finding a baby before?'

'We checked it out, something of a sad coincidence. A stillbirth at a relative's house.'

Kavanagh grimaced, dismissed them with a salute and headed down the corridor alone.

'Have a good lunch, sir.' Barrett called after him.

Barrett was getting on his nerves. And for all her brightness, Considine was getting nowhere with her social work contacts. Ach, that wasn't fair. They just needed a break. It would come.

If they could find a realistic suspect, the forensics could probably do the rest. Otherwise they were going to be reduced to sampling every blue carpet in south Dublin or seeking permission to do physical check-ups on likely women. Starting with the two unfortunate families in Dodder Vale, then the girls of the gardening club and the younger nuns. But they couldn't go round palpating women without solid reason. He could just imagine what Mary O'Shea would do with that.

'Boss?'

Barrett interrupted his thoughts.

'I forgot to say your wife rang. She been called away to her aunt's.'

'Oh. Thanks.' Why did she have to go and do that? She could have just left a note at home, didn't need to talk to anyone here about anything.

'I hope everything's alright,' said Barrett

'What do you mean?'

'With her aunt, boss, I hope it's not serious with her aunt.'

FIFTEEN

She had come to look, that was all, just to see the place where Joan was. The mental hospital, that's what they used to call it. Or the nuthouse. A long grey building at the top of a grass bank. The window bars were painted white, blending in tastefully with the multi-paned windows behind. She imagined Joan appearing at one, dishevelled in a nightdress, white fingers raking at the pane. It gave her the creeps.

The big gates to the grounds were open, and as she watched, a couple walked out through them, chatting in an ordinary way, not hurrying or throwing fearful glances over their shoulders. The driveway climbed steeply up the bank and ran level along the front of the building. Maybe it would be okay to take a closer look, now that she had come all this way.

The front of Damascus House was flat, except for a glass entrance porch with a niche above it where a statue of Mary opened her arms to all comers. Ali walked slowly forward.

'Excuse me.'

A woman pushed past her from behind, carrying a cone of yellow flowers, clacking her way inside on stubby heels. So they allowed visitors. She'd just check if there was a notice saying what the hours were. Mary O'Shea would never be this timid. Mary O'Shea would have phoned, demanded information, be sitting on Joan's bed by now.

She didn't want much, just for Joan to tell her a bit

about the baby, to explain how it came to be under that bed. Then the thing would be done. She brushed her hands over her hair, pulled her ponytail tighter.

There were no details about visiting hours inside the porch. Beyond a second set of glass doors, a man sat behind a reception desk. He looked up and beckoned her.

The inevitable smell of chemical pine threaded through blousy heat. The man at the desk was busy with some paperwork. When she got close, she realised it was only a newspaper.

'Can you help me?' said Ali.

'Only if you can help me,' he replied, sucking on the end of his biro. 'Five letters, second one O, last one S — *weaver appears mistily.*'

'Sorry?'

He pushed the paper towards her and pointed at the last blank squares on his crossword puzzle. Ali shook her head.

'You should get into it. Keeps the old brain together...' His eyes drifted up toward the ceiling. 'Looms!' He scribbled the letters in, quick heavy strokes. 'Got ya!'

He flung the paper aside and gave her his full attention.

'I was wondering, is it possible for me to visit Joan Dempsey sometime?' said Ali.

'And you are?'

'A friend.'

'*I've* never seen you before.'

'An old friend. I don't live round here.'

He leaned forward over the desk and pointed. 'She's on the open ward. Down the corridor, up the end stairs, turn right and she should be somewhere around the west wing.'

'Does she have a room number or something?'

'Well, she won't be in it. She busies herself about the place. A busy bee.'

He looked down at the empty desk in front of him.

'Don't know what I'm going to do now,' he said pleasantly.

Ali walked down the wide corridor, her sandals chirping on the vinyl floor. There were doors on either side, all identical, with small windows of meshed glass beside each handle. One door was open and as she passed she caught sight of someone lying on a bed, an arm flung over her eyes, body covered with a flowery duvet.

As she climbed the stairs, her doubts multiplied. It was very likely that Joan wouldn't know her, or wouldn't welcome her if she did. A woman in a white overall banged through the fire doors at the top of the stairs, her head tilted to one side to see past an armload of sheets. She passed Ali without acknowledgement. Ali went through the doors and found herself looking down another corridor. On either side were large wards where people sat on beds or circulated slowly in dressing gowns. It looked like an ordinary hospital. She wanted to ask someone where to go, but the only official person she could see was a woman mopping the corridor ahead.

The woman was facing away from her, and as Ali approached she noticed she was wearing ordinary clothes, pale tight jeans and a baggy jumper. She was humming a song, something just beyond naming, but familiar.

Maybe it was the tune, or something in the way she moved, or just the way her curly hair piled together in defiance of gravity, but before she was within ten feet of her, Ali experienced a rush of recognition, as if her heart had pumped out a blast of hot water. She stood still and watched Joan move the mop to create shining figures of eight across the sea-green linoleum.

'Joan?'

The mop turned first, skimming round in a semi circle, Joan turning neatly behind it as if executing some kind of dance step.

'It's you!' Joan smiled and fine lines radiated from the sides of her eyes and bracketed her thin mouth. Otherwise she seemed not much changed. Smaller, certainly. Just tiny. Ali was more than a head taller than her now.

'I didn't think you'd know me.'

'Didn't I see you the other night?'

'You haven't seen me in years…'

'You were with that man — Gay Byrne.' Joan's smile faded and her eyes grew wide. 'Oh God.'

'What is it?'

'Something bad happened to you. I forgot.'

'You saw me on the telly — is that it?'

'The telly. Yes.'

'I'm visiting Buleen, so I thought I'd come and see you. Is that all right?'

'I suppose I can finish this later.'

Joan put the bucket and mop away in a cupboard, and led Ali to a large room full of vinyl armchairs and smoke, occupied by half a dozen people. A woman was lying on the floor. Sleeping, Ali presumed, since no one seemed concerned about her. Two men in shirt-sleeves were hunched over a card game. Joan proudly showed Ali a big television that was set into a cabinet on the wall.

'That's what I saw you on.'

'I'm still amazed you knew me. It's been so many years.'

'She's on the telly!' Joan announced to the room at large. Heads turned to them and quickly away. The woman on the floor slept on.

'Do you have a job here, Joan?'

'I like to help out.'

'But you stay here all the time, do you? As a...' Ali searched for the right word. *Patient* or *inmate* seemed too direct.

'Oh yes, full time.' Then, in a low voice, looking round as if worried the others would hear, 'They take care of me.'

'Should I tell someone that I'm here with you?'

Joan shrugged. 'What's Gay like? Is he very short?'

'He's normal-sized, I guess, and just like himself.'

'He looks short on the telly. Have you got cigarettes?'

Ali reached into her jeans pocket and pulled out her packet of Silk Cut.

'I don't think I have a light.'

'I can get you a light,' said a voice behind her. She looked around to see that a young man with a straight fringe had crept up on them. *Weaver appears mistily*, she thought. Other faces had perked up hopefully around the room. More impressive to have cigarettes than to be on the telly. She gave the boy a cigarette, then one to Joan and took another for herself. The boy walked over to the card game.

'Tony, can I have a light?'

Tony took a lighter from his jeans pocket, and as he did so, Ali noticed the bunch of keys hooked to his

144

belt. He winked at her as he put it back.

Over by the window, a girl her own age with a bad complexion was staring at her. Ali waved the packet of cigarettes in her direction and the girl approached with all the brash confidence of a woodland creature. They lit their cigarettes one by one from the boy's fag, drawing in deeply to make the glow catch across. The timid girl pressed the lit cigarette to her own so hard that the tip of the lit one became unhinged. The boy grabbed it from her, cursing.

'Watch it, Peter,' said Tony, never lifting his eyes from the cards. The boy shuffled off to sulk in a corner, holding the cigarette pointed to the ceiling. The timid girl sat in the chair beside Ali, a little smile on her face. Ali smiled back awkwardly. The lounge felt like a cross between a youth club and an old folk's home. There was a pool table on one side of the room, but no sign of any cues or balls. Instead, the surface was covered with boxes of jigsaws and piles of scuffed magazines.

Joan leaned across and poked the girl's knee.

'Go on with you.'

The girl moved away, and Joan leaned closer to Ali.

'You've gotten very tall. Have you heels on?'

Ali showed her the flat soles of her sandals. 'My dad was tall.'

Joan bit her lip and put her hand to her chest.

'Your poor Daddy. God, I remember you coming to Caherbawn with your Mammy and the tears still wet on your cheeks.' She looked as though she would cry herself.

'You weren't too happy either, were you, Joan?'

Joan shot a look around, settling on the card players.

'I have to be careful. They rely on me to be cheerful.'

Joan picked up an ashtray and motioned to the window with a jog of her head, and they strolled over with exaggerated nonchalance. The view outside was of a brutish tarmac yard stretching away from the back of the hospital. Cars were parked along its far edge where it butted up to a field dotted with black cattle.

'Do you remember me finding something that Christmas day?' ventured Ali.

Joan shook her head, looked out at the hot cars.

Ali moved an inch closer, 'You know there was a baby. It wasn't alive. It was in a box, up in the back bedroom. And I wondered... was it yours?'

'You found a baby in Dublin. I've never even been to Dublin.' Joan wouldn't look at her. As she lifted her cigarette to her mouth Ali noticed a tremor in her hand.

'Not that baby. I'm talking about before.'

'Boxes. Bedrooms. I don't know what you're on about.'

'You *were* expecting, weren't you?'

There was a tiny flicker from Joan, a tightening of the corner of her mouth.

'T'was a miscarriage.' She hissed the word out.

Ali looked out the window. What she had seen couldn't be a miscarriage, could it? A miscarriage would be unformed, would look like something from that abortion film that the nuns had shown them with the bin full of discarded foetuses; a red galaxy swirling with the soft outlines of frog legs and newt palms among nameless clots of matter. Girls had fled the assembly hall, retching as they went.

Joan flicked rhythmically at the cigarette butt with her fingernail. Ash flakes sprinkled the windowsill.

'The baby was wrapped in a towel,' Ali persisted. 'It was a small baby, but it looked perfect.'

On the word *perfect*, Joan froze. She addressed the windowpane.

'Not a miscarriage, the other thing. When it doesn't live. Your aunt said that there would be other babies. But she was wrong, I tried and no others came. I gave myself to men I didn't even like. A stone birth — I mean *still* birth — that's what they call it.' Joan's voice was getting unsteady. 'Sometimes I think God must hate me. He just hates me.'

She crossed her arms and put her chin against one shoulder.

Ali wished she hadn't mentioned the baby. She didn't know how to do this, not without upset. A whole world of upset. She had a nerve coming here, bothering Joan. If the people who ran this place knew why she was here they would keep *her* in, her and her dead babies. And Tony would wink at her as he tucked her up in her narrow bed, keys jingling at his hip.

'I'm sorry. Nobody ever explained it to me. I'm just trying to make sense of it.'

'You said it was perfect. Was it really?'

Ali nodded, put an arm round Joan's waist.

'I'm sorry.'

'What did your aunt tell you?'

'I didn't ask her.'

Ali had never sung songs with Una, never run her hands through Una's hair. She couldn't even re-member speaking to her aunt when there weren't other people present.

Joan turned away from the window, smoothed out her cheeks with her palms.

'You used to drag that black kitten about — remember?' said Joan, 'Carried it all over the place with you like a dolly, never mind the fleas on it. You had bites all over your arms.'

Ali smiled. Remembering it now. 'You put calamine lotion on me.' Chalky streaks of it, crackling when it dried.

So odd to think of this tiny woman taking care of her, the substantial presence of her then compared to now. She had been queen of the kitchen, the heart of the house for Ali, but Joan had owned nothing but her labour.

A woman wheeled in a trolley of blue cups and handed strong, sugary tea to everyone, Ali included. She and Joan sat in chairs near the window. The boy called Peter turned on the television with the sound down, and everyone looked at the screen for a while, supping their tea. Onscreen, a man in yellow dungarees was talking to a red haired puppet. The card players took a break from their game. It was sort of cosy.

'I went to visit but your aunt shooed me off. They won't give me my job back.'

'It was a long time ago, Joan.'

'Well she used to be very good to me. And then she wasn't.'

'When you were pregnant?'

Joan frowned and checked that no-one had heard. The card players were talking. The sleeper on the floor slept on, a cup of cooling tea by her head.

'You and your Mammy as bad as the rest.'

'What did we do?'

'You passed me on the road, me and my brother, like we were too dirty to pick up, like we were tinkers.'

As Joan said it, Ali had a vague memory of being in her mother's new car, starting the trip back up to

Dublin, and Joan on the grass verge of the road, holding a yellow-haired boy close in to her body as their car drove past them.

'Did you leave Caherbawn the same day as us?'

'Thrown out, more like.'

Joan was as cross as if it was yesterday, screwing the butt of her cigarette into the ashtray, mashing it.

'You know, there really isn't much of a job to do anymore. There's hardly anyone to cook for,' said Ali.

'How d'you mean?'

'Roisín, the twins and Davy are gone. They have their own homes. There don't seem to be any farm-hands, either. It's only my aunt and uncle there now. And Brendan.'

The anger drained from Joan's expression. She looked confused and her mouth writhed, trying to form some word. Ali got out of her chair and stooped down in front of Joan, catching her small hands together in her own, trying to soothe her. She looked over at Tony, but he didn't seem to notice Joan's distress. Only the shy girl looked over, scratching her cheek rhythmically.

'You were very good to me,' Ali said, searching out eye contact. 'I remember that. You were kind.'

Joan looked at her, uncertain.

'You sang me the farting song that Auntie Una banned. You let me plait your hair, and you made me show you my Irish dancing up on the kitchen table and clapped out the beat for me. Do you remember?' Joan nodded, a suggestion of a smile on her face now. 'I didn't come to trouble you, Joan, I'm sorry if I have.'

'I can't believe where the time goes,' said Joan, 'I lose track.'

'Why are you here, Joan?'

Joan looked around the room, and back at Ali.

'I needed to feel safe,' she said, 'but I didn't mean to stay so long.'

'Things can change.'

'Would you do something for me?'

'Yes,' said Ali. 'I'd be happy to.'

'Take me out.'

'I don't know if... I wouldn't be allowed.'

'I go out all the time. We could go on a jaunt — just for an afternoon.'

'Okay. If they let me.'

Joan's smile was broad now, and she brushed Ali's hands away from her.

'We'll have a picnic.'

'Let me ask at the desk if that will be okay, first, Joan.'

'It will, it will.'

'I'll think of somewhere nice. If it's allowed.'

Tony was on the reception desk when she came down, and he said that it would be fine for Ali to take Joan out on Thursday. For however long she wanted. It all seemed rather casual.

SIXTEEN

Swan drove along the north quays then headed over the river towards Ranelagh. He wanted to drop in on the Hogan girl again, make sure she had no more media appearances planned. Perhaps she'd still have that mortified look about her, the one she wore so well on *The Late Late*. And that slimy doctor who spent his time teaching twelve-year olds the facts of life. Something creepy about that. If he ever had a daughter, he wouldn't want her taught by him. A daughter. Elizabeth's voice cut in to his thoughts — *If we don't try again we'll never know.*

He braked as the car in front of him slowed. The traffic looked knotted all the way up Camden Street. The radio news was talking about the recession and unemployment, but it didn't seem to stop people buying cars.

He parked on Sandford Road and walked up the narrow passage to the Hogan's front door. He had been taken aback on his previous visit by the scruffiness of the place, forced to revise his notions about St. Brigid's girls and their cushy backgrounds.

It was the kind of house he often had cause to visit, tall old terraces divided up badly into bedsits, usually home to the young and the transient. A line of plastic doorbells hung to the side of the door, the names in the little windows faded to sepia scratchings, cut wires hanging below. He knocked on the blistered paint and waited some time before he heard steps approach.

'Who is it?'

He recognised Deirdre Hogan's voice. As soon as he announced himself, she opened it, all smiles.

'You've good timing. Coffee's on.'

He followed her down to the kitchen. She seemed to be dressed in night clothes, but she had mentioned before that she was some kind of artist, so perhaps she wafted around like this all day.

'Is Ali at home?'

'She's not,' she said, leaning into a cupboard for mugs. 'But I'm sure I can help you with whatever you want.'

Swan took a chair at the big table. Mrs. Hogan reached over his shoulder to put the coffee down and a layer of silk brushed his cheek. Sometimes he found the attentions of women uncomfortable, like now, the way Deirdre Hogan was smiling at him, her head tilted away while her eyes slid back to find him. She took a chair directly opposite and leaned forward on the table so that her crossed arms framed her cleavage. It would be easy to misread the situation.

The coffee was strong and slightly gritty.

'I can guess why you're here — it's *The Late Late*, isn't it? I'd be annoyed if I were you — I told her so, but she was determined to go on.'

'I take it you tried to discourage her.'

'What powers have I against Mary O'Shea? Ali's only young. Think of the excitement, the attention.'

'She didn't seem too excited by the end of it.'

Deirdre Hogan looked uncomfortable. 'Well, you don't have to worry about it anymore. She's had enough attention to last her for years.'

'I thought she might. Where is she?'

Mrs. Hogan opened her mouth to speak, closed

it again and smiled. She gave him a look that seemed to convey a great intimacy, as if the two of them were beyond simple whys and wheres.

'You know, when Ali's Dad died, my life fell apart. A heart attack, it was. He was playing rugby at the time, only forty-two. How could you expect something like that? My sister down in Buleen took us in and I stayed there licking my wounds for quite a few weeks. I was so wrapped up in my own grief, I couldn't see what Ali was going through. She was only six — she acted normally, played, laughed — I thought she hadn't taken it in. But now I see it wasn't the right place for her.'

'I don't understand what you're getting at.'

'Well, a farm is a harsh place, you know... ailing lambs by the cooker, crows strung up on the barbed wire, baby pigs rolled flat by their sow. All the shit and blood of it.' Mrs. Hogan wiped a single tear away with the side of her palm, 'and then that bloody box. It had to be her that found it.' She sighed. 'Ach, I'm just indulging my own guilt, detective.'

'I just want to have a word with her.'

'That's what I'm getting at, she's gone down to stay with my sister.'

'Right now? We're in the middle of an investigation.'

'She's refused to go back to the farm for twelve years, wouldn't even enter the house after her Grandad's funeral, made me drive straight back to Dublin. Now, she's somehow found the strength. Sure, didn't you want her out of the limelight.'

The mother was right. Surely the girl would cause less trouble down there. He managed to squeeze an address and phone number out of her. Caherbawn Farm, Buleen, near Kinmore. He'd need to look it up on a map. He didn't know his own country as well as he should.

His visit had been a waste. Then he thought of something Mrs. Hogan could do for him.

'While I'm here… could I borrow one of Ali's school blouses? One was found in the shed, and we're trying to gather a few comparisons. I'd be obliged.'

He followed Mrs. Hogan — *call me Deirdre, please* — up two flights of bare stairs to the top of the house and into the girl's bedroom, while she flung apologies over her shoulder about the state of the place.

The room looked like someone had stolen half the furniture then exploded a basket of clothing, kitchenware and toiletries over the remains. Painted floorboards were visible here and there through the wreckage. The lilac walls were decorated with posters and leftover blobs of blu-tack.

Deirdre Hogan rifled through a chest of drawers, then rooted through a dirty clothes basket.

While she searched, he examined the pictures of pop stars, their young faces twisted in sneers and dumb, malevolent stares. He wouldn't be young again for anything. All that yearning. All that pretending you didn't care. He winced at the ramshackle shower cubicle festooned with clothes and the old sink unit in the corner. On the floor beneath the sink an electric kettle shared a tray with some mugs and a jar of instant coffee. This room had been a bedsit — a complete home to someone. He looked at the door and saw there was a lock still on it. A tingle ran up the back of his skull.

Was it possible for a girl to deliver a baby and conceal that fact from other people for some time? If she had a lock on the door, didn't have to share a bathroom, it would help a great deal. But could she be as cool as Ali Hogan was after the fact? That would take some acting. He recalled the first sight of her, the clownish clothes, her eagerness to help. But now he was remembering other things. That big baggy dress she had on. He'd seen other girls in dresses like that. He knew it was the fashion, but it could serve another purpose entirely.

For those two or three days that constituted its brief life, its only life, the baby could have been kept somewhere like this, out of sight, out of hearing.

Mrs. Hogan was picking up clothes at random from the floor, stirring some larger piles with her foot. There was no carpet here though, no blue carpet fibres. Though a rug would be easy enough to roll up and remove.

'This is impossible. There might be one in the laundry room.'

He followed Ali's mother down the stairs. When they got to a landing, he asked where her own bedroom was. He wanted to judge the distance between the two.

She stopped still and gave him an amused, searching look. 'Just down here at the front.'

'And this laundry room?' he asked quickly.

'By the kitchen,' she said, turning from him.

She led him to a narrow room under the stairs that was made even more constricted by the heaps of stuff massed against the walls or piled onto shelves that rose to the ceiling. Useless looking stuff — stacked yoghurt cartons, jars, bags full of more bags and folded wrapping paper, stacks of magazines. Mrs. Hogan was standing by an old ceramic sink, so big you could stand a child in it, sorting though one of several plastic baskets massed on the metal counter beside it.

'This one's the ironing,' she said. 'Sorry about the

mess, things are always going missing on me... Ah!'

She pulled out a crumple of white.

'We got there at last.' She handed the shirt to Swan, showing her dimples. 'How about some more coffee?'

'Why not? May I take one of these bags?'

He pulled a yellow bag from a clutch of plastic bags stuffed into a cardboard tube, and put the blouse inside it.

As Deirdre Hogan made coffee, he asked more about the house, how long they'd been there, and who else shared it.

'The lodgers are all gone now,' she said. 'Just the separate basement flat rented out now. It seemed like a good idea at the time to buy this, and it did keep us afloat. I practically evicted the last tenant a year ago, but, do you know, now they're gone, I just don't know where to start with it. Ali and I rattle about in it. Maybe I'll get lucky and she'll marry a builder.'

Swan stirred his coffee. Pretending concern for Ali's state of mind, he got her to go through her daughter's movements before the finding of the baby. Mrs. Hogan was happy to talk. She said she was away with friends on the Sunday, the day before Ali found the baby, the day the pathologist determined it was killed. Ali had been home when she got home, she thought, but that was late. She said Ali had been hanging around the house mostly since her school term ended.

'She complains she has no money, but does nothing about finding a job. My young brother's the same.'

There was nothing in what the mother said to contradict his tenuous new theory. For all her warmth, Deirdre Hogan didn't keep very close tabs on her daughter. Ali had the means to conceal a baby, she wore baggy clothes, and she was on the spot when the child was found. Was that because she had recently concealed it? Guilt drawing her back? He remembered the large patchwork bag of hers they had taken from the shed. The one she tried to get back from them. Big enough for a child. The convent was just around the corner. Maybe the attention seeking was actually part of it, some twisted form of remorse.

Deirdre Hogan released her hair from its metal clasp and started to twist it into some new arrangement at the back of her head. As she held her arms up, her wide sleeves fell down to her shoulders, revealing plump, pale arms.

'And what about yourself, any children?'

He recoiled inside. He didn't want to tell her about his marriage troubles nor did he want to take her upstairs to some sagging clutter-draped bed. Not in this life, at least. He tried to imagine Elizabeth in a dressing gown, entertaining some caller with a glimpse of her breasts over burnt coffee. Never.

Deirdre Hogan took his silence to be an admission of romantic failure.

'I'm sorry,' she said, 'If you don't want to talk about it, that's fine.'

His disdain crumbled. What was the good of having such an admirable wife when she was rarely at home, and hardly spoke to him when she was. They had a chasm between them. That's what it was getting like, a black pit with no crossing place.

'Tell me, Deirdre,' he said.

She smiled at the mention of her name.

'What would you do if your daughter came to you and said she was pregnant?'

'Oh God, is that your trouble?'

'No it's just a question, I don't have children.'

If we don't try again we'll never know.

'Oh. Well I always say to Ali, she should come straight to me if anything like that happens, and God, it can happen so easily, but I would never kick her out.'

He was inclined to believe her good intentions, but intentions weren't the same as facts. He had a feeling the mother didn't know the daughter that well.

SEVENTEEN

Butterflies skittered about the purple shocks of thistle that rose here and there above the grass and frothy meadowsweet. The sun came out between clouds and Joan looked around and smiled. Beyond Joan's curly head Ali could see the line of trees that marked the river.

Joan paused in her tracks and held her free hand behind her to signal Ali to stop too. There was someone walking along the riverbank, a man, too distant to recognise. They stood silent, watching him grow smaller, headed for the town. Ali looked back towards the road. She could make out the whole top floor of Caherbawn rising above the surrounding hedges. She wished that Joan hadn't been so insistent that they come here for their picnic, so close to her aunt's. She walked on through the meadow, following in Joan's steps until they reached a bend in the river, screened by saplings.

A crescent of butterscotch-coloured sand jutted into the slow dark water. The opposite bank was undercut, a ledge of rough grass hanging over a mud wall pocked with holes and burrows above the waterline. In the shadows of the trees, midges swirled like sparks.

Ali kicked off her sandals and bundled up the skirt of her dress, tying it in a knot in front so that it hung in a baggy puff above her knees. Joan sat cross-legged on the dry river sand, squinting up at her, smiling.

'It must be nice for you to be out here. In the open air.'

'I've been out loads,' said Joan. 'My mother takes

me shopping on Fridays, and I've been home for a few Christmases. I've even tried to stay out a few times, but something always happens.'

'Like what?'

'I lose the run of myself. I get panicky, and they bring me back.' She shrugged, then flicked her chin up. 'Hey, do you see that rope?'

Ali turned to where Joan was looking. A frazzled grey rope hung over the water from a nearby branch.

'That was your cousins' swing. They'd stay down here for whole days in the summer, and me minding them if your aunt could spare me. *Make sure they don't drown,* she'd say. I hadn't the nerve to tell her I couldn't swim meself. But sure, they all grew up, didn't they, though the twins had me terrified. Savages, they were.'

'I remember Roisín talking about the river,' said Ali. 'But I never came down here.'

'Were you never here in the summer?'

'No, this is the first time I've stayed with them since, you know, my Dad…'

Ali stepped into the water. It was the colour of strong tea, giving her legs an orange cast. Muddy sand oozed between her toes. She walked back and forth, calf-deep.

'Are you coming for a paddle, Joan?'

But Joan was off on more memories, suddenly streaming with talk after her silence of the bus — things that the twins did to scare her, Brendan's fishing exploits, how, if Roisín got splashed, she would squeal in a way that would make you deaf.

'Did Davy not come down?'

'Too grown up he was. Or thought he was.'

Ali's feet had numbed, so she came out of the water and sat down to unpack the picnic onto the fringed scarf she had brought to serve as a rug. Joan talked on. Two boiled eggs. Ham sandwiches that she had made behind her aunt's back and wrapped in a bread packet. A bottle of lemonade and a yellow brick of Battenberg cake she had bought from the shop. Nothing looked as nice as she thought it would.

'Have something to eat, Joan.'

'In a minute. I've something to tell you.'

'Oh?' Ali rearranged the food and waited.

'It wasn't until I saw you. Standing in that corridor tall as a woman — I realised how much time had passed. And now that it's sunk in, well, it's all different.'

'How do you mean?'

'You saying there was no job at Caherbawn for me. I was waiting to get back to it all this time, waiting for your aunt to give in, waiting to get better. I spent years up in Damascus House thinking they'd get me right to take up my life again. But there's no life to take up. Everyone's changed or grown except me.'

Joan got to her feet and started pacing, hands dug into her jeans pockets.

'You weren't well, Joan.' Ali watched her walk to the water's edge. 'Was it the baby… was it that, that put you in the hospital?'

Joan stooped to pick up a stone and flung it into the water.

'It's not a hospital, you know. It's a residential facility.'

'Sorry. You don't seem so bad to me.'

'I'm not well.' Joan turned to look at her directly. 'After the baby and losing the job things were hard. I fell out with my family.'

Joan dropped down to sit on the other side of the picnic cloth and hugged her knees tightly to her chest, squinting at the light that flashed from the river.

'I didn't know the baby was coming. I should have known, but my monthlies were never regular. Then there was the pains, and I was trying to keep quiet.'

'Was this in Caherbawn?'

'In the kitchen. I was scared I would die.'

'Oh, Joan. Did no one know?'

'The dog was there for the first bit. Looking at me.'

'What?'

'That old dog, Brownie. I was scared he would eat it.'

'Jesus. Why didn't you get some help?'

'I shouldn't even have been there.'

'Didn't you go to the hospital?'

'There wasn't time. Then it was too late.'

'Why did you hide it?'

'I didn't — it was taken away. You can't have seen it.'

'I did! And so did my Ma and Una, and Joe I think, he was there too —'

'Shut your mouth, you.'

'I'm sorry,' said Ali. 'I just need to get it straight in my head.'

'Don't bother yourself.'

Joan took a sandwich, tore at it quickly with her mouth. Ali tried to look like she wasn't scared of her. She lifted one of the boiled eggs and rolled it against a flat stone, the shell crackling to mosaic.

They stayed for a while in silence, Ali concentrated on peeling the egg, bit by bit, revealing the shine. Joan threw a hard end of crust at the water. Immediately there was a 'plop' and a flash of silver. Joan and Ali looked at each other and rushed to the river's edge.

Three dark torpedo shapes moved in the depths. Joan was suddenly gleeful — clenching and unclenching her hands as if she wanted to clap, urging Ali to go in and try to catch one. Ali laughed and shook her head, but to please Joan she bundled up her skirt in one hand and tiptoed back into the water, trying to move her feet as smoothly as possible. As her shadow fell over the trout, they shot off downriver, scarcely moving a fin to do so. They were there, and then they were gone. But the mood had lightened, and they returned to their picnic as if starting over.

Ali had forgotten to bring a knife and they had to squash the pink and yellow cake into slices with a thin driftwood stick. They passed the bottle of lemonade between them. Joan told proud stories now about her three brothers — how they could tickle trout with their hands, how the youngest had tamed a crow to sit on his shoulder. Later on, Ali tried to swing on the decaying rope swing, pressing her feet tight against the knot at the bottom, leaning back to get it moving, imagining her cousins all playing here, while she was stuck on her own in Dublin.

Every so often, Joan would ask what time it was.

'What does it matter what the time is?' Ali said finally. 'You said the doors don't close until eight.'

'No, really, what time is it?'

'Quarter to three.'

'I've got to go.'

Joan went over to get her jacket and the sports bag that she had brought with her. When Ali had gone to pick her up from Damascus House she was sitting in the foyer with the bag between her feet. Ali thought Joan might have brought some picnic things of her own, but she had just dumped it on the grass. Now she put the jacket on, picked up the bag and headed back through the field. Ali shouted after her to *wait*, but she kept on going, leaving Ali to bundle the picnic things into her basket and buckle her sandals before setting off in pursuit. As she ran towards the road, she thought she saw something moving behind one of the bedroom windows at Caherbawn, but when she stopped to look properly, there was nothing there, just darkness.

She caught up with Joan at the field gate.

'Wait for me.'

'I'm not going back,' Joan said, 'and don't worry, I'm not going to hang around your neck neither.'

'But the people at the hospital… I signed my name in the book!'

Joan laughed and reached up to touch Ali's hair. 'You're awful chicken for such a big girl.'

They walked along the verge, past the entrance for Davy's bungalow and on until they came to a forestry road. Entering the shade of the trees, Ali immediately felt chilly. She followed Joan uphill on the yellow clay track, trying to think of ways to talk her round, to get her back to Kinmore. Little stones kept flicking into her sandals, and she had to stop and shake them out while Joan kept walking further ahead. One time, she looked up and Joan was gone.

She called her name and listened to the sound die in the trees. There was only the creaking of boughs and the dull wave of a car engine passing on the road behind. It was tempting to go back, to leave Joan in the woods, but the moment Ali thought it she felt ashamed. She hurried towards the spot where she had last seen Joan.

The trees thinned to the left of the track and tire marks led off into what looked like a clearing. She could see far ahead on the forestry road, and it was empty. Joan must have turned off here. Ali hurried down the new path, passing a tumbled wall of mossy stones. She entered a clearing where a ruined, roofless cottage stood among rusting bracken. There was someone talking inside the ruin, it was Joan's voice. Moving towards the cottage, Ali noticed a blue van parked at the back of the building. Sunshine still caught on the tops of the trees, but at ground level the air was shaded, almost foggy.

As Ali stepped through the entrance her eyes took in several things at once; that there was an odd little corrugated shelter at one end of the enclosure, and that Joan was not alone and raving but chatting happily to a young man who was sitting on the sill of a gaping window, a can of lager in his hand.

'Ivor wouldn't mind a sandwich if we have one left,' said Joan.

The boy nodded at her. She had seen him before, outside Melody's on Sunday, the one she thought looked like a viking. Joan was talking about Ivor at the river. The little brother that had tamed the crow was now six feet tall, incongruously large beside his sister. Ali unwrapped a sandwich for him and handed it over, not knowing what to say.

He offered her a drink from his can. She shook her head.

'I'll have some,' said Joan.

'You won't,' said Ivor, 'God knows what kind of drugs they've been giving you up in that place.'

Joan looked delighted at his bossiness. Ali took out the lemonade and passed it to her.

'I'm going to stay with Ivor.'

'You can't stay in this place,' said Ali, looking at the rusting patchwork of the lean-to hut.

Joan goggled like Ali was the one who was crazy.

'No, in the village! Ivor's got a flat above the garage. I'm going to look after it for him and cook.'

'Do you think I look like I live in this dump?' said Ivor.

Ali stuttered. 'Sorry. No offence.'

'It's true we used to stay here the odd night when we were young. This was our grandad's place, before the Forestry bought the land.'

'Ivor was only ten when he put that shelter together,' said Joan. 'He was always good with his hands.'

'When times got a bit wild up at our house, Joanie would take me down here. *Going camping* she'd call it.'

He smiled then, a brief flash of sunshine across the dour plains of his face, revealing one gold incisor among the white of his teeth.

Ali wanted to see him smile again, just to see the flash of gold. She talked about their picnic at the river, making fool of her own attempts at paddling and swinging, claiming she had stolen the picnic food from under her aunt's nose. Every time he smiled, she felt she had won something.

Ivor finished the last swig of his can and threw it in the fireplace where it joined a heap of other cans and a mess of ash and twisted wire. Ali noticed that Joan looked exhausted, had been quiet for some time.

'Sorry. You'll be wanting to get on to your new home, and I've been prattling on.'

Joan came over and hugged her, the top of her head bumping off Ali's chin.

'You were good to take me out. I couldn't have done it myself, and Ivor won't go near the place.'

'They might keep me,' he said.

'I said to myself you coming was like a sign.'

'I'm sorry I upset you,' said Ali.

Joan's eyes shifted briefly to Ivor, then back. 'We'll not mention it again,' she said quietly, then lifted her voice, 'There's a marquee dance on by the school tomorrow night, Ivor says. Maybe I'll go. Maybe I'll see you there.'

'Oh, I'll be there,' said Ali, 'Brendan's doing the disco.'

Ivor rose from the windowsill and brushed invisible crumbs from the front of his thighs. He gave his sister a little smile and she returned it and lifted her sports bag. Now that Ali realised it was all that Joan packed for her new life, it seemed terribly small.

At the doorway, Ivor hesitated, waited till Joan went on, then came back to stand in front of Ali. The blazing sky cast him in silhouette, the edges of his crinkly hair on fire, his face unreadable.

'Who's taking you to the dance?' he demanded.

'I'm taking myself to the dance. It's the twentieth century.'

He just looked at her for a moment, not saying anything. She held a hand up to shade her eyes, to try and read his expression, but he was already leaving.

She listened to the van fire up and drive away, wondering why he had sounded angry.

The lean-to was a strange little construction, a bit like a metal tent. She strolled over to an open end and saw an old mattress lying there, smeared with mud on top and a blue bloom of damp rising up its sides. Some animal had been chewing at a corner. She hoped it had been nicer back when Joan and Ivor used to camp here.

She threaded her way to the forestry road, glad that Joan would be living in the world again, but worried about her own name lying in the register at

Damascus House.

As she walked on, she found herself wondering what Joan meant when she said her baby was *taken away*. Who took it? Why was it under a bed?

A gust of wind nudged her and she walked faster, forcing herself forward, back to Caherbawn. Crows argued above her. She told herself to stop fretting at it.

EIGHTEEN

The security guard at the back gate of Trinity College examined Swan's ID carefully before waving them through. They controlled the most desirable car park in the city centre, but did they have to be quite so up themselves? Those porters with their stupid frock coats and riding hats, like they were off to a hunt, when they were from the same plebeian stock as himself. Never so much as sniffed a horse, except for the ones that pulled the knacker's carts.

'Boss?' said Barrett.

Swan realised he had been muttering. He pulled into a parking space near the cricket pavilion. Sports fields spread out in front of them, and beyond, the stately quadrangles and cobbles that featured in a hundred thousand postcards.

'Why weren't we born to this, Barrett?'

'Did you apply, boss?'

'Did I biffo. My parents wouldn't hear of such a thing, and the bishop's ban was still in force. I hear its mostly southside types now, the cream of young Ireland'

'I got in. Did a year of economic and social studies. Loved it.'

Swan carried on as smoothly as he could manage, 'Why didn't you graduate, so?'

Barrett shrugged, looked at his watch. 'Circumstances. The need to get a job. I think we're a bit late.'

Swan let it alone. A rustle of applause greeted

them as they got out of the car. Young ones sat about on the steps of the pavilion, at their ease, drinking, watching lean boys in whites play cricket. They couldn't even play an Irish game here, loping around like Brideshead fops with their little red ball. God, he was getting like his father, disgusted at whatever was put in front of him.

They passed behind the pavilion and entered a nondescript building that was part of the science department. Four flights up was the office of the State Pathologist, a man who combined an academic career with intimate examination of the country's dead. He was a well-known figure throughout Ireland, striding across newspaper photographs — out of court, into court, or entering a tented area in some newly blighted place.

The room they entered hummed with fridges, freezers and extractor fans. The whiff of formalin brought Swan's nostrils to attention. The muddle of the place reminding him of Deirdre Hogan's, but here the clutter was elevated to a professional level. Slide carousels, files, shelves of reference books, microscopes and other precise-looking instruments he couldn't put a name to crammed the room. Stacks of tupperware boxes filtered the light from the attic windows. Of course it probably had a different name when put to scientific use — *plasticeptacle* or *polyquarinator* or something.

Among this attic of delights stood the Edwardian figure of the pathologist, leaning on his knuckles over one of the island counters that sliced the room, half moon glasses balanced mid-nose as he stared at something in a white plastic box in front of him. He wore his lab coat open, displaying a tweed suit, check shirt and knit tie. He looked like a man who might go and shoot some grouse when the office day ended.

As they approached he pulled a lid onto the box and pushed it to one side. While they made their pleasantries Swan eyes kept wandering towards it, imagining lurid contents — a severed body part or some naked, quivering organ.

'Vincent, do you bring me news or are you wanting something from me?'

'I had a question,' said Swan, 'It's going to sound a bit naïve.'

The State Pathologist folded his arms and leaned back in readiness. 'It's the simple ones are the tough ones,' he said, '*Who made the world* and all that.'

'How can you tell if a woman has carried a child? Internally, I mean.'

Swan got a smile for his effort.

'Hmmm... pregnancy shifts the pelvic girdle, widening and loosening the joints to a certain degree. It also stretches the womb, naturally enough, and even though it contracts again, you can tell the difference at post mortem if the deceased is still of child bearing age. After the menopause it's a bit more difficult. Of course in cases where there was a subsequent hysterectomy, the difficulty is obvious — just the bone girdle to go by.'

'What if the woman is still alive?'

'I don't get you.'

'If she's walking about saying that she hasn't had a baby at all, can you prove she has?'

'There would commonly be signs from such a major event, of course, trauma... scarring... suchlike... It depends on how much time had passed between delivery and examination.'

The pathologist reached over and pulled the plastic box an inch towards his body, then poked it so it lay exactly parallel to the desk edge. Swan felt the silence between them like a great fog of uncertainty. Three men talking wombs.

'I think you should be talking to an obstetrician about this,' said the pathologist, 'but I imagine the accessible signs to look for are stretching of the skin, scar tissue from tearing at the mouth of the vagina and changes in the os.'

'The what?'

'The os. The opening in the cervix — becomes distended into a line rather than a dot. And a scan would probably reveal womb changes.'

Barrett had pulled out his notebook, was writing 'OZ?' on a blank page.

'What about the psychological effect? Do you think it would be possible for a woman or girl to deliver a baby and then sort of forget about it? Or not really forget about it, in the ordinary sense, but blank it, act as if nothing at all had happened. Even tell herself that nothing had happened?'

The pathologist pulled over a stool and sat down.

'Psychology's not my field. But I remember a case in England, about eight years ago, still sticks with me. A young guest at a wedding delivered herself in a toilet cubicle during the reception, then placed the baby and the afterbirth in the sanitary bin and rejoined the party. People were coming and going all the time, and one witness saw the girl retouch her makeup before leaving the Ladies. And none of her friends or even her boyfriend admitted to noticing she was pregnant.'

'Complete denial?'

'Yes, or at least a sense of putting things back to how they should be, *sans* baby.'

'And just carry on normally.'

'Exactly. Unless you've come across yet another

dead infant, I presume we are still discussing your Rosary baby?'

Swan nodded.

'In cases of denial you don't take the time to wash, feed and clothe your baby before killing it. Though you might take into account the possibility of puerperal psychosis — there is often a strong urge to harm the child, which is why we separate infanticide from murder.'

'Do you think its possible for a girl to deliver and look after a baby on her own, to keep its existence from anyone else?'

'I'm flattered that you seek my opinion on such a wide range of things.'

'Have a go —'

'Probably. Maybe. Women have delivered on their own throughout history, I'm sure they still do, though few would actually choose it. There's a good man at Holles Street I can recommend for all this stuff.'

Barrett wrote the good man's name in his book. The pathologist reached out for his plastic box again, pulling it directly in front of him and pausing to look at them with his thumbs hooked under the lip of the lid.

They said their thanks and goodbyes quickly.

In the stairwell, Barrett started to pester him.

'You've got a theory, haven't you? Is it the Hogan girl? The blouse you gave me for forensics, it was from her house, wasn't it?'

Swan didn't answer, just led the way back to the car. They stood on either side of it, looking at each other across the roof.

'If it was her, how could she act so cool?' Swan offered.

'Cool indeed,' said Barrett, 'one of the guards said she asked for a last look at the baby when they were taking it from the garden. Did you know that?'

'I didn't... that bag of hers that was in the shed — bring it up to forensics for a check on the inside. And ask Considine to get in touch with her friend again, Carmen Fitzgerald. Have a little chat.'

Barrett looked happy as Larry then, jiggling his knees all the way back along the quays, eager to get on with his messages.

As Swan drove across the Liffey, Barrett turned abruptly to him.

'What the hell was in that box?'

NINETEEN

Their footsteps boomed on the wooden floor of the empty marquee. Davy did a little run around the pillars with the loaded trolley; *brumpa brumpa brumpa* across the boards. Ali thought this was hilarious and probably would have been pretty funny even without the cans of cider they had shared in the van.

'Watch out for the whirly light cupboard thing,' she said.

'Oh we wouldn't drop the whirly light cupboard,' Brendan said from the empty stage, and Ali bent over, jack-knifed on a wave of giggling that was almost annoying in its intensity, like being tickled by someone who wouldn't stop. Brendan jumped down and patted her head in passing, dislodging one of the combs that held her hair in a whirl on top of her head. A hank of it fell over one eye. She cursed, he laughed.

Father Philbin appeared at the marquee entrance and squinted across the gloom at them.

'Are you not set up yet, lads? The band's due for the sound check.'

Not waiting for an answer, he crossed the floor and disappeared into the side tent, where refreshments would be sold. Brendan and Davy quietened and started to connect their speakers and decks. The wall of the tent behind them lifted at the bottom and a thin man in a boiler suit and flat cap crawled through, holding a cable and plug board, which he handed to Brendan.

'Good man!' Davy called after him. From outside the tent came the wheeze and splutter of an engine cord being pulled. A low thrum started up, followed by a click, and the tent was cheered with light from the strings of coloured bulbs that hung across the space.

'Hey, Ali — whirly light for you.' Brendan had the light box working, kaleidoscope patterns pulsing across its square screen like fast-blooming flowers. An insistent beat burst from the speakers and Ali was on her feet. The bass was so loud she could feel it vibrate her kidneys. She shut her eyes and danced. She hadn't felt this good since — she couldn't remember. When the last bars faded away, the music seemed to drain through the floor.

She opened her eyes to find five men in matching jackets staring at her. One of them started to clap slowly.

'You the floor-show?' said another.

'Just, ah, testing the boards.' She stomped her heels in a little tattoo, looking down at her feet to hide her embarrassment.

The one who had clapped stepped forward. He had ink black hair in a style that could only be described as a pageboy. The oldest pageboy in the kingdom — close up he looked about fifty.

'We're the Corvettes' he said with a smile and held out his hand to her. He couldn't be prouder if he was saying 'We're Roxy Music.'

More wires and sockets were brought in for The Corvettes to do their sound check. Brendan and Davy were sorting out their record boxes, so Ali stood against a pillar and watched the band run through a few numbers. What they lacked in originality, The Corvettes made up for in versatility. They raced through versions of 'Karma Chameleon' and 'The Hucklebuck' before the singer produced a *bodhrán* and someone else got out a fiddle and they were whooping up a jig and a reel. Two of them never even moved the fags from their lips.

The man with pageboy whispered closely into the mike,

'And this one is for the be-yootiful girl in the tight red trousers', and they swung into 'Three Times a Lady' before deliberately fluffing it and breaking down into a tumble four bars in, the bass drum whacking alone into the empty tent like an amplified heart.

Some women came in carrying crates of teacups and an urn the size of a rubbish bin. Drink wasn't allowed at the dance, which was why Davy was now pulling her outside — so they could get a pint in at the Red Rock Saloon before things got busy. Brendan left a cassette of party music playing, just to fill the space.

'The machine plays both sides, so we've got 60 minutes and counting,' he announced, gunning the accelerator in the van.

+

By those calculations, the tape ran out ten minutes before they made it back to the marquee. A dozen quite elderly people sat on the benches that lined the edge of the tent while two children practised their spinning on the empty boards.

Brendan hopped up on the stage, mumbling words of welcome and apology into the microphone, while shaking a twelve inch single from its sleeve.

'Here's one I *know* you're going to like'. Bouncy electro-pop streamed out of the speakers.

Ali sat on the side of the stage. It was good to have a pseudo occupation, to pass the occasional record up to Davy for him to pass to Brendan, to put things back in the boxes in order. Around eleven, the marquee started to fill up in earnest, people drifting in, the men bowed by the weight of bottles in their jacket pockets, the girls carrying clinking shoulder bags. Ali noticed tight huddles where she could just glimpse something being added to the bottles of Fanta and Coke that everyone clutched.

Four girls drifted out into the middle of the floor and started to dance, smiling only at each other or down at their shoes, pretending not to be aware of the crowd that now ringed the hall, three or four deep as closing pubs swelled the numbers. Brendan turned up the music to rise over the sound of the talking. In response, people raised their voices, yelling conversations into their neighbour's ears. Ali looked around to see who she recognised; she saw Roisín's husband Colman, roaring drunk and hugging an equally red-faced buddy by the neck — Cathal, the arsehole with the foetus feet badge. Roisín would be home with the baby. More girls were dancing now, sedate little shimmies set against the wild gestures and stumbles of the roiling crowd ringing the floor. It was either going to be a brilliant night or a riot.

Davy hopped down from the stage and grabbed her wrist, pulling her out into the centre of the sparsely occupied floor. He was the first man up, and what he lacked in rhythm he made up in enthusiasm, twirling her about, playing various invisible instruments, winking at the other dancers. They danced for four songs, by which time the floor was packed. Brendan gave them a thumbs-up from the stage.

'Want a soft drink?' said Ali, 'I'm parched.'

Davy signalled that he had another source of drink up by the decks, so she threaded her way to the refreshment tent on her own, squeezing her fingers into her pockets to find the fiver she'd stowed earlier.

Things were quieter in the side tent. Women poured tea and offered Club biscuits or packets of crisps from big tin boxes. As she stood in line for her lemonade Ali noticed Joan over to one side, standing with a couple of older women. After she bought her bottle, she wandered over, noticing as she drew close that Joan wasn't doing any of the talking, was in fact smiling past the women's heads at the blank wall of the tent, jiggling her head from side to side. The women eyed Ali with suspicion.

'Alright?' she called to Joan. Joan didn't seem to hear, so she tapped her on the back. She swung round quick as a flash, something like fear widening her eyes then settling into pleasure as she recognised Ali.

'Look at you — and that hair — you've mad style.'

'I wouldn't get looked at twice in Dublin, but here… anyway, how are you settling in at Ivor's?'

'Yea, yea, its good,' said Joan, dismissing the question. Her eyes were raking the crowd behind Ali's shoulder. 'Is your aunt not coming?'

'She's a bit old for this, eh? Not much of a groover, Aunt Una.'

'I need to talk to her. Sort things out.'

'Tell me, I'll pass it on.'

'Nope,' said Joan, and turned back to the whispering women. Ali wandered back into the main hall. She hoped it wasn't her old job that Joan wanted to ask Una for. She thought they had gotten beyond all that.

Ali found a quiet spot by the marquee wall and took the combs out of her hair, shaking it down and raking it through with her fingers.

She looked up and saw Peggy Nolan standing alone in a big rosy dress at the edge of the light, watching the dancers. Her expression was as miserable as the pattern she was wearing was merry. Some people could make you feel guilty just by breathing. Perhaps she should go and talk to her. But as Ali moved forward she saw a hand reach out and touch Peggy's shoulder from behind. Peggy looked round at the man on the end of the tapping hand, her dulled expression unchanging. But the man must have seem some form of consent in her eyes, because he guided her out into the swarm of dancers, an arm firmly around her middle. Ali moved to the little gap Peggy had vacated. Davy was close by on the floor, dancing slowly with a tall girl Ali hadn't seen before — elegant, with dark sleepy eyes and high cheekbones, like a girl in a magazine. Davy was talking close into her ear, but the girl hardly seemed to listen, looked bored with him.

Ali squeezed her way back to the stage and asked Brendan to top up her lemonade with the Bacardi she'd seen him buy at the Red Rock.

'The lovely Valerie,' Brendan said when she pointed to Davy's dance partner. 'And he's still trying to get her back, poor sucker.'

So this was the girl he had built a house for. Ali found it hard to believe anyone would turn down Davy, even a girl who looked like that.

Then the Corvettes took to the stage and the marquee jumped and sweated to a ceilidh set. Davy re-appeared to persuade her up for the Walls of Limerick. She hadn't ceilidh danced since she was thirteen and spent three unhappy weeks down in Irish college in Spiddal. They skipped and spun, passing under the facing couple's steepled arms after each bout to meet a new pair to in and out with. Half way round the hall they ducked under and came face to face with Ivor Dempsey holding hands with a small busty girl who seemed to be unable to dance without holding her mouth open in a delighted silent scream.

'Teresa, darlin', ' said Davy and kissed her hand as he sidestepped her away.

Ivor looked either furious or embarrassed as he offered his hand, it was hard to tell which. Ali was just plain embarrassed. Why had she acted like such a stuck-up tit yesterday? It had taken her until now to realise that he had, perhaps, been asking her out.

'Howya?'

'I'm grand, Ivor' said Ali and gave his hand a little squeeze.

He stood still for a moment and looked at her. Everyone around them was spinning, and he belatedly caught her elbow and whirled her so hard that her feet lifted up from the ground.

He laughed and brought them to a sudden stop. Her head kept twirling, even as Davy danced her on to the next pair.

'Lovely girl, that,' said Ali.

'Oh yea, Theresa's a panic.'

'Does she go out with Ivor?'

The steel-haired woman that Ali now faced grabbed her by the waist and whisked her around grimly, prompting another bout of dizziness. She hoped Davy would remember the question.

They came together again and held their hands high for the pair of women to pass under.

'That big galoot? I doubt it.'

The jig squealed to an end, but most people stayed in their places for the next one to kick off. Ali dragged Davy away from the floor, needing air. They went out the front entrance of the tent where a man stamped the back of their hands with an indecipherable blotch.

Figures milled in the dark. You could see the street lights of the town away to the left, but here in the school grounds there were just a couple of floodlights over the playground, lighting empty tarmac beneath and making the surrounding darkness blacker. The marquee itself glowed dim yellow behind grimy canvas. Over to the right, a line of girls was queuing for the three portaloos. Men were pissing against the yard wall beyond that, legs spread for balance, chatting. The field across the road was full of cars and vans now where there were none earlier. Dozens of bicycles leaned in the ditch.

Ali took out a squashed packet of cigarettes and removed an oval cigarette.

'That your idea of fresh air?' asked Davy, but he left the nagging at that. They stood in silence watching people come and go, disappearing into the dark, or looming suddenly back into the glow of the marquee. Ali asked about the girl was that he'd been dancing with earlier. He pretended not to know which girl she was talking about.

'Brendan said you used to go out with her.'

'Brendan's got a loose gob.'

'C'mon Davy, tell.'

'Nothin' to tell. My own fault, that's all. Got caught looking the other way. Nobody does that to her ladyship.'

'God, she sounds a nightmare,' said Ali. A man was shouting beyond the circle of light, up the road or in fields beyond. Hard to tell if it was serious or just tomfoolery.

'What's it to you?' His voice was teasing.

In Dublin they had spent a lot of time together,

out in the night air, with candles and moths and strange drinks. It was just the two of them — no Valeries, no tragedies. She wanted that feeling back.

'Remember that night you made us Harvey Wallbangers?'

'Ah, now,' said Davy.

'I can't remember a thing after the second drink.'

'That's convenient,' said Davy, and there was something hard in his voice, no teasing now.

Ali gave a weak laugh and stepped away from him, confused. A car drove past slowly and came to a stop just by the school building.

'Back in a minute,' said Davy, and went over to the car, leaning in the passenger window to talk. The queue to the portaloos was getting shorter, she might as well join it. She called out to Davy, to point out where she was heading, but he didn't hear. The car engine was revving loudly, the smoke from the exhaust drifting up against the brightness of a broken brake light. Everyone drove wrecks around here. She took her place behind two girls. To one side of the queue, a metal stand held a spotlight that pointed right at the toilet doors, dazzling all who exited.

When Ali came out of the toilet, Joan was in the queue.

'Joanie!' said Ali, enfolding her in a hug.

'Stop it, stop it.' Joan pushed her off and glanced around to check who was looking at them.

'I'm just being friendly.'

'Well I'm tired. I should be in bed by now, you know.'

'You've got to tell me one thing, though — honestly.' Ali waved ahead the person behind Joan in the queue.

'I don't want to talk about that.'

'No, no, not *that*. You've got to tell me, do you think I look like a freak?'

Joan said no, but Ali told her how everyone kept staring at her clothes. She was stroking Joan's arm to get her to listen. Joan suddenly slapped her hand from her.

'You know nothing about being looked at funny. You know nothing about nothing.'

'Don't be like that.'

Someone called Joan's name then, and she pushed past Ali, swallowed up by the dark after a dozen strides. Ali looked around and noticed the women in the queue staring at her.

'Is it the red trousers?' she asked.

+

Inside the marquee, the band were taking a break, and Brendan was dancing on the stage behind his record decks, urging people to keep going. *Too shy shy hush hush eye to eye, Too shy shy hush hush eye to eye.* Ali waved and did a little imitation of his moves. Laughing, he held a hand up at the side of his face to block out the sight of her.

She decided not to drink any more. For one thing, she didn't want to have to visit those loos again. Brendan put on a slow song, and she went up to sit on the edge of the stage, in front of him. All the couples who had been flinging their arms and legs about suddenly fell on each other as if delighted to have something to lean on. One couple stood stock still, French kissing studiously, like they were working their way into each other's mouths. Ali's view of the floor was

184

blocked by some idiot standing right front of her. She tilted to one side before realising that the idiot was Ivor Dempsey and that he was holding a hand down towards her.

She met his eyes and slipped her hand into his, to see how it would feel to touch him again. Then she was on her feet and Ivor's arm was around her, drawing her out into the middle of the shuffling dancers. She rested one hand on his shoulder. His shirt seemed such a thin barrier to the body beneath. He pulled her close and she moved her hand to the back of his neck. His hair touched her cheek. She felt him inhale, his nose just behind her ear, and she hoped there was something pleasant to smell there, not the reek of fags and booze. He smelt lovely, sharp. She was allowing herself to relax into it when there was a scraping shriek across the record and some manic Madness track kicked in, leaving the dancers as disorientated as if someone had flung a bucket of water on them. Ali looked up to the stage and saw that Brendan was grinning, looking straight at her.

She tried to guide Ivor to the back of the marquee, but he had seen.

'They're great jokers, your family' he said, and his face was like granite. He put his hand against the curve of her spine and steered her towards the refreshment tent. She wasn't sure if he was angry with her too, but they could have a sit down in the annex and maybe sort it out. But just where one tent led into another, Ivor drew aside a flap of canvas and pushed her out into the darkness. She stumbled over the muddy grass, his hand still pressing against her waistband. It was quiet behind the tent, though she was aware of huddled, possibly embracing, figures here and there in the shadows. She stopped walking and turned to face him, put her hand flat against his chest. She could feel the pump of his heart under her palm.

'I don't want to be rolling around in some ditch,' she said. He put his hand out and rubbed his fingertips slowly across her lower lip.

'Would a van do?'

A moment went by, and then she said yes.

They drove a mile or two out along the road, turned down a lane and parked. He collapsed the back of the bench seat so that it formed a kind of cushioned recline for them. He did it in so practised a way that Ali flickered with doubt, thinking of other girls in this same place. He brushed a hand over the surface and smiled at her.

Everybody thought she was a slut already. Even Davy. She didn't want to try to remember what it was that Davy had been hinting at. She wanted to be only her body, not thoughts or memories. She took off her top and sat before Ivor in her bra. There was only one thing.

'Do you have something?'

He smiled and patted his shirt pocket, then reached for the button of her trousers.

They wrestled each other out of their clothes, laughing and straining. The image of a smiling, approving Mary O'Shea came into her head and she pushed it away.

Sometime later she was on her hands and knees and he was covering her. There was a slick of sweat between his chest and her back. He reached a hand around to touch her, and pressed his teeth against her neck. Her body shook, her arms suddenly unable to support her. Ivor groaned and collapsed onto her.

'Fucking hell' he muttered and rolled onto his back, one hand fumbling at his groin, taking care of the condom. She nuzzled into his side, trying to keep the feeling going, sneaking looks at his body through half-closed eyes, the dim light barred by shadows of branches around them. He looked like he was sleeping, but his fingers moved slowly back and forth through her hair, keeping her quiet. Owls called in the woods.

+

The marquee was still alight when they got back. Ali wasn't sure how much time had passed. They parted outside the van.

'I need to find Joan,' he said.

She slipped back in the way they had snuck out. All the refreshments were packed up. Sleepers and snogging couples occupied the benches. Half the dancers had gone home. The Corvettes were playing *Spancilhill*, and a scattering of people were lurching around the floor to it. A circle of six men, including Roisín's husband, rotated drunkenly at one end of the floor, arms around each other's shoulders like a rugby scrum.

Brendan was putting the records away.

'Where's Davy?'

'Fucked off somewhere. Just like you. I'll need your help with this lot.' He wouldn't look at her.

'I met some girls outside,' said Ali, acting more pissed than she was.

'Did you now?'

'They were such a laugh. I lost track of time,'

'And which one of those charming ladies gave you that big hickey?'

Ali clamped her hand to her neck.

'Other side.'

She wrapped both hands round her neck.

'Must have got your head stuck in a tent flap,' he said, but he wasn't smiling, and wouldn't speak to her on the way home.

TWENTY

Joan came over when Una called but refused to get in the car. He had told Una she wouldn't want to, but Una never listened.

'Tell her it's just for a moment.' She hissed the message from the drivers seat, and he turned to Joan.

'Just a quick chat,' he said, 'in private, like. You *said* you wanted to talk to Una. Well, here she is.' The chug of dance music started up again in the marquee behind them.

'She can talk to me up there.' Joan pointed up the road to where the village started, sodium light falling on darkened housefronts and empty pavements.

She turned and walked away, up the middle of the road, towards the lights. Davy got into the car with Una.

'What's she playing at?' she asked.

'I don't know. Maybe she's drunk.'

'You're pretty well on yourself. She shouldn't be out of Damascus House. I told Peter Nolan, they should keep her in. She's not right, she's been making threats.'

Joan was a smoky flicker in the darkness. Una started the engine and eased the car along the road in her wake. She didn't turn the lights on.

'What threats?'

'Letters. At least one a day.'

'Is she saying she'll tell on you?'

Una gave him a disgusted look. 'Tell on *me*? You don't know what you're saying.'

Joan looked back over her shoulder. Davy rolled down the window and stuck his head out.

'Come here for a minute, eh? Just — come on,' he called.

A wash of light fanned through the car as a vehicle appeared behind. Una pulled into the side and ducked her head low. He copied her, not really knowing why they were playing this game. The other car swooped past, then braked hard as it lit up Joan in the centre of the road. She scrambled to the side with one hand shading her face.

'Maybe you should do this another time,' said Davy.

'I don't want her coming to ours, for Joe to get wind of it. I need her alone.'

'I've an idea,' said Davy. 'You drive on past her, and let me out. I'll talk to her, take her to Olohan's lane. You come join us. It's be quiet there.'

'I'll come too.'

'No. Wait and I'll talk to her. Give me a head start.'

She was standing at the little triangle, the one with the tub of flowers and signpost on it. She was looking down towards the bridge. He stuck his hands in his pockets and sauntered over.

'Nice night for it,' he said.

'Is your sister coming?'

He slid his hands out of his pockets and transferred them, gently, sliding, over her shoulders.

'Joanie.' He purred it. She met his eye only briefly. She was such a little thing. Big trouble in a small package. 'Come away to the lane with me.'

She looked at him again, examined his face as if trying to remember something about him that wasn't coming back to her.

'No,' she said, and his hands tightened.

Down by the old bridge a figure appeared and stood watching them. He stepped away from Joan, but it was only Una, come round the back way. Davy put his arm firmly around Joan's shoulders and marched her down that way. When they got to Una, he gave her a little push and backed off. He'd got them together, he could go now, back to the dance, but still he stood, curious to see how Una would handle her.

'What do you think you're playing at?' said Una in her familiar scold.

Joan just blinked at her then walked slowly to the centre of the bridge. 'I want to show you something,' she said. Davy could only just catch her words over the sound of the river rush. He moved with Una to flank her. Joan pointed over at crumbling bulk of the old chapel ruins.

'Do you know what's there?'

'What's there?' asked Una tightly.

'It's the *cilleanach*,' said Joan. 'My mother told me about it. It's where the unbaptised babies go.' Davy shifted to see exactly where she was pointing. It wasn't the chapel, it was the little walled plot beside it, frothing with brambles and bracken.

'It's not used anymore, Joan, it's just stories,' said Una.

'That's where he should be... my baby.' She sagged as she spoke. 'I'm very tired.' She turned so that her back was against the wide bridge wall and tried to push herself up on to it.

'Why don't you and me talk about it,' Una said, 'Davy doesn't know about these things.'

That was so typical of her. Make him help when she needed him, then try and wave him off like a he was still a boy. In a moment she'd say it was women's things, women's business. Well, he wasn't going anywhere. He stepped in and put his hands under Joan's arms, gave her a *hoosh* up so that she could sit on the wall. Now she was at an even height to Una, eye to eye. This would be interesting, he thought.

'Your child's at peace, Joan. You need to understand that,' said Una.

'You told me he went to limbo. Someone at the place told me there was no limbo anymore,' said Joan. 'I hate to think he might be floating alone in the dark, the cold.' Davy made a small, involuntary sound. She wasn't so far from the truth of it. Una shot him a fierce look, put her hand to Joan's arm.

'Don't talk like that.'

'You said there would be other babies, but none came.'

'You've been unlucky.'

'If his remains were in the right place, then he'd rest. Maybe another child could come to me then.'

'That's a bit morbid now,' said Davy, trying to lighten things, but Una looked murderous, no appreciation for his efforts. Well all right then, she could handle it herself. He turned from them, ran his eye over the backs of the houses. Dark windows, everyone asleep or at the dance.

'He *is* at rest,' Una was saying, 'On the farm.'

Joan started wailing then. 'I'm not asking much of you, missus.'

He was vaguely aware of Una reaching out for the girl, then a flurry of fast movement. Una knocked into him, holding her jaw, and Joan — Joan was gone.

He threw himself across the width of the stone wall, looked down into the dark. He could make out nothing, just some smears of river scum scrolling by.

'*Jesusgodnojesusno…*' Una's voice ran out over the flowing water.

'What have you done?' he said.

'She kicked me! She flung her leg out and kicked me!'

'Did you push her?'

'Of course I didn't. She toppled herself!'

Una grabbed his hand and pulled him after her, over to the chapel and down the riverbank, sliding on the muddy grass. She hadn't held his hand since he was a child. It was so strange, like a game. He was aware of wanting to laugh, to just scream with laughing. They were feeling their way along the outside of the bridge, down to the arch, the stone damp and gritty under fingertips. He kept looking at the surface of the water, its even drift. No splashing, nothing moving in it.

'Are you sure she fell in?' he asked.

'Don't be a bloody simpleton,' Una said.

'I can't see a thing.'

'She's probably hiding. Call her name, would you? Quietly.'

'Joan?' his voice was tentative.

They stood and listened, there was only the river's steady flow.

Una shook his hand off, drew herself up and stepped off the bank, into the water. It was waist deep at edge, and her coat floated out around her, like a lily pad.

'She'll be hiding,' she said, and waded her way under the arch.

Davy looked at her stiff neck as she disappeared into the shadow, her awful determination. What had just happened could not have happened.

He scrambled back up the bank. Far off on the

main street, a pair of drunk women were singing, holding each other up as they walked along.

He started to run, away from the town, the bridge, the lights. He clambered over the first gate he came to and ran up two fields before he let himself stop. He flung his body down in the lee of an old wall, panting. Close by, a cow wheezed and he jumped with fright. It was a wonder his nerves still worked at all. He remembered the naggin of rum in his jacket pocket. It hadn't broken. He clamped it to his lips.

TWENTY - ONE

It was pathetic to admit, even to himself, but Swan quite enjoyed Saturdays in the office. The drive into work was clear, and a sunnier air was discernible amongst his colleagues — dress code loosened by one button. The overtime helped, of course. A packet of chocolate biscuits lay open beside the coffee machine. He took two and balanced them on a saucer on top of his coffee cup. Breakfast.

Half of the others were in already, Considine frowning at her desk with the phone jammed to her ear, Barrett scooting his chair across the aisle to pass him a sheaf of messages. The top one said Dr. Flynn from the technical bureau wanted him to call. The number was an internal extension, not the one for the state lab at Abbotsford, so he guessed she was upstairs. He felt invigorated for the first time in days, things were starting to move. Hopefully, Goretti could provide another piece of the jigsaw.

Dr. Goretti Flynn's office was crisp and organised, as was the woman herself. Her hair bothered him — a perfect dome of it floating about her skull as if it had never met with the resistance of a headrest or pillow. He imagined her sitting bolt upright in bed in a frilly nightdress, fast asleep. In other respects she was a very attractive woman. He was once tempted to comment on the hair, but stopped himself in time. It was hard enough to get forensics results through at the best of times.

Goretti was at her desk, a china cup in one hand and a pen in the other, making marks in a grid on a large sheet of paper. Swan rapped gently on the glass door and she looked up and smiled. As he entered, she put her cup down and wiped her fingers on a tissue from a box on her desk.

'I've something to show you,' she said.

She unlocked the door of the small lab behind and brought him over to a counter where three zip lock bags lay.

'These are your three blouses — the one on the right is from the crime scene, the one on the left Declan Barrett gave me from the convent laundry, the one in the middle you brought in a few days ago. The blouse from the convent has a name tag sewn in at the neck, and Declan said all boarder's shirts were required to have the same. Neither of the other two blouses has a name tag or signs that one was ever attached.'

Goretti was on a roll. She had that clipped quality to her voice that usually boded well.

'So, taking the name-tagged blouse out of the equation for the moment, I compared these two. If you washed out the fluid stain you would be hard put to tell them apart. Identical material, identical size, and as far as I can tell, identical wear and tear.

'This type of blouse is made in Birmingham and imported by one Irish wholesaler. It's sold in places like Arnotts, Clery's and Roches Stores. Since it's a standard piece of school kit, the wholesaler estimates they shift thirty thousand units a year. But that's predominantly at primary school level, in smaller sizes, so there's only about one thousand sold per year in this size.'

'*Only* a thousand? That's a lot of blouse.'

'Yes — were it not for two things. Now neither is conclusive, but put them together and they are... well, pretty interesting.'

She shook both blouses out of their bags and showed him the right cuffs — both were frayed along the edge in exactly the same way, in exactly the same place.

'Probably from rubbing against an edge or surface while writing, but interesting how the wear is identical.'

'A common thing, though.'

'Okay, but look at this,' Goretti swung a lamp out over the counter and switched it on. 'Look closely — just above the pockets.'

On both blouses there were several holes pierced through the fabric in the same position on the right breast, the tight weave of the polyester pulled open at minute entry points. Something had been pinned there.

'Could be from some badge or religious medal the girls all have.'

'Not in St. Brigid's they don't. Prefects wear a sash, only one medal or cross on a chain around the neck is allowed. All else is considered jewellery and Sister Mary Paul would kill you if she found it.'

'Your research is formidable.'

'Sure they drilled it into me.'

'Ah, for god's sake Goretti, why didn't you mention it?'

She shrugged. 'It's not important. Let's just say my days at St Brigid's weren't the happiest of my life. I'm sure whatever was attached to the shirt would have been hidden by the tunic bib that covers it — so it was something clandestine.'

'So, badges or brooches aren't allowed, but Ali Hogan wore some under her uniform, as did the owner of the shirt in the shed.'

'Or they're both Ali Hogan's.'

'Do y'know, that's a possibility that's looking

stronger by the minute. Did you have time to look at that bag Barrett brought up?'

'That's why I'm in here on a lovely morning and not on the golf course.'

The bag was over on the central table, pulled inside out on a sheet of white card, so that only its black cotton lining showed.

'You wanted a check for blood?'

As he walked towards it, Swan could see that the lining looked spotless except for some wrinkles of lint in the corners.

'Nothing?'

Dr. Flynn nodded, not breaking eye contact.

Perhaps a stain of bloody fluid in the bag to match the one on the shirt and paper bag would just be too neat. The baby could have been wrapped in some other layer that they hadn't located, or she brought the baby to the garden in just the paper carrier at an earlier time. The misty woman or girl in his imaginary scenarios now wore Ali Hogan's face.

There were no leads yet from the towelling or blue carpet fibres, difficult without a scene to match them to. He urged Goretti to get out and grab what was left of the weekend.

'If I served only you, Vincent, I'd be happy to, but there are others in line. Thanks anyway.'

Half way down the stairs, Swan met Gina Considine striding up to get him.

'Managed to track down Carmen Fitzgerald,' she said, 'her mother had taken her on holiday, South of France, no less. She brought her in this morning.'

'I told her to tell Rathmines if she left the city.'

'Do you want to hear it or not?'

'Anything good?'

'Well, she's flabbergasted at the idea that Alison might have been pregnant. Says she didn't have a boyfriend, they told each other everything and shared rooms in each other's houses, so she would have noticed if she had a bump.'

'Is she plausible?'

Considine shrugged. 'I think so, but then she told me something else.'

She jigged her head towards the corridor of interview rooms and Swan followed her.

Carmen Fitzgerald lit up the dreary room with her red jacket and electrocuted yellow hair, but her face was ashy.

'Tell him what you told me,' said Gina, 'about the night before.'

'Can I go home if I do?'

Swan looked to Gina, she nodded at the girl.

'We were at the school the night before — near the hockey pitch. We go there sometimes… to drink. It's just round the back of Ali's house.'

'What time was this at?'

'Dunno. About nine or ten. We met two blokes we knew from Rathgar College, so we went for a drink. But we weren't near the Rosary Garden.'

'She says they didn't see anyone else,' said Considine, 'that they drank some beer and went home by eleven.'

'And Ali was with you all the time?'

Carmen chewed her bottom lip into a small sideways loop.

'She went off for a little while with Ronan — they didn't go far away.'

'And you were involved with the other boy.'

'God no! Bobby Kinsella, you must be joking.'

'I thought you said Ali didn't have a boyfriend.'

'She didn't — that was just, y'know, a little bit of messing. Ali always had a soft spot for Ronan. He used to go out with Eleanor Glenn.'

She spoke as if Swan would have foreknowledge of her social scene, of the repulsiveness of Bobby and the cachet of Eleanor Glenn.

'Was Ali a virgin, do you know?'

Carmen blushed as red as her jacket.

'I don't know!'

'Don't you talk about those kind of things?'

'I don't know. Honest.'

They let the girl rejoin her mother, but asked them to stay to have a statement taken.

Considine and Swan regrouped in the stairwell. Carmen's hotly claimed ignorance of Ali's sexual experience wasn't particularly convincing. And the fact that they'd been in the grounds of St. Brigid's around the time of the child's death was unsettling, to say the least.

Swan told her the pathologist's story about the girl whose boyfriend didn't even notice she was pregnant. Wasn't it possible that a best friend mightn't notice either? The blouse pointed clearly to the Hogan girl. They couldn't ignore it.

'We're going to have to move this forward, Gina, fast. I'll get Barrett to track down the two boys this morning, but more importantly we need a to recruit an expert — a thingammie — gynaecologist — can you take care of that?'

TWENTY - TWO

Ali had slept badly. Despite the amount of drink she'd taken, her mind kept churning awake with thoughts of Ivor and what had happened in his van. The shame and the wonder of it. How different it felt compared to every fumbling misadventure she'd tried before. But on the way back to the marquee they found nothing to say to each other. Maybe they never would. It was just a one-night stand, she told herself, trying out the phrase she knew from magazines, flicking it away.

Ali swung her feet to the floor. This swoony feeling was exhaustion, not emotion. She had slept naked, and now peeled the sheets from her body, pulled on her pyjamas and an old jumper and went downstairs.

The house was strangely silent, the kitchen empty. Toast crumbs littered the oilcloth and the teapot felt warm. She checked the immersion was switched on for a bath, and went to the scullery to get milk for cornflakes from the big jug there. It was so fresh from the cows, it was still lukewarm and frothy. She changed her mind about eating.

As she filled the kettle she wondered if Davy was up and about in the bungalow. Maybe she could bring coffee up to him, try to get back in his good books after the coolness they parted with last night.

The lovebite. She tried to see it in the small rectangle of mirror that hung over the sink. It was hardly anything, just a purple smear. If she remembered not to push her hair back, it would stay hidden. She met her own eyes. She could go out for a walk later. Down through the village maybe. Joan said Ivor's flat was above the garage.

There was a sudden movement in the background of her reflection, and she turned. Someone had passed by the window, and was opening the door in the scullery. She heard rustling among the jackets there.

'Hello?'

Brendan appeared in the doorway. He looked shattered, and she smiled at him, thinking of a joke to make about hangovers. He didn't smile back, just stared at her like he wasn't sure what she was doing there, and hurried up the hall to the front door. Something wasn't right.

She followed up the hall. By the time she got to the front door, Brendan was halfway down the drive, running. Two Garda cars were parked in the road, their blue lights flashing silently. There was a tractor in the field, and a couple of Gardaí were trying to connect a flatbed trailer to it. Down by the river were more people. Near them she could see the bright flash of sand where she and Joan had picnicked. You could see it so clearly from here.

Joe and Una were standing down by the gate, looking over at the Garda cars. When Brendan reached them he stopped briefly and pointed back up at her, at the house. Joe turned, started to make his way up the drive.

Brendan reached the tractor and pushed past the guards to quickly finish hooking the trailer to it, using something he had brought from the house. He got into the tractor cab and drove off to the river with both guards sitting on the back edge of the trailer, feet dangling like children. A car passing on the road slowed right down to have a look.

Her uncle stood below her on the path.

'Something's happened,' he said, and her first instinct was to laugh, but nothing came out of her mouth. She had the strangest sensation that the inside of her body was completely hollow, that she was a thin shell holding on to nothing, brittle and light.

'Kevin Lawlor, from next door. He was out walking his dog. He found someone in the river. Drowned. Dear God.'

The hollowness swirled in her chest.

'Do you remember Joan, who used to work for us? I didn't even know she was let out, but he recognised her straight away.'

'Who? Recognised who?'

'Kevin. He recognised Joan. She was caught on a branch in the shallows, lying on her back, you see. Not a mark on her.'

Ali put one hand out to catch at the door jamb, and the sharp corner of wood became the only solid thing in the whole world, an axis around which everything spun. Joe caught her by the waist and steadied her.

'Joan was at the dance last night,' she said. 'We were talking.'

'She shouldn't have been out of that hospital, let alone at a dance. You go inside while they bring her up.'

'Bring her up?' Ali saw a vision of Joan rising through dark waters, a rope wrapped around her waist. None of it made any sense. The memory of Joan pushing past her in the dark outside the marquee, just hours ago, angry with her, telling her she knew nothing. What was it she didn't know?

Down in the field the tractor was returning, heading for the road, the two Gardaí jogging along behind, hands on their batons. She couldn't see what was on the trailer, it was hidden by the cab of the tractor. Joe had turned to look now too.

The tractor turned into the road and now they could see another man, hunkered down beside a long black bag on the trailer. The bag undulated in shallow mounds over its contents. Over Joan.

An ambulance had appeared from nowhere and waited on the roadside behind the police cars. Another car drew up to join the vehicles on the roadside. Father Philbin got out from one side, wearing his black rain-coat. He took a rolled up length of green material out of his pocket and hung it over his shoulders, hurrying to the thing on the trailer. Doctor Nolan emerged from the other side of the car and Aunt Una turned quickly and started to walk back towards the house.

Joe had an arm round Ali's shoulders, was turning her round, urging her into the house. The last thing she saw was Doctor Nolan unzipping the top of the bag, revealing a flash of Joan's face, white and sharp-nosed, nesting in brown curls. Father Philbin was making the sign of the cross in the air above her. Joe gave her a final nudge into the hallway and pulled the door closed between them.

She wavered in the middle of the hall, air sucking around her. Maybe she would lie down here on the tiles, the diamonds of brick red and black that were so familiar. She tilted down to sit on them. The tiles were so cold.

Here was where the box had lain. Ma had taken it from her arms and bent down to put it right here. Ali moved her hand over the tiles as if they retained the print of it.

What have you got there love? Ma in a crouch,

lifting the lid. Ma putting her hand to the grubby towel then falling back like she was bitten, falling right there, thumping her back against the stair post. Someone shouted from the kitchen passage, Aunt Una, bearing down on her like a storm. So fierce that Ali had covered her face against the blows she thought were coming. Feeling the spittle on the palms of her hands as Una shouted close to her head. *What in Christ's name have you done?* The shame and the fear of it. Everybody looking at her, Una grabbing her wrist in her hard fingers, pulling at her. Nobody stopping her doing it. Ma looking away. Ashamed, it seemed.

The shifting blackness that was always inside her. This was the place it had come from. The front door opened and Joe came to stand over her.

'Get up now, we'll go down and have a drop of tea.'

Brendan was already sitting at the table, still as a statue. Ali took a chair opposite. His eyes were red rimmed, but dry. Joe ran the tap, rinsed out the teapot and mugs, bustling and clattering.

'Did you see her at the dance?' Ali kept her voice low.

Brendan shook his head.

They heard the front door open, and Una came down to the kitchen. She looked as if she had somehow lost weight since the day before, a scrawny strained look to her face and neck. She went to the scullery to take her jacket off, still in Ali's line of sight.

'Father Philbin and Kevin are coming here for a cup of tea. Maybe some of the guards too.'

She wiped down the table, brought out good cups. Ali watched her move around and thought of the terrifying aunt of memory. Una was solemn and frail in the wake of this horror; hard to believe she ever spat curses or lifted a hand to anyone.

Father Philbin blessed the air as he entered the kitchen. Kevin Lawlor, the neighbour, was behind him, cap in hand, his expression caught between embarrassment and woe, but also, Ali could see, just the edge of excitement too. He was the man of the hour, the one with the story to tell. He met their eyes boldly, even as he received commiserations from Una.

The tea cooled while Father Philbin led them in a series of prayers — an Our Father, the Confiteor, and one she didn't recognise that began *Out of the depths we cry to thee, oh lord...* Out of the depths, where Joan had been, the girl who couldn't swim.

The others blessed themselves as he finished, and Una passed round a plate of biscuits.

'Take some sugar in your tea, Kevin,' she said, 'for the shock.'

It was all the cue he needed.

'I don't know how I'll ever get over it, missus. The dog was whinging to get out, and I couldn't sleep on for her noise. So I took her out the back of the house and felt a bit brighter myself for the morning air, so we went on along to the river. It was a beautiful morning.'

He shook his head, took a sup from his cup.

'It was a rag of pink I thought I saw, just near the bank. But when I got up close I could see it was a woman in a pink blouse lying stretched out by the side of the water. Her curls were blowing in the wind. The sun must've dried them.

'When I was about ten yards away I recognised who it was, and, God forgive me, my first thought was that it was typical mad behaviour to be sunbathing half in, half out of the water. At that hour. But she didn't wake when I shouted her, and when I got as close as we are now, there was no mistaking that the life had gone from her. Her shoulders had caught on a branch just under the surface. She didn't look too bad though. Not bloated or anything…'

'Jesus…' said Brendan.

'Sorry — but you know, I don't think the sight of it will ever leave me. The Gardaí said she was probably carried down the river from the town, or even as far up as Ennisbridge.'

Ali clamped her jaw against the confession that rose in her throat, that wanted to surge out of her mouth, spilling her guilt across the cherries printed on the old oilcloth. Joan was her responsibility. She had signed the book at Damascus House for her. People would know that.

The back door slammed and Davy came in. His hair was tousled and the collar of his pyjamas stuck out of the neck of his jumper.

'A Garda came to the bungalow and told me. Why didn't you come and get me? It's mad isn't it?' And he gave a little high laugh. 'Unreal, man.'

'Say hello to Father Philbin, Davy,' said Una.

'Father. Kevin. Unreal, eh?'

'Twas me that found her,' said Kevin. 'She looked very peaceful — like your one — Ophelia.' Kevin spread his hands wide on the table. Davy shook his head quickly, like he was trying to flick something out of it.

Father Philbin said he needed to go to Ennisbridge, to comfort Joan's parents, and that Kevin should come with him. He turned in the doorway to give Brendan a hard look and said that perhaps the marquee dances had gotten out of hand. Brendan didn't bother to answer.

'Sit down and have some tea,' Una said to Davy, but he ignored her and leant against the sink twisting a tea-towel between his hands.

Ali thought of Ivor. He was looking for Joan when they parted. Maybe he had never found her. Not only had Ali made Joan angry, she had taken away the person who protected her.

Joe and Brendan started to swap theories. Joan had been drunk. Joan had been suicidal. Joan had been unlucky, tripped and fell.

'Do you remember,' Joe said to her aunt, 'when those two boys from Galway drowned in Lough Dreena. Went for a midnight swim. Both of them drunk as it turned out. Drink makes you think strange things of yourself, gives you the inclination for adventures, but takes away your judgement.'

'Joan wouldn't have gone for a swim,' said Ali. 'She didn't know how.'

Everyone looked at her.

'You hardly know her,' said Una

'I saw her at the dance. I don't think she was drunk, either.'

'Don't say you met her at the dance,' said Una, 'or the police will want to talk you. You've had enough of that, surely.'

'Una,' said Davy, flicking his towel in her direction, 'don't work yourself up. She was a depressive — cracked you used to say. At least she won't be bothering you anymore, eh?'

'Steady on,' said Joe.

'You should have more respect,' said Una, her colour rising with her voice.

'Should I?'

The doorbell trilled, breaking the argument, and

they fell silent while Joe went to answer it. Una got up to put the kettle on once more. It shook in her grip. They heard mumbled voices, and Joe returned.

'There are a couple of Gardaí here.'

Una banged the kettle onto the range. 'Show them down.'

'They just want to talk to Ali.'

It was going to come out now. How she had brought Joan out of the home, stirred up the past and then abandoned her.

A tall Garda dipped his head as he entered the kitchen, removed his hat. Ali looked at him in astonishment. It was one of the guards from Rathmines. She had met him in the Rosary Garden. How could he be investigating Joan's death?

'We can give you a few minutes to pack a bag, but we have to hurry,' he said. 'We need to get back to Dublin before teatime.'

'You can't take her away,' said Joe, ' Something happened here this morning, she's very upset.'

'Sorry, I'm afraid our thing trumps yours for the moment, Mr. Devane, we need her in Dublin.' He turned to Ali. 'You're not under arrest, but DI Swan would be obliged if you'd come back with us to help with enquiries.'

'Is it the baby?'

The guard's expression changed, shifting from formality to a kind of regretful softness.

'Yes, Ali,' he said gently, 'it's the baby.'

As they drove away from Buleen, she asked the policeman whether they had somebody under arrest, but he said he couldn't tell her anything. He suggested she take a nap meanwhile, and Ali obediently curled up on the back seat, her seething head cushioned on her rucksack.

+

'This is where I was told to bring you.'

The late sun glinted off lines of parked cars and spread a mellow light across the old stone of St. Enda's hospital. Ali had woken as the car stopped. Her tongue felt sticky and she had a headache.

'But it's a hospital.'

She thought she would be brought back to the station at Rathmines, or maybe home.

'This is where Detective Swan said. He's probably inside.'

He helped her out of the car, and shoved the rucksack under his arm. A bunch of nurses smoking by the hospital entrance gawked. Inside the panelled entrance hall a young woman in a belted mac stood waiting. Beyond, through glass doors, Ali could see the over-lit glare of the hospital, trolleys and oxygen tanks parked against the walls of a long corridor.

The woman nodded at the Garda. She had short black hair and quick expressions. She smiled at Ali.

'I'm Detective Garda Gina Considine. DI Swan asked me to meet you. Everything okay?'

Ali nodded back automatically, though nothing was okay.

The woman's handshake was strong, not exactly a shake, but a steady, held grip as if she was trying to communicate trustworthiness through her skin.

'I'm sorry about all this,' she said. 'There's no other way to be sure.'

'Be sure of what?'

Detective Considine glanced at the policeman

210

who gave a brief shake of his head in response.

'Thanks Liam,' she said, 'I'll take it from here.'

She took Ali's elbow in a firm hold and led her to a corner of the entrance hall.

'I'm sorry nobody explained things. It's a bit sensitive.'

Ali had an urge to tell her about Joan, to blurt out everything that had happened, to make this woman understand that she was not up to whatever it was she was asking.

'We've got to a stage in our investigation where we need to clear certain people from our enquiries. The only way to do it is to ask them to give a blood sample and have a quick examination.'

'Okay. But why do you need me?'

'You're someone we need to clear,' said Considine, looking at her intently, something like a warning in her eyes.

A yelp shot out of Ali's mouth, 'It wasn't *my* baby!'

The policewoman held her gaze, let a moment pass before speaking. 'I'm sure that's what the doctor will say.'

'Someone I know killed herself last night.'

Considine frowned. 'Well — I'm sorry to hear that. We won't force you to cooperate right now, but if you don't, we'll just have to bring you here again tomorrow. It will happen, Ali, easier to just get it over with, eh?'

Considine looked past her, as if waiting for someone to appear in the car park.

'Is my mother here?' asked Ali.

'No, though I did speak to her this morning. The thing is — your mother says she doesn't know

211

where you were at the time of the murder. Your friend Carmen says you were in the convent grounds. And you managed to discover the body in a place that you had no real business being in.'

'I didn't, Fitz did.'

'There's other things too.'

Ali looked behind her. There was nobody but the two of them in the big hallway, but she felt crowded in. She hadn't had the chance to have that bath. The sweat and alcohol and smoke fumes of the night before would still be clinging to her skin. She was in no state to be peered at, or poked at or whatever. Despite the half-sleep in the car she felt frayed, like she might cry if someone said boo to her. She needed to be home, she needed to be clean and alone and have a think about what had happened to Joan.

'I can see you're upset,' said Considine.

Ali bit the inside of her cheek hard to stop the tears from coming.

'Would it be you that examines me?' she asked.

'No, we have a proper doctor for that.'

Ali didn't remember saying yes, but neither did she say no, and somehow she found herself in a cold room, sitting on a paper sheet on an examination bench while a nurse in a plastic apron opened cupboards and set out small implements. She had been told to take off her 'lower things', so she removed her jeans and pants and then her socks because they looked odd on their own. She was glad that her t-shirt was long, and pulled at the hem of it with both hands until it was tented over her knees.

The nurse approached with a syringe and asked Ali to look over at the door. The policewoman's face hovered there, framed in a small glass window. Ali felt the prick on the inside of her elbow, and the sensation of a needle stretching the underside of her skin. She was starting to feel wobbly, and was aware that the nurse kept shooting her hard little looks. Once, she heard her click her tongue against her teeth.

'Sorry?' said Ali.

'Nothing. Doctor's on his way.'

Ali was staring at a metal bin, fixing on it as a still point that would save her from nausea, when the door swung open and the doctor from *The Late Late Show* walked in, Doctor Beasley, a determined smile on his face. This couldn't be right, thought Ali, all queasiness banished by the shock of seeing him here, of the dawning realisation of what an examination might entail. She reached out for her folded clothes, but the nurse was already carrying them to the far side of the room.

'Hello Alison. Quite a different setting we meet in this evening.' He pulled on some thin latex gloves that the nurse handed him. 'Did you enjoy your television experience?'

She remembered him stuttering and irritable under Mary's barrage.

'Not really.'

He worked the gloves down between his fingers.

'I'm surprised. You got quite the easy ride, I thought. If you would be so good as to lie back and relax?'

'Wait,' said Ali. 'I need to talk to that policewoman.' But Considine had vanished from the doorway.

'It's seven o'clock, I'm sure we'd all like to go home soon.'

Ali heard the nurse 'tsk' behind Beasley's back.

'I don't think I want to do this right now. I don't

feel well.'

'It won't take long. The Gardaí need the information to do their job, that's all. Nothing personal.' He pulled over a curtain to block out the view from the door.

She was lying back now, following the nurse's orders to put her feet flat on the bench, to bend her knees. She felt her will give way, a falling sensation.

Beasley stood to one side of the bench, level with her waist. He kneaded her stomach and asked her about sex. How often she had it. Not if.

'Not often. Three times is all.' Beasley raised his eyebrows and waited, as if another answer might follow. Ali said nothing.

'Okay so, when was the last time you had sex?'

A flash of herself rolling around in the van, Ivor laughing and reaching for her hips. She couldn't say *last night*.

'A while ago, a few months ago.'

'Hmmm.'

He moved down the bench, asked her to part her legs a bit. She felt cold rubber fingers on her, poking. She looked right into the bulb of the big lamp that hung over her until black blobs obscured her vision. The nurse handed him something metallic. As he put it inside her, she felt it as angular, cold as ice. The blood drained from her head and saliva pooled in her mouth. Then he did something that made it push her apart inside. It wasn't sore exactly, but it felt wrong, like something that happens just before something very painful. Her whole body was tense as bone. The stretch became an ache.

She glanced down and saw that he was leaning right over her with a torch, looking inside her, his brows clamped in concentration. Minutes seemed to pass.

'Please…' Ali said.

In answer, he raised one rubber-clad finger, indicating she should wait a moment, never taking his eyes from his task.

Ali looked beyond the light to the white tiles that covered the ceiling, the galaxy of tiny holes that perforated each of them. She imagined she could float up and crawl into one of those small holes, hide away in the darkness there.

She was aware of something scraping her inside, of sticks and swabs being dropped into plastic bags and vials.

'What are you doing?' her voice came out shaky.

Doctor Beasley sighed elaborately.

'Alison, If I do a full range of tests now, the police will have all they need, and you won't have to come back to me.'

They left her lying there, a cold draught across her naked thighs, while they went to the other side of the room and muttered together with their backs turned.

At last he came back over, released the pressure and took the instrument out of her. He dropped it into a dish on a trolley beside him. The nurse looked at her as if she had produced something filthy.

'You shouldn't be let near anyone.' Ali's words were brave, but her voice still wavered.

The nurse came over to the bench as Beasley retreated.

'The doctor is just doing his job. If you don't like it, you should of thought of that before you did what you did.'

This woman knew nothing about her, nothing. Ali stood up, inches from her.

'What is it you think I did, you stupid cow?'

The nurse looked around, but Beasley had left. She flared her nostrils and clamped her mouth, gathering the roll of paper towelling from the bench.

'That's for the guards to decide, darlin',' she said finally, stepping on the pedal of the bin so hard that the lid clanged against the wall.

TWENTY - THREE

Swan set off for the hospital the minute that Considine phoned. He met his wife coming up the garden path, her blue overnight case in her hand.

'Better?' he asked.

'So-so,' said Elizabeth and bent away from him to tickle the cat who was lying on the hot dirt of the flowerbed.

As he started the car he realised she might have been referring to herself, not Auntie Josie. But there wasn't time to go back and check.

The hospital was strangely deserted, fluorescent light falling in the empty corridors, dusk pressing at the windows. At last he spotted Considine looking through a door into a room beyond. He called her to him.

'The doctor's in with her,' said Considine.

'Did you find a good one?'

'Goretti Flynn gave me the name, says he's very well regarded — Donald Beasley.'

'Beasley. The name's familiar all right. Well done.'

'The staff said we could make use of a room down here.'

Gina led the way to a side room. The lighting tubes rat-tatted on, revealing two formica tables and a scatter of chairs. Health service posters lined the walls; a smiling skeleton with a red heart hovering in its ribcage, an old man sitting beside an electric fire with a Thermos flask on his blanketed lap. Dominating one corner was a human-sized cardboard cut-out of Postman Pat.

'How's our girl?'

'Looking a bit shook — she said something about someone she knows committing suicide. I didn't know whether to believe her.'

'But she agreed to be examined,' said Swan.

'Well, I persuaded her.'

There was a knock on the open door and Swan turned to see an oddly familiar face.

'I've completed the examination. Do you want me to run through the initial findings?'

'Yes, please,' said Considine.

'Just give us a minute,' said Swan.

Doctor Beasley agreed to come back shortly.

'Jesus, Gina!' Swan hissed as the doctor's footsteps faded, 'Him! Did you not see that *Late Late*?'

Considine stood her ground while Swan ranted about how it could taint the evidence, the bastarding smallness of Dublin and their generally atrocious luck on this case.

'Flynn said he was the top man,' she said. 'Done dozens of expert witness slots for the force — sure, his evidence will stand up in any case. How was I to know the girl made him look a tit on the telly?'

Beasley re-appeared with a camel-coloured coat over one arm and a snappy, un-doctorly attaché case.

They sat at one of the tables for Beasley to talk them through his examination of Ali.

'There are certain signs to support your theory — the extra weight carried on the abdomen, slight swelling of the uterus, the evidence of recent abrasion at the mouth of the vagina. Also I'm certain that she lied to me about her sex life. She's certainly no virgin.'

'Her virginity wasn't the question. We just need to know if she was recently pregnant,' said Swan.

'Well, it's difficult to be definitive on this. As

I say, she's young, very healthy. Things can return to normal quite quickly. There's little research to measure it against, so I don't want to rule anything out.'

'What about the cervix?'

Beasley's eyebrows crawled up his forehead. 'What *about* the cervix?'

'I believe it changes, or the entrance does — something about a slit, not a dot.' Swan could almost feel Considine gawping at him. Heat rose from his collar.

Beasley brushed the back of his hand over the table, as if wiping away these hypothetical body parts. 'It's not as simple as that.'

'Okay, Doctor, this is what it sounds like you're telling me. There's no evidence that she was recently pregnant, but at the same time you won't rule it out. Is that it?'

'What I'm actually telling you is that I will prepare a full report as requested, and I'm happy to testify in court that a pregnancy can't be ruled out. If that's what you're after. I'll write up my notes tonight and telex you a copy. And I'll send the invoice to the finance office.'

Top man indeed. The baby was born two weeks ago. Surely that would do something to a woman's insides that you'd notice. Swan was a great admirer of the resilience of women, but Christ, that would be some bounce-back.

'What about a scan?'

'Yes, a scan, as I said, would be helpful but the machine operator won't be in until Tuesday, unfortunately. If you would like to bring the suspect back then...'

'We'll let you know,' said Considine, and showed him to the door. Swan stared at the innocent face of

Postman Pat across the room.

'What do you think, Gina? From a woman's point of view?'

'I think he's a prick,' said Considine.

'I mean about her being pregnant.'

'Dunno. He says he won't rule it out. And there's all the other stuff — the blouse, the fact of her being on the spot. But you'd think a doctor could tell.'

'You would,' said Swan.

'Are we going to get her scanned?'

'I think what we need is another doctor.'

'Sorry.'

'Sorry for biting your head off.'

+

Swan found Ali alone in the examination room, sitting stiff-backed on a chair behind the door, a pair of socks in her hands, tears wet on her face. He squatted down in front of her, wondering if it was Beasley that had upset her.

'Can I go home?' Ali asked, her voice polite but strained.

'Garda Considine told you why we had to do this.'

'What did he say? Did he say I had a baby?'

'Did you?'

'No! Is that what he said? He hates me.'

'He'll do a report for us. Is there anything you want to tell me?'

Ali shook her head vigorously. As her dark hair swung back he spotted a mark on her neck — a smudge of bruising with a dotted crimson centre. The mocking voice of Beasley came back to him. *She's no virgin.* Well she mightn't be a virgin, but it didn't mean she was a mother. He felt that familiar deflation of a neat theory beginning to disintegrate.

'Am I under arrest?'

'No. I'll get a car to bring you home. We'll have a chat tomorrow.'

The girl bent forward to put on her socks with shaking hands. Pink socks, dotted with little hearts.

TWENTY - FOUR

Swan caught himself smiling at some children in their mass clothes outside Rathmines church. He was sitting in traffic, waiting for the lights to turn, and a tiny girl with a ponytail sticking up from the top of her head raised a little hand and wiggled her fingers at him. Without thinking, he grinned like a cretin and waved back. A bigger boy behind her put a protective hand on his sister's shoulder and flicked a V-sign at Swan. That was more like it. He laughed and drove on.

By the time he had gotten home from the hospital the night before, Elizabeth had made house cosy again, the way he never could. Table lamps glowed, Benny purred on a fringed cushion. They didn't discuss his work and they didn't discuss her time in Kilkenny. Their sparse chat was about what was on the radio, how well the garden looked. The stuff of strangers at a bus stop. It was only when she sat at the piano, at his urging, and music flowed about them that he felt they existed in the right realm together, romantic, emotional, speechlessly close.

He drove on to Ranelagh and parked outside Hogan's. Considine was standing by the gate. Before they reached the front door, it opened and Deirdre Hogan, dishevelled in that dressing gown yet again, drew him in by the sleeve, leaning close to whisper that Ali wasn't herself, would hardly budge from her room.

He refused her offer of coffee.

'We'll just go on up to her room, if that's okay.' As they walked through the hall, he noticed that the receiver was dangling down from the payphone. He looked at Considine, and was pleased to see she had noticed it too. She was in asset, this one.

The bare steps squeaked and bowed as they climbed the curved staircase. It could be such a lovely house. He imagined the home that Elizabeth could make of it.

Ali was standing in the doorway of her bedroom wearing men's striped pyjama bottoms and a baggy jumper.

'A woman from the Gay Byrne show has been calling here all morning looking for me,' she said, 'one of your lot must have said something, because I didn't.'

Swan immediately thought of Beasley. 'It wasn't us. Maybe someone in the hospital recognised you from *The Late Late.*'

'Oh, my fault, is it?'

'I didn't mean that. Look, I'm sorry about yesterday.'

Ali turned and walked back into her room. He took it as an invitation.

'Doctor Beasley took things further than required,' he said, as they followed her. Strictly speaking, he shouldn't be admitting any fault to her, but the guilt was itching him. He'd been taken aback at the full gynaecological detailing of Beasley's report which had arrived promptly that morning.

He hadn't really thought it through, had left it to Considine and the doctor and allowed himself to assume that there were less invasive ways to determine these things. Considine managed to get him the home number of the consultant at Holles Street that the pathologist had recommended. Swan read Beasley's findings over the phone to him before he showed the report to anyone else. The consultant laughed off the idea that the girl described had delivered a full term child a fortnight before.

It was just as Swan suspected. After Elizabeth's last miscarriage she had been in bed for a week and the bleeding had gone on and on. That was after just four months, and the baby would have been no bigger than something that could be in your palm, perhaps. He hadn't seen it himself, just stood outside the locked bathroom door as Elizabeth wailed with a ferocity that made her a stranger to him. That was when the cool had come down between them, that second time.

The consultant from Holles Street said a scan wasn't even necessary to clear Alison Hogan, but Swan was wondering if it might be still useful to kill Beasley's report. Close the door on it.

'Why did it have to be him?' said Ali, ' And that nurse was horrible — '

'I think maybe we should get another doctor — perhaps a woman doctor — to look at you. Give you a scan.'

'How could I have a baby and not know it?'

They were standing in the middle of her bedroom, facing each other.

'Can we sit down?'

There was more floor showing than before, an attempt at tidying, but no surface was completely clear. Ali walked over to a mound of clothes and produced a little basket-weave stool from underneath that she brought back to the middle of the room for him. She flounced down on her bed and started to comb her fingers through her hair, inspecting the ends. Meanwhile Considine had drifted off to lean against the shower cubicle in the corner, out of the girl's line of sight, disappearing her presence.

'Do you know what a poltergeist is?' Swan asked.

'I saw the film.'

'It was a little girl in that film, if I remember right, but your paranormal experts would claim that poltergeists are more attracted to teenage girls, that the power of adolescence stirs up all kinds of commotion.'

'Is this about the state of my room?'

Swan laughed. 'No, no… what I was trying to say — badly — is that you remind me of one of those girls, so many bits of this case keep leading back to you. See, I don't believe in poltergeists, Ali, but there's a hell of a lot of disturbance happens around you.'

She shifted her eyes slightly to meet his, and he saw an edge of fear.

'I want to show you something.' Swan opened his briefcase and took out a transparent envelope.

'You said the baby was wrapped in a white cloth.'

'Is that it?' said Ali.

'You tell me.'

He placed the envelope on his knees and slowly drew out the white blouse her mother had given him.

'Could be,' she said.

'Actually, this is one of your own school blouses.'

'Oh. But blouses are all the same.'

'Not quite… there's something I need you to explain.' He beckoned her over, tilted the material towards the light of the window.

'What are these?'

At first she seemed to be just staring at his fingertip moving over the material.

'These little holes,' he persisted, and she bent closer. She lifted one hand to the left side of her chest.

'Badges.'

'What badges?'

Ali walked over to a gaping chest of drawers and took out an old leather collar box. She sat cross-legged on the floor in front of him and opened it, dipping her fingers into a tangle of plastic beads, outsize rings and knotted chains, selecting four round badges from the bottom which she held out on her palm like coins. Swan put the blouse back in the envelope and took them from her.

One was very small, the size of a five pence piece. It depicted a feminist symbol of a clenched red fist inside a circle with a cross at the bottom. Two middle sized ones said *Free Nelson Mandela* and *Art is Revolution*. The last was largest — a scrawl of punkish writing against a black background; 'SPUC OFF' it said.

'A little bird told me that the school doesn't allow badges.'

'They can't see them under my tunic.'

'What's the point of that?'

She shrugged. 'I know they're there'.

A very timid rebellion, thought Swan.

'Do other girls do the same?' He willed her to say yes.

'I don't know. Maybe'

He held up the SPUC OFF badge. The initials stood for Society for Protection of the Unborn Child.

'Does this mean that you're pro abortion, Ali?'

'I think women should have choice.'

'Is it what you would do?'

'Depends. Maybe.'

'How would you know where to go? There's a ban on information now.'

'The small ads in any women's magazine from Britain have numbers. I've seen them.'

'Have you now? And what if your pregnancy had gone too far?'

'What did Doctor Beasley say to you?'

'He said he couldn't rule you out.'

'I didn't have a baby. Jesus. Look at me.' She stretched her arms out from her body. Swan wondered what he was supposed to be looking at; what he saw was a well-built girl in a jumper so baggy she could be concealing a toddler.

'Look,' said Swan, 'lets talk about the blouse. How could a blouse of yours have got into the shed?'

'Dunno.'

'Did you ever change your clothes in the shed?'

'Yea, we could wear rough clothes for gardening. But I don't think I ever left anything there.'

'And what were you doing in St Brigid's that Sunday night?'

Ali went back to sit on the bed, started fiddling with her hair again. The colour rose in her face.

'I was with my friends. We were drinking in the trees by the hockey pitch.'

'And you saw nothing?'

'No. And I didn't give birth between beers.'

Her expression had grown bullish; she no longer bothered to meet his eye.

'Garda Considine here mentioned — last night — some trouble down in the place you were staying.'

'Someone drowned after a dance?' added Considine. 'Someone you knew.'

The girl met Swan's eye.

'It was Joan,' she said, 'Joan Dempsey. She used to cook for my aunt. Then she was in a mental home, a hospital, until last week.' She made a little broken noise like a hiccup. 'They say that she jumped into the river. I don't know.'

'Why was she in a home?'

Ali looked towards the light of the window, the fingernails of one hand raking red lines down the pale inside of her opposite forearm.

'The baby I found... before, you know... it was Joan's. She told me so last week.'

Swan and Considine looked at each other for a minute. Jesus H Christ. There was the distant sound of footsteps climbing the stairs.

'You see, Mr. Swan, you're not so far off with your poltergeists — I do have special powers — ' The person coming up the stairs was humming now, signalling their approach.

' — people die around me.'

The door swung open to reveal Deirdre Hogan with three mugs and a packet of biscuits on a tray.

'I know you said not to, but there were these jaffa cakes just staring at me from the shelf, and I thought, well if they don't eat them I might, so I better bring them up to the guardians of the peace and my slim daughter *toot sweet*. And a cup of coffee to wash them down. Only instant, mind.'

Throughout this patter she wandered deep into the room, trying to clear a surface for them, tutting and laughing. But her eyes kept checking on her daughter. Ali had fallen back into herself, staring down at the mug her mother had passed her.

'You're not going to take her anywhere are you? I'm a bit concerned about what happened yesterday... and the phone keeps ringing.'

'I took it off the hook.' Ali said. Her mother nodded. A trust seemed to have grown between them.

'We were just here for a chat, Mrs. Hogan.'

He got to his feet. 'Get some rest, Ali.'

+

'That's that, don't you think?' said Considine when they reached the pavement. 'She didn't have a baby. And there's an innocent reason her blouse could have been lying in the shed.'

'I just don't know. What are you up to?'

'I'm going to go back round doctor's surgeries. Some woman might have come in by now.'

Swan sat in his car for a while before turning the engine on. To believe Ali Hogan or not.

He counted up the infanticide cases he'd had experience of — the baby by the canal, the one under the garage in Clondalkin two years back. Oh, and there was that case in Drimnagh — two tiny skeletons in a boarding house cupboard, ribs like fish-bones covered in paper-thin skin. The woman from Achill who had put them there twenty years before said she hadn't know anyone in Dublin at the time. That was her only explanation.

He remembered the words of a farmer he'd met once in a bar in Athlone. He'd said that it used to be a common thing for the bog strippers to turn up the remains of infants. The little bones of them scattered over the flayed land.

He thought the man was being morbid in drink, but maybe it was himself who was naïve. Perhaps the whole country was dotted with tiny corpses waiting to be found — babies tucked behind gateposts, eased under floorboards, or thrown into sacks with the company of stones to take them down into brown water. An Irish solution to an Irish problem. Grown secretly

229

in the dark, and to the dark so quickly returned, some never surfacing at all to feel air inflate their lungs, the trickle of warm milk filling new stomachs.

And what of his own babies — would they ever make it into the world or would there just be more pain? Two conceived, both faltered in the womb. Two months. Four months. He was forty-three. Elizabeth thirty-eight already. Perhaps they were too old, or a bad match. All he knew was that he couldn't bear it to happen again. She wanted to try — said they didn't have the luxury of waiting — but he couldn't go near her for fear of it.

He wiped a hand over his eyes and turned the ignition, driving without focus until he was away from Ranelagh, waking again to the world beyond the windscreen only as he turned down by the canal.

He noticed a woman sitting on a bench in a short skirt and boots, her hair dyed a chemical auburn, her mouth clasped passionately around a cigarette. It reminded him of Sister Bernadette and her good work with the working girls of this area. The ice queen moving among them. Community projects, the old nun had said. Not a great distance from the convent, really. He wondered if anyone from the team had checked it out yet.

Percy Place was where she said the drop-in centre was — just nearby. He took a left fork out of the main traffic flow and cruised slowly to where the handsome Georgian terrace faced on to the canal. Half way down he spotted a round plaque on the wall — a famous writer remembered.

Swan parked. It was a lovely street, especially in the quiet of a late Sunday morning, like a film set the way that the whispering trees watched over the little stone bridge. The start of a Kavanagh poem learned at school came to him —

Leafy-with-love banks and the green waters of the canal, pouring redemption for me...

Ah, redemption. A pint of that would be welcome.

The house was tall and wide, and a little brass sign at the top of the steps said 'Order of the Annunciation' in letters you would have to be closer than two feet away to read. Very discreet. He knocked. Nothing happened. He knocked again.

A door opened somewhere below and Swan looked down over the railing into the paved basement area. A young woman with very short hair walked out and put something in a bin. Even from above, he could see how her stomach domed out.

'Excuse me? Do you know if there's anyone in up here?'

She looked up, shading her eyes with a hand. She was much younger than he had first thought.

'It's all the one. Who are you looking for?'

'Sister Bernadette?'

'She's had to go away.'

'Do you work here?'

'Naw. I'm a *resident*.' She didn't look like a prostitute, not at all. She looked more like a schoolgirl.

An awful thought struck him.

TWENTY - FIVE

After Swan and Considine left her, Ali collected up their mugs, and put the tray outside the door. She turned back to the mess of her room, a mess she had only become aware of through strangers' eyes. Clothes spewed from the rucksack she had brought with her from Buleen. It was a place to start.

When she shook out her jeans, the little medal that Joan's mother had given her fell out of the pocket, followed by the flutter of Mary O'Shea's business card. Ali picked up white rectangle and stared at it, sat down on the bed once more.

She rubbed the edge of the card back and forth against her lips. Mary would be very interested in what Beasley had subjected her to. There might even be a story in it, but how could she control where that story went? How could she be sure she wouldn't come out of it looking suspicious, stupid, both? She couldn't trust Mary, and she couldn't trust the police. The police thought she might have had a baby. Beasley had looked inside her and thought so too. Swan was talking about poltergeists and dark forces. She felt drenched in guilt, but couldn't attach that feeling to anything in particular. All of it was awful. Everything that had happened since she stepped into the garden, or was it the night before that when things started to fall apart?

She should have told the police about being at St. Brigid's that night, it just never occurred to her. It was nothing to do with that baby. They had met up with Bobby and Ronan outside the Berrybush pub while

Davy had been inside buying a naggin of vodka for her and Fitz. The boys had beer, and it was their idea to go to the school grounds, not hers. Ronan had been paying her a lot of attention, slagging her, pretending to be interested in her bangles, that kind of thing. Usually boys paid more attention to Fitz.

He stole one of her bracelets and she had chased after him, running over the grass in her bare feet, leaving Bobby and Fitz behind at the hockey pitch drinking beer. When she caught up with him, he grabbed her, pressed her into the bark of one of the big cedars. They were only messing about, nothing serious. He was kissing her neck, and she was starting to feel kind of floaty with it, watching the branches above her moving against the darkening sky — that deep, deep blue that comes just before black. One of Ronan's hands was at her chest, twisting the buttons of her shirt. She wasn't wearing a bra. Ronan laughed and stepped back from her. She looked down and saw with a shock that one breast was exposed, lolling out, almost luminous in the dusk.

It was then she heard the footsteps on the path, a soft gritty rhythm coming towards them. Ali turned quickly and hugged the tree, signaled to Ronan to hide too. She didn't dare move until the sound had faded well beyond them. Ronan claimed it was a nun who passed, perhaps a ghost nun, but that wasn't what she had seen. The half-glimpsed figure looked more like a man.

She couldn't tell Swan she had gone off with Ronan — he thought she was a right tramp already. She'd caught him staring at that damn love-bite on her neck. Anyway, she couldn't really be sure she had seen anything.

It was her that deserved to be locked up some place like Damascus House. She couldn't imagine Joan ever feeling more crazy than she did right now. She tore Mary's business card into little pieces. It was better not to have the temptation after what happened last time.

She didn't know what to do with herself. The muffled sound of the radio floated up from the room downstairs. Her mother would be sitting there among her broken things and saucers of glue. A spider in her web, fiddling, mending.

The gate to the passageway squeaked. Ali went to her window and looked down. A familiar bright head bobbed up the passageway.

As Ali ran down the first flight of stairs, the doorbell rang.

'I'll get it!' her mother shouted.

'It's okay,' Ali called back, 'it's only Fitz.'

When she pulled the big door open, Fitz was picking at the labels on the rack of old bells.

'When you going to get rid of all these?' she asked.

'Hello to you too,' said Ali, giving her friend a quick hug and pulling her inside. Her mother was moving around on the landing.

'I wanted to say sorry —' Fitz began.

Ali pushed her into the front room. She didn't want her mother hearing any more than was necessary, especially now that she was being so nice, treating Ali as lovingly and carefully as a piece of her broken porcelain.

'Have I been in this room?' asked Fitz, looking around at the stripped single bed, the tilting empty shelves.

'Davy was staying in it last,' said Ali.

'The foxy uncle,' said Fitz, and ran a palm sensually over the striped mattress before sitting down on it.

Ali laughed obligingly. This is how they always were together, joking, mock sophisticated, but it felt awkward today, like she couldn't find the rhythm of their usual dance.

On the wall over the bed, Davy had stuck pictures from newspapers, a collage of faces that he had added to day by day like a flat bulging cloud. He stuck them to the wallpaper with toothpaste. She noticed Mary O'Shea's picture in the centre, little fangs and horns drawn on in black felt tip.

Fitz followed her gaze.

'Did he do that? He's funny. Where's he gone?'

'He had to go back down to Buleen. Work.'

'Pity. I think he fancied me.'

Fitz was probably right, but Ali wasn't going to tell her that. When she'd brought Fitz home with her that night she noticed him flustered, tripping over himself to bring them out for a drink. If only they'd managed to get served in the Berrybush, they wouldn't have ended up going to St. Brigid's with the consolation prize of the vodka he'd bought them and those stupid boys. Davy wouldn't come with them. Why would he drink like a kid when he could sit in a pub? That's what he said.

'Anyway,' Fitz was saying, 'I'm sorry I said anything to the guards about the boys, but they kept on at me. I was worried they'd do me for underage drinking.'

'It doesn't matter,' said Ali, 'but it is creepy, don't you think? I mean... someone else was there that night. I just don't know. Maybe it *was* me that did it and I've blacked it all out. Have you noticed anything strange about me in the last few months?''

'No, but I'm noticing it now.'

'I'm serious.'

'Unless you're completely schizophrenic, or something. Ali, you'd *know*. And I'd certainly know.'

'You'll testify in court, then?'

Fitz laughed and rolled her eyes.

She wanted to tell Fitz about Joan, but how could she even start to explain it all?

'Aren't you're worried about the results?' said Fitz.

Ali's first thought was that Fitz somehow knew about Beasley and all the tests they did on her, but as Fitz went on to say how she hadn't done enough revision, Ali realised she was only talking about the Leaving, the exam results, the thing she'd been so obsessed about before all this. Her future.

'They'll be here next week. I can't believe it. Do you want to meet up? We could go into town…'

Ali imagined sitting with Fitz on a red settee in Bewleys, eating almond buns, laughing about nothing and watching university boys go by.

'I can't go out, Fitz, I can't see anyone.'

'I guess I could come over here… maybe.'

'Don't worry about it. You go out. I'll phone you.'

'Do that.'

Ali walked her to the door.

When Fitz reached the bottom of the steps she turned and cocked her hand like a gun. 'Ciao baby. Don't take any shit.'

Ali stood for a while with her forehead against the closed door. She missed the way they'd been.

She went back into Davy's room. She missed him too. Maybe when all this was past, he would come back and get a proper job in Dublin. Anyone could see there was nothing for him in Buleen, just an ugly half-finished bungalow. And the place did something bad to him, made his humour bitter and careless. She stood and looked at the pictures he'd put on the wall until her mother called her to the kitchen.

Ali sat and ate the soup her mother put in front of her. Tomato, sweet and bland.

'I talked to Una on the phone just now. She says Joan's funeral is tomorrow. So quick. But I don't think she was suggesting we should go.'

Joan's funeral. Coming back to Dublin had been forced on her. She should be in Buleen, should be there to acknowledge all that she hadn't done for Joan.

'I think I need to be there, Ma. I spent time with Joan in Buleen. I even spoke to her that night she died.'

'I'm concerned about you, pet. You've been involved in too much — too much grimness.'

'We could go together. You haven't been back in a long time.'

'Hah!' said her mother, 'I don't care if I never see that hole again.' She quickly put her hand up to her mouth. Ali stared back at her. It had never occurred to her that her mother didn't love the place she came from.

'Why not?'

'Oh, I don't know, lots of things. Bad associations. Do you remember your Granddad at all?'

'Sort of.' What Ali remembered was an old red-faced man propped in an easy chair in Una's front room. His stillness and silence had been frightening.

'He was fairly diminished when you knew him. When I was a girl, he was a bit of a brute to be honest. No affection. Thought a father's role was to toughen you up.'

Her mother pushed her half-finished plate of soup away to one side.

'I remember once — I'll never forget it — he had this notion that being able to deliver a good death to a beast was an essential skill. He thought the whole family should know how to do it, even his children.'

Ali put her spoon down. She wanted to tell her mother to stop talking, but no words came.

'One of the cats brought a bird into the kitchen, maimed. It was a little wren, hopping around under the table with it wing sticking out. I was only five or six. My father fetches a bucket from the scullery, fills it with water. Then he bends down and catches the bird, calls me to him. I thought he was going to mend it somehow, so I wasn't scared until he presses the little thing into my hand, tells me to hold it under the water. I wouldn't do it, no matter how he argues that it's the right thing, the kindest thing.

'So he puts his hand around mine and forces them both into the bucket, and I can feel the little thing fluttering inside my fingers, panicking, but I can't open my hand. Finally it stops moving, and I look at my father. He takes our hands out of the bucket, pulls my fingers apart, and the bird is stretching out in my hand, its little claws uncurling.

' "See," says my Da, "You've stopped the suffering." And although it's dead, I know it's looking at me with its black eye and it knows that I caused it to suffer something worse than a maiming. In his book it was the right thing to do, but, you know, I don't think I ever felt the same about him after.'

'Did he make the others do that?'

'Oh yes. He made Una kill a lamb that was ailing, but she would have done anything for her Daddy. Davy went trapping rabbits with him from the time he could walk, learned how to dispatch them. A chop to the back of the neck. But it was different for him.'

'How different?

'Ach, he's a boy, it doesn't seem to go so hard with them. He was never upset about it. Anyway, it was enough to give me a stomach full. I never miss the place at all. But if you want to go back, I won't stop you.'

Ali went upstairs to pack. As she changed her clothes, she spotted the little Lourdes medal on the floor. She picked it up it and put it in her shirt pocket, happy to take any protection that was going. From somewhere in the chest of drawers she found a black skirt to wear for the funeral.

'There's a train in an hour.' Her mother was standing at the phone. She put the receiver down and turned to take Ali into her arms for the first time in years. Ali hugged back.

'Be careful,' said Ma. The phone started to ring again. Neither moved to answer it.

'If my Leaving results come,' said Ali, 'don't open them. Wait till I get back and we can open them together.'

TWENTY - SIX

Swan took his badge from his inside pocket and held it out towards the pregnant girl. She squinted and shook her head. It was too far away. Swan went down to her, could hardly ask her to climb the steps for him.

'Someone was supposed to meet me here,' he lied. 'I need to take a quick look round. Are any staff about?'

'One of the nuns'll be coming to make the dinner, but there's nobody here now. Never is on a Sunday.' Her accent wasn't Dublin, more southerly — somewhere near Cork. She inspected his ID diligently and smiled a cheeky smile.

'I'm not in trouble am I?' Flirty, despite her condition. Swan held his tongue.

He stepped towards the open basement door, peered in — he could see a washing machine and a chest freezer.

'Can I just—?'

'I suppose its alright — but don't go into any of the girls rooms, they're private.'

'How many?'

'Many what?'

'Girls are staying at the moment?'

'There's three of us.'

Swan followed her into the house, through a large functional-looking kitchen. Beyond that there was a sitting room. The curtains had been drawn to block the light from the TV screen, but even in the blue-washed gloom, the pregnant state of the two young women slumped on the sofa was the first thing he noticed. They were planted deep in the cushions as if their distended bellies had fallen on them and rooted them there. The girls stirred at his entrance, and one drew a hand up over her stomach in a protective gesture.

'He's just having a look round,' said the crop-haired girl and shot him a grin as though his motives were slightly suspect. She went over to an armchair and descended into it slowly, taking the strain on her arms. It seemed he was free to wander. Through the next doorway a staircase led up to the rest of the tall house.

On the floor above, next to the main entrance, he found two nicely proportioned rooms furnished with bland desks and filing cabinets and those low easy chairs with no arms — perhaps this was the drop-in centre that Sister Bernadette had mentioned, but the two floors above that looked like an upmarket B&B — nice carpet, another living room or parlour and a series of gleaming doors with numbers on them and tiny brass frames below. A few of the frames held yellow cards with names inked on them in cramped gothic calligraphy — Jenny Mooney, Esther McDaid, Sharon O'Higgins — just like the writing on the Reverend Mother's door back at the convent.

He tried a door with no name on it and peeked into a simple bedroom. The single bed was stripped back to its floral mattress. The white wardrobe and matching bedside and dressing table all had the same gold squiggly handles. If not exactly luxurious, it was comfortable and fresh, a lot better than most charity gaffs.

What were those bloody nuns at — not telling them about this place? He was sure it hadn't turned up in their checks of maternity homes.

'Are you finished yet?' The girl had come

to keep an eye on him.

'Seems a nice place.'

She made a non-committal noise and leant a shoulder against the wall. She didn't seem worried by him, more curious.

'Are you from round here?' asked Swan.

'Naw. I'm from Clonakilty.'

'How are you liking Dublin?'

'We don't go out much. They think someone might spot us. From home.'

'Which one are you?' Swan pointed to the doors with names on them.

'Esther McDaid. No longer a maid.' She gave a little laugh. 'You got any money?'

'What do you need money for?'

'They don't let us have any. They say it might be stolen if we had it.'

'Maybe I have. Tell me, who was the last girl here to have a baby?'

Her bold smile dimmed and she examined him closely. He stared her out, trying to look kindly, trying to hide the excitement he felt. He wondered whether he should be so blatant as to take out his wallet.

She turned around and headed for the stairs, looked back at him over one shoulder. He followed her down. On the return of the last flight of stairs she stopped and opened a door he had presumed was a bathroom. It led to a corridor, an extension on the back of the original house. Holy pictures lined the wall, and the end of the corridor opened out into a little chapel with miniature pews for about eight people. A hanging candle in a small red glass signalled Christ's presence. Esther bobbed a quick genuflection, leaning back to balance her heavy bump.

She led him to the left, to a blunt little offshoot passage with a door at the end.

'She stayed here, not for long. A couple of weeks ago. We weren't even supposed to know about it, but she came out some nights and talked to us, once the nuns were gone or asleep. One day I heard a baby cry in there. She didn't give it up. I heard her arguing with Sister Bernadette about it.'

'Are you going to keep yours?'

'They won't let me. I told Bernadette it wasn't fair, and she told me that I would spoil the baby's life if it grew up as a bastard. She used the B word.'

There was a name holder on this door too, but the little card was blank. Swan tried the handle. It opened into a bedroom larger than the ones upstairs, with a sofa and a double bed. The carpet that ran seamlessly between the skirting boards was a rich cornflower blue. Swan let out a whistle then walked to the centre of the room and slowly looked about. His veins hummed with excitement. There were no personal belongings, nothing that drew his eye. He opened the wardrobe door. It was empty, except for a padded plastic rectangle with teddy bears on it. Inexperienced as he was, Swan recognised it as a changing mat.

He closed the wardrobe and looked around. Esther had disappeared. Instead, Sister Dreyfus stood there in a grey anorak, her habitually tense expression turned to frank alarm. He suppressed a terrible urge to laugh.

'Can I help you, detective?'

He backed her out of the room, closed the door behind him. Esther McDaid was sitting on one of the chapel pews, pretending to pray. He would have to remember to slip her some money. At least enough for a train fare.

'I need a telephone, and then I need to see Sister Bernadette. Here. Now.' He tried not to shout it.

+

Mother Mary Paul was having extraordinary difficulty backing the convent's station wagon into a quite generous space across the road from St. Jude's. He watched her efforts through the window of the front office he had commandeered as his own.

More than an hour had passed since he hit the phone. Sunday was a bad day for excitement — the world wasn't geared up to cope. Considine was at home, and offered to locate Barrett and come to Percy Place as soon as they could manage. Rathmines Garda station would send two uniforms over to secure the scene. There was nobody in the technical lab, so he left a message at the duty desk. He was tempted to phone Goretti Flynn at home, but she would just tell him to lock the bedroom door and wait for morning.

The nuns had been elusive too. Nobody answered the main phone in the convent, and it was only by bullying Sister Dreyfus for information that he managed to reach Mother Mary Paul on a private line. Mary Paul said Sister Bernadette was on retreat across the border in Newry, but she would come herself right away, didn't bother to fake surprise or ask why. Sister Dreyfus was supposed to be downstairs making lunch for the residents, but kept appearing at his elbow with cups of tea. Hovering.

Mother Mary Paul finally gave up her struggle with the car, leaving it at an angle to the curb. She slammed the driver's door with surprising force and shifted her shoulders back, military style, before heading towards the house. Swan opened the front door and directed her into the front office. The cloying smell of packet minestrone permeated the hallway.

'Monsignor Kelly is on his way,' was the first thing out of her mouth.

He was about to shut the front door when he heard a little skid of tires, and Considine jinked her mini into a small space at the kerb. Barrett was with her. Swan asked Mary Paul to wait in the office and went to fill them in.

They clustered on the pavement. He turned to Considine first, couldn't resist a bit of finger pointing.

'You were supposed to check out every lying-in home and refuge in the land. Remember this one? Run by the nuns from St. Brigid's?'

'There's no central register, boss. This place wasn't on the adoption board list, so they must be operating outside the system.'

'Someone must have known. We've wasted a lot of time. I want you to go in there and talk to the residents. They're down in the kitchen. Don't let the nuns at them. Get me some background on the girl that stayed here two weeks ago and left with her baby.'

'You're joking,' said Barrett, 'fuck's sake.' He looked accusingly at Considine.

Considine flared her nostrils slightly and walked stiffly up the steps while getting her notebook out of her shoulder bag. Barrett straightened his tie and followed Swan in to talk to the Reverend Mother.

'So...' Swan settled into a chair opposite the nun, 'when were you going to let us in on this little secret?'

'It wasn't — isn't — a secret. We've nothing to hide.'

'Did you not think that the fact you were running a home for pregnant girls might interest us?'

'It's nothing as grand as that. The few residents here are in a fragile state, there was no point in putting them through police questioning. There's no connection between St. Jude's and the child in the garden, I'm perfectly satisfied with that, and you will be too.'

Mother Mary Paul's hand disappeared into the folds of her habit and emerged with a ring of keys. She rose and went to a quaint sideboard in an alcove beside the fireplace. She unlocked one of the cupboards. It was empty except for a couple of files, a book and what looked like a petty cash box. Mary Paul pulled out this book — a hardback black ledger, the paper dyed a rosy pink along the edges. She flicked through it, arriving at the place she wanted, handed it to Swan.

'I checked this myself. Afterwards.'

The list of names ended half-way down the left page. In the columns to the right there was the name of a town, a priest, then two columns of dates. At the top of the first column of dates it said 'arrival'. Above the second column were the letters DLV. The most recent entries were the same names as those he had read on the doors upstairs. They only had an arrival date next to them, nothing in the column marked DLV.

'The second column… ?'

'That's the date of the birth.'

The latest delivery date recorded was 3rd June 1984, more than six weeks before the Rosary baby was born. Swan flicked back through the earlier pages. The register went back seven years. The busiest year was 1978, when twelve girls stayed. Not exactly an avalanche.

The information here seems a bit minimal,

mother. What about the girl's addresses, the details of adoption?'

'We just provide a place for the girls to stay. They are referred by their parish, and all adoption details are dealt with privately.'

'Privately between who?' he asked.

'I think you need to talk to Monsignor Kelly if you wish to pursue this.'

The doorbell rang, and he answered it to two flush-faced young guards from Rathmines. Swan sent one down to the back door and told the other to stay on the steps and prevent arrivals and departures.

He sat down again to face the nun.

'The thing is, mother, a girl stayed here recently who isn't on this register. She had her baby in her room with her, and now she's gone. Disappeared about the time that the baby was found in your convent grounds.'

'She must be on the register. Sister Bernadette wouldn't allow it otherwise.'

'Well, she's not. It's a pity Sister Bernadette's not here to explain. We've sent a car up to Newry to collect her from the retreat house. Seems they don't believe in answering phones there either.'

'It's a silent retreat,' said Mary Paul. To one side of her, Barrett rolled his eyes.

'I'll leave you here with detective Barrett,' said Swan, ' just in case anything pertinent comes to you.'

In the basement kitchen, Considine sat at the table with the three pregnant girls, while Sister Dreyfus busied herself by the stove, a big blue apron practically brushing her sensible shoes. A plate of white sliced bread and some industrial-looking cheese were laid out on the table.

'What have we got?' said Swan, taking a chair.

'The girls say she arrived about a month ago, and mostly kept to her room.'

'Do we have a name?'

'Peggy!' said a girl with very fine blond hair.

'Did Sister Bernadette bring her here?'

'Don't know,' said Esther, 'She just came down to the kitchen one day…'

'And she had a baby with her?'

'Not when she arrived,' said Considine. 'As far as I can establish, cries were heard from the room two weeks after, not long before she left.

'We never saw the kid,' said Esther. 'I think she was keeping it away from us, you see, out of kindness.'

'What did she look like?' Swan asked.

'She was about nineteen or twenty, I'd say. Lovely thick hair —like a conker.' This from the blond girl. Considine scribbled away on her notebook.

'Was the baby delivered here or in hospital?' Swan was wondering if this girl could be someone they had already accounted for, someone that came up in the hospital searches. He needed to keep a lid on this exultant, headlong feeling.

'Sister Bernadette would know. I think they got on well.'

'Who got on?'

'Sister Bernadette and the Peggy girl. I heard them talking in her room a few times — when I was praying in the chapel.' The two other girls looked at Esther sceptically.

Swan had managed to get hold of TP Murphy in Dundalk. The investigation into the creamery shooting was going slowly and he had agreed to go and fetch Sister Bernadette from Newry. He would be there within the half hour. With Sunday traffic, he could get back to

Dublin with Sister Bernadette by four or five.

'When did she leave here? Tell me about that…'

The girls looked at each other.

'Dunno,' said Esther, 'It was about two or three weekends ago, we just sort of realised she'd disappeared. Gone home.'

'Home to where?'

Esther checked silently with the other two. 'Dunno. Country girl, anyway. Nowhere near me. Galway, maybe?' The quieter girls just shook their heads.

Swan became aware that Sister Dreyfus, standing with her back to them at the kitchen sink, had given up an semblance of lunch preparation and was listening intently, completely still.

'Sister?'

She turned slowly, clutching a dish brush in her yellow gloved hands.

'Did you see this girl?'

She nodded.

Considine asked the girls to wait in the TV lounge, assuring them that they would get their lunch soon. Sister Dreyfus removed her rubber gloves and sat at the table, simultaneously hesitant and determined.

'I know it was a Sunday, because there was only me here. I was on my way upstairs, after the girls had their tea, and she came out of her room. She had a big coat on and she had a bag. She was holding something inside the coat — I thought it might be the baby. She didn't notice me — it was almost dark. I followed her up the hall. There was a car outside. She got into it and drove off.'

'When you say she drove off — did she drive the car herself ?'

Sister Dreyfus thought for a moment, her face a scowl of concentration. 'She can't have. She was holding the baby still. There must have been someone driving. She just went away'

'Was Sister Bernadette here at the time?'

'No'

'Did you see the baby move, or hear it cry?'

Sister Dreyfus's eyes grew large behind her glasses as she realised the implications of what he meant. She shook her head.

'I went into the room after. It was like she'd never been there.'

Above them he could hear male voices, raised. The guard at the door fending off Monsignor Kelly.

'Did you discuss this with Sister Bernadette?' A quick shake of the head, a cowed look.

'Did you not think, when the baby was found in the convent, that there might be a connection?' said Swan.

'No, I thought she had decided to keep her child. That was why she sneaked off. By rights she should have left it with us.'

An idea was beginning to form in Swan's mind, something that would make sense of the convent's secrecy.

'Who adopts the babies, sister?'

'I don't know anything about that. Mother Mary Paul, you should talk to her.'

Swan waited for Considine to finish her notes, thanked the nun for her time.

Sister Dreyfus held a pale finger in the air. 'Wait!'

'What is it?'

'Her name!' The nun went to a drawer in one of the kitchen cabinets and took out a notebook. Several nibbed pens were bound to it by a thick rubber band. Sister Dreyfus brought it to the table and opened it. It was a kind of copy book, where names and letters were drawn in the familiar, mannered thick-and-thin stroke calligraphy Swan recalled from the name signs upstairs. Sister Dreyfus flicked through the pages and stopped, put her finger to a name repeated three times in three varied styles — Peggy Nolan. Peggy Nolan. Peggy Nolan.

'That's her. I make the name signs. I made one for her door, but she took it off.'

It was a common name. There must be hundreds of Peggy Nolans throughout the land. Maybe it had already come up in the investigation.

'Familiar?' Swann asked Considine.

She frowned. 'I'd have to check.'

'Please go ahead with your lunch, sister, and thank you. Your help has been invaluable.'

Sister Dreyfus smiled, a mercurial spasm.

Up in the front office, Swan found that Barrett and Mother Mary Paul had run out of conversation. The nun gazed anxiously out the front window.

'Monsignor Kelly is outside, waiting,' she complained.

'How much do they pay you for the babies?' asked Swan.

She glared at him, full beam. 'How dare — Nothing! That's not the way it is — even slightly! If the parents choose to show gratitude, that is completely —' she jerked in her seat, 'I think you should talk to Monsignor Kelly about this.'

'We can't let anyone else into the house now, mother, we need to search it. In fact, it might be an idea for you to take the girls back to the convent with you.'

'I can't take them back to St. Brigid's, it's not suitable.'

'I'm sure you'll sort it out. By the way, does Sister Bernadette drive?'

'Yes she drives. And I hope she gets back soon to help me sort out this… *misunderstanding*.'

'We'll be first in line for Sister Bernadette. Tell me, is the name Peggy Nolan familiar to you?'

'It is not.'

Swan showed Barrett and Considine the back bedroom where this Peggy had stayed. They didn't enter the room, but stood close together on the threshold.

'Can you find out about locking this, Declan? And supervise the exit of the girls and nuns. I'm thinking the baby could have been killed right here, in the bedroom. There's no immediate signs but it would account for her hiding it under her coat, wouldn't it?'

'Could be,' said Barrett.

'Gina?'

Considine was frowning at the carpet, miles away. At the sound of her name she quickly met his eye.

'It's odd, but I'm pretty sure there was a girl down in that town, Buleen, called Peggy Nolan. The guy I met was Doctor Nolan, right? And his daughter, the receptionist, she was a Peggy. I remember thinking it was and old fashioned name for a girl.'

They looked at each other for a few seconds. Weighing the idea.

'Sister Bernadette,' said Swan, 'where would you say her accent was from?'

'I'd say Tipperary,' said Barrett.

'Could it be east Clare? It's soft, though.'

'It could be Clare,' said Barrett.

Considine shrugged.

'If the nun was from the Buleen area, maybe she knew your Peggy Nolan already. Did your girl have hair like 'a conker'?'

'Yea,' said Gina, 'dark reddish. She was the right age too.'

A phone was ringing upstairs. Swan took the steps two at a time. When he got to the office, Mother Mary Paul was holding out the receiver to him. TP Murphy was on the other end..

'You've got the nun?' asked Swan.

'You little bollix,' replied Murphy, 'A complete wild gooser. And now I've got the RUC on my back. They insisted on accompanying me to Newry, and now they want me to fill in a stack of forms, threatening me with cross border infringement. It's going to take me hours to get home.'

'Where is she?'

'She wasn't there at all. The priest who finally deigned to break his silence said she phoned last week to cancel. You owe me.'

Damn. Where had she got to? Swan's mind raced as he went back down the stairs to his colleagues.

'Barrett — stay here until it's secure and empty. Make sure the tech bureau are coming soon as. Gina, I want you to put out a call for Sister Bernadette, but also I want you to get the team to trace all the Peggy Nolans you can find just in case your one's too good to be true. Then come join me.'

'Where?'

'Buleen, of course! Wherever the hell that is. Oh, and give that girl with the short hair a tenner — no make it twenty. I'll see you right.'

On the doorstep, Monsignor Kelly was pacing

and smoking — an expensive looking brand with a gold band around the filter. He threw down a long butt as Swan emerged and came forward to shake his hand. Cufflinks in the shape of a cross.

'Bit of a mix-up with your officer here,' said the monsignor, as if they were old friends temporarily kept apart by a harsh world.

'Sorry about that, Monsignor, thing is, I've got a bit of business to do, so perhaps we could catch up later.'

'Is everything alright?'

'Smashing, Father. Lovely place they have here, beautifully kept.'

Monsignor Kelly looked relieved, grateful.

'My officers are taking a few statements from the nuns and residents, so Garda O'Malley here can keep you company till that's finished.'

'But it was you I needed to — '

'No can do — *father*.'

Swan set off down the front steps. At the bottom, he turned back.

'Must take a good lot of donations to keep a place like this in the style, eh?'

Monsignor Kelly's determined smile dribbled off his face.

'But as I said to the reverend mother, we'll talk later, eh? After I've seen the adoption board.'

+

Swan headed home. He couldn't see the end of it yet, but he was starting to see the beginning. Peggy Nolan could've known Sister Bernadette of old, and persuaded the nun to help her, to let her stay at Percy Place. She delivers the child there, with the nun's help, because

254

the nun knows nursing, but three days later the child is beaten to death. The nun sneaks her away. Bernadette knows the Rosary garden well. It's her idea to bury the child there, but for some reason it gets left in the shed.

But *why* — why kill it? Was it an accident?

At home, he poured himself a finger of whiskey, searched out a couple of clean shirts, underwear, toiletries. He had hoped, without too much hope, that Elizabeth might be there. The only sign of her presence was a small sheet of paper torn from a notebook, the left edge frilled where she had ripped it from the spiral. Auntie Josie had taken another dip, it said, she was needed there, it said. With luck she'd be back tomorrow.

He made some calls, and packed his things in a briefcase, sat on the bed for a time. He didn't want to go away with things as they were between them, without doing some little thing to thaw the ice, though he wasn't sure how.

He woke before dawn, relishing the idea of driving the empty roads west as the sun rose behind him. He made a cup of coffee and fed the cat, stood looking at Elizabeth's note on the table as he supped. Just as he was leaving, he turned the note to the blank side and wrote quickly.

It's not just there you're needed. I need you.
I'm sorry for any coldness. We'll do as you want.
I love you,
V

He stared for a moment at his hokey words. She'd think he'd gone mad. Fuck it.

He left the note on the table and ran out the front door before he could change his mind.

TWENTY - SEVEN

Father Philbin's homily didn't mention Joan's time in Damascus House. He also avoided anything particular to the circumstances of her death but opted instead for generalised gravitas and veiled allusions to 'a young life snuffed out in its prime' and 'which of us knows the time and the place of our calling'. Under this roof, in these circumstances, there was no question of Joan having had a conscious role in the slip or fall that took her into the river's flow. If her death was suicide, they would not be having this mass; therefore it was not suicide.

The church was packed when Ali arrived. Many more than at that Sunday mass Una had dragged her to when she first arrived. A little over a week ago, but felt like so much longer.

At first, an uneasy silence reigned among the congregation, torn here and there by muffled coughs and shuffling footsteps. Finally the moan of the organ washed down on their heads and she turned to see the small coffin being carried in on the shoulders of six men, one of whom was Ivor. His hair was combed back and flattened with some lotion or oil that darkened it. His expression was full of effort. She looked down at her hands as he came level, couldn't bear the chance that their eyes might meet. All through the mass she thought about Joan, how unbelievable it was that she lay inside that box. How she herself may had some part in it by making Joan angry outside the dance. It would be easier to think it an accident, join in the church's version, but she just could not.

The choir of reed-voiced pensioners struggled into the sweet first lines of *Bring Flowers of the Fairest*. The coffin was hoisted once more and the men stepped it back down the aisle. Ivor was on the opposite side of it now, screened from view. After the coffin came Joan's mother, who had pressed the medal on her, not knowing she'd need all the compassion of Mary for herself. A ruddy-faced man in a tight black suit walked in line with her, presumably Joan's father. They didn't touch or lean on each other. The space between them was marked.

Ali joined the rest of the congregation to follow the coffin as it was carried down the street, an empty hearse driving behind the crowd. The graveyard was new — a field at the edge of town occupied by only two and a half rows of shining stone tablets adorned with wreaths, small statues, domed displays of plastic flowers. The rest was mown grass, waiting for the dead to come, many of them breathing now in this gathering. Two mounds of earth marked the hole where the procession would end.

The women gathered close around the grave, murmuring Hail Marys together, a decade of the rosary. The men were scattered to the periphery by some invisible force, many solemn with clasped hands, just observing the backs of the women, others starting to chat in low voices, just like they were attending any village occasion, the perpetual banter. A soft, sieved rain billowed down the valley, but few took shelter under umbrellas. Coat shoulders darkened. Ali hadn't even a jacket to protect her, was soon soaked through in her black cardigan and skirt.

She caught sight of Roisín and Una on the other side of the crowd, but otherwise did not know many people there. Joan's family came from Ennisbridge, two miles up the road and a world away. At the edge of the graveside, she recognised Peggy Nolan's pale blue mac. The woman beside her shared her umbrella, holding the big black wing of it low over both their faces. Doctor Nolan stood several paces behind them, straight as a soldier.

Ali wondered how well the Nolans had known Joan. She thought of Doctor Nolan on that Christmas day, the present in his hand, the daughters in their good coats. Had he been brought into the secret of what had been found? She vaguely remembered the two Nolan girls sitting side by side in the living room, obediently bored. Their father out of the room, possibly with Joan.

The first note of a laugh broke through the air and was immediately stifled. Ali wheeled round to see Davy looking down at the ground, kicking a stone away. The man beside him had a guilty hand near his mouth, and his eyes checked the crowd. They couldn't just keep quiet for ten minutes, always the jokes, always the bit of crack, even here. She turned back to the gathering at the graveside and noticed that a few of the women were also looking over to Davy and his crony, among them Peggy Nolan, whose placid face was unusually alive, eyes burning as she looked at the boys. Ali thought of Peggy standing at the edge of the dancefloor in the marquee, that same still attention. At that moment the woman beside Peggy lifted the umbrella that hid her face.

It was just for an instant.

The woman's eyes met Ali's and the umbrella dipped down again. She was wearing her veil as usual, looked no different than when she stalked the corridors of St. Brigid's, but Ali's first shocked thought was — *Antoinette Nolan*.

It was as if two different photographs — one of Peggy's prim teenage sister and one of Sister Bernadette standing at the front of her classroom had been superimposed and found to be identical. Sister Bernadette was who Antoinette Nolan had grown up to be, the colouring, the stature, the pale hand that still rested on Peggy's shoulder, all so vividly obvious now. Peggy had said her sister was in Dublin, that was all. She didn't say she was a nun.

The prayers ended and the crowd loosened, moved away from the grave as two men with shovels came forward. Ali pressed through the shifting bodies towards the spot where Sister Bernadette and Peggy had been standing, but when she got there, they were gone.

Most of the mourners had regrouped around the Dempsey family, queuing to shake hands and express their sympathies. Ivor was standing beside his mother, his tallness marking him out. Ali wanted to leave, but she knew the right thing was to pay her respects, to let him know she had shown up. She pulled her damp cardigan around her and pressed into the thickest part of the gathering.

She was an arm's length away from him before he noticed her, his eyes locking onto hers as he reached for her hand, pulling her close.

'You. You're here,' said Ivor.

'I'm so sorry —'

An old man pushed in beside her and started to talk close into Ivor's face. He was saying how Joan was in a better place now and Ivor was answering, but his fingers held Ali's firmly, keeping her close to him. On the other side of Ivor stood his mother, her eyes bloodshot, her expression congested with grief. A woman was talking to her, head nodding sadly, yet Joan's mother suddenly turned as if Ali had called her name and looked straight into her eyes, then down to where Ivor's fingers were entwined with hers. Mrs. Dempsey's mouth opened, lips wavering.

Ali tried to pull her hand from Ivor's, but he would not let go. The old man moved on and Ivor bent his head to her ear.

'I couldn't find her,' he said, his voice cracking.

He released her hand and she sank back into the crowd. She had no right to be upsetting these people. No right to push herself into their lives. If she hadn't taken Joan out of Damascus House... hadn't brought up the idea of the lost baby... Tears blurred her view as she hurried down the wet path to the cemetery gate.

She walked away from the town, over the bridge and out towards Caherbawn. The rain blew off. She didn't want to go back to the farm, she wanted to go somewhere she could be alone, where she could try to forgive herself. A beam of sun caught the tops of the trees beyond the farm and she remembered the ruined cottage, the place where Joan had been full of hope and Ivor had smiled his gold-flecked smile.

TWENTY - EIGHT

There wasn't a living creature to be seen on the streets of Buleen. Swan finally spotted the blue Garda sign over one of the doors on the main street. The station was locked. A handwritten note simply said that Garda Fitzmaurice would be back after the funeral.

He walked along the wide pavement, peering at the few dark shops until he came to the doctor's surgery. Doctor Nolan was not in residence, another door locked against him. It must be a popular funeral. Then Swan remembered the Hogan girl distressed about the woman who had drowned herself. That must be it. A tragedy would always fetch a crowd.

Patience, he told himself. The previous evening, Garda Fitzmaurice had confirmed by phone that Peggy Nolan was in Buleen with her family — *Where else would she be?* — there was no reason to think she'd fly the nest. And, no, there was no sign of a baby.

He walked all the way down one side of the street and up the other. He noted the press of cars around the ugly pink church.

That was all the patience he could tolerate. He needed a phone. In the comfortable-looking hotel, Swan asked for the use of a room. The German proprietor showed no particular surprise, just walked him upstairs to a high, simple bedroom whose two windows overlooked the main street. With this view, he'd be able to see Garda Fitzmaurice return. Swan picked up the telephone in one hand and leaned against the window casing.

Barrett was in the office. He said Sister Bernadette had not turned up yet. He also said that Considine was on her way, that she would arrive at noon at Birdhill.

'Birdhill?'

'There wasn't a car to spare. Kavanagh's on an efficiency drive — he told her to get a train…'

'How the hell would that be efficient?' Swan said.

'It wasn't me told her!'

'Just tell me how to get to this Birdhill place. Never heard of it.'

Swan hung on the line while Barrett consulted a map. Down in the street, men in sombre clothes gathered outside a pub. The funeral aftermath. He leaned closer to the glass, looked sideways. The cars were gone from outside the church. Below him, a dark-clad figure appeared around the corner, arms wrapped around herself, hair bedraggled.

Swan cursed, hung up and ran downstairs. He arrived on the pavement in time to touch her shoulder as she passed.

Ali Hogan jumped at the contact, and the face she turned to him was full of fear.

'Aren't you supposed to be in Dublin?' he said.

'Have you come to get me?'

'Get you for what?'

'I don't know…'

Clots of cobweb adhered to the sleeves of her cardigan and the front of her skirt was streaked with mud and grass stains.

'Are you alright?'

She looked down at herself, started to wipe ineffectually at the stains on her skirt.

'I — I was in the woods. There's an old cottage — I think I found something. Will you come with me?'

'I'm waiting to meet up with someone.'

'Oh.' She didn't seem curious about what had brought him there, caught up in her own drama.

'What was it you found?'

She shortened the distance between them, looked full into his face and said, 'I think it's a grave.'

The Garda station was still closed, Considine wasn't due for an hour and a half.

'Is it far, this place?'

'Not very.'

'I've a car near here.'

'It's just a walk.'

Swan followed the girl back over an old bridge and out of the town, towards scattered houses and patches of woodland. He should have insisted on the car.

'Does your mother know you're here?'

An impatient nod. He took in her black clothing. A car came towards them, and they stepped onto the grass verge.

'Were you at the funeral?'

'Yea.' She stepped back onto the tarmac and walked off at a lick. Swan hurried after, regretful now about this country detour, unsure of how to manage the girl.

She led him up a rough track that cut through pine woods, then along a path to where the remains of a cottage stood in a mossy clearing. It looked like it had been abandoned before the trees had been planted around it. A few jagged stubs of beam were all that was left of the roof, the walls were starting to fall in.

Swan followed Ali into this derelict enclosure. The girl stood in the middle and started to talk.

'This was where Joan brought me the day she

got out — so I came back to remember her because we were happy that day and I was looking at that hut that she said Ivor built and I noticed that there was a bit on the end that was planked up, and I don't know why but I just thought I'd have a look, and the planks came away…'

As she spoke, Swan walked over to the bit that she had described as a 'hut'. It was just a lean-to of corrugated iron and wood cladding resting against an end wall. The kind of thing you would build to shelter a few sheep or some fodder.

One end was open, and a filthy mattress lay inside, as repulsive as a carcass.

' —they used to stay here, the two of them, she said, when there was trouble at home. It was their place, so she must have made the grave too, don't you think?'

Swan stooped and made blinkers with his hands to see better into the dark. Beyond the head of the mattress was a wall made of short lengths of horizontal planks. He stood and cast his eye over the outside of the shelter. Sure enough, it was longer than the space he had just looked into. Ali waited for him at the other end.

The boards that clad the outside of that end were vertical, and two of them were now lying on a flattened area of nettles and grass, leaving a gap into the dark space.

'They were loose,' Ali was saying, 'I just put a hand to them…'

Kneeling on the bruised ground, Swan twisted his shoulders and pushed his head through the gap. The air was colder inside, heavy with the smell of damp clay. The space was small as a cupboard, no more than three foot deep, and empty.

Light crept in over his shoulder and his eyes adjusted. He hadn't noticed the slate propped against the cottage wall. It was an ordinary slate, might have been part of the cottage's roof once, but the bottom of it was embedded in the earth. As he tipped his head nearer, a little light struck it and he could see marks scratched into it — the spidery double outline of a cross, and beneath it a heart. The ground in front was just slightly mounded.

He pulled back out of the small gap and started to wrench away the other planks. They came easily, the old wood crumbling away under force.

'And what exactly do you think is in here?'

'I think it's Joan's baby, it must be,' said Ali.

Swan thought they were more likely to find someone's dog or kitten beneath the slate than a child.

He was so close to solving the mystery of one dead baby, but had somehow let himself get diverted into this other tale. The wise thing would be to leave this little slate as it was, get on with the matter at hand. Fitzmaurice could come and check it out another day.

'I'll run back and get more help,' said Ali.

A fuss was the last thing he wanted. He was only a couple of hours away from moving in on the Nolan girl.

A flat stone lay in the weeds beside him, the size of his palm. He picked it up and started to scratch experimentally at the earth in front of the little slate.

'I can't watch.' Ali walked away.

Hopefully there would be nothing at all here, thought Swan, scraping methodically now. He was only an inch down when his makeshift spade encountered a small, pliable obstruction, a pale nub that had an odd pinkish tinge to it. He put aside the stone and took his penknife out of his coat pocket. By prodding about, he loosened the earth about this small protrusion and brushed it away in one movement. There, in the scooped out hollow, a perfect little hand emerged.

Swan's heart missed a beat. Each wormish finger was less than an inch long. Tiny pricks of clay filled a row of four dimples on the back of the palm. Warm relief trickled through him as he made sense of it. He pushed a finger against the flesh-toned — it was obvious now — plastic.

As he started to dig out the rest of the doll, he called Ali to him.

'It's only a doll.'

She came to kneel beside him as he uncovered the whole arm, and next to it a forehead started to emerge. Here and there the plastic was marked with bright yellow streaks, some kind of aging. Once the head was free, he prised the rest of it from the soil, shook it free of insects and dirt and handed to her. The body felt heavier than it should, as if soil had gradually sifted inside during the time it lay in the ground. The doll had a flannel nappy still wrapped around its bottom, a filthy scrap.

Swan poked around below where the doll had lain to check there was nothing else there. Behind him, Ali muttered something.

'What's that?'

'Baby Joy,' she repeated, 'this is Baby Joy.'

'Was it yours?'

'No, but it was supposed to be.' Ali brought the grubby body up to her chest, embraced it. He should get her back to her family. The girl wasn't right, it was plain.

'I need to get on,' he said, 'I'll walk you back to town, to where you're staying.'

'My aunt's house is just down the road.'

'I'll walk you to that, then.'

He was glad to get away from the desolate cottage. As they walked, he rubbed his hands together to get rid of the soil that stuck to them. His trousers were mucky too. He offered to take the doll, to get rid of it for her, but Ali wouldn't give it up.

Half way down the forestry track, Ali stopped still.

'Have you come here because of Joan?'

'Joan? No.'

'You have, haven't you?'

'I don't know your Joan, Ali. I'm still after the mother of the Rosary Garden baby.'

'So what are you doing here?'

Swan hooked his hand into the crook of Ali's arm, forced her to carry on walking.

'There's someone here we need to talk to.'

'Oh,' said Ali, looking down at the movement of her feet. Then she said in a small voice, 'Is it Sister Bernadette?'

'What about Sister Bernadette?'

'I saw her this morning.'

It was Swan's turn to stop walking.

'She's here?'

'Yea, it's stupid, but I never realised before that she's from here — I even met her when I was small, only then she was called Antoinette Nolan.'

'Antoinette Nolan. With a sister called Peggy?'

'You know Peggy?'

'Not yet,' said Swan.

Now it made sense. Nuns had families, you forget that. Mother Mary Paul even talked to him about nuns taking new names. And families had their loyalties; a girl in trouble would naturally seek out her sister.

Garda Fitzmaurice must be back at station by now. They needed to make a plan for handling the whole Nolan family, get in some extra guards from Kinmore. And there was Considine to collect.

'Is your aunt's house near?' They had reached the roadside, and the town was in sight.

Ali nodded, raised a hand slightly from her side to indicate something not far away. The other arm still cradled the filthy doll. She looked a forlorn sight.

'A bath is very good for the spirits,' he said, hurrying away, 'ask your aunt to run you a bath.'

TWENTY - NINE

Cathal Hayes was talking on about some woman he'd met in Limerick, about the unusual sexual offers she had whispered in his ear at some drinking dive. Davy clutched his pint and watched the Dempsey family gathered on the other side of the pub, the centre of attention. It wasn't the usual post-funeral lark of ham sandwiches and plates of biscuits in someone's tidy front room. There was nothing to eat, and the Red Rock Saloon was the roughest of venues. Perfect for the Dempsey family. He hadn't really meant to come, had sort of drifted in with the crowd.

Joan's brothers kept throwing filthy looks at him. He had the feeling that a fight was brewing, and he welcomed it.

Some aul' fella appeared at his side.

'Your sister says can you come outside.'

Davy squinted at him. 'Right you are.'

The old man moved off.

'I'm thinking maybe now she was only a prostitute,' Cathal was saying. Davy studied the crush of people around the Dempsey family, offering their words of wisdom about death. Their tiny ignorant opinions. He looked at their mouths, their flapping wet lips. He understood so much now about the rottenness of it all.

He tipped his glass to his lips, swallowed deep. Cathal had disappeared without him noticing. He was standing alone and people were staring at him openly. The old man reappeared.

'Go on now, son. You're not wanted here.'

Una was waiting outside in her car, clutching the wheel even though the engine was still. He walked over and put his palms on the car roof and hung down from them to peer in at her.

'What's up with you?'

'You're drunk. Get in,' she said.

'I've got a pint on the go.'

'Please, Davy'

'Oh, please, is it?'

The man who had ushered him out of the pub was standing in the entrance way, barring it. Davy started to laugh as he made his way around to the passenger side of the car. When he got in, Una rolled her window down, as if he stank, and maybe he did. She looked all keyed up, like she could snap if you twanged her.

'This feels familiar,' said Davy.

'Don't bait me,' said Una. 'It's not right for you to be in there.'

'Free drink and weeping — it suits me fine.'

'Who's in there? Did anyone say anything?'

'Ach… everyone's scrambling for their bit of the blame. The Ma's not there, but the men are. I'll bet you a quid there's a fight before closing.'

'Do they think she jumped?'

'Sure isn't that what happened?'

'Don't mess me about.'

'I wouldn't dare mess about with *you*. Someone told me Ned Greevy's saying he spotted her alone on the bridge that night. What do you make of that?'

'My nerves are in bits. I didn't push her, you know that.'

Davy combed his hand through his fringe, cleared it from his eyes.

'I was looking the other way.'

Her mouth opened in protest, but she seemed to change her mind and swallowed it back. She turned the key and the engine shuddered into life.

'Hey, let me out,' he said.

Una pulled out of the car park, her hand clumsy with the gears.

'I can't trust you not to say something stupid when you're like this.'

'What you going to do — *kill* me?'

The old Ford barrelled up the road towards Buleen, Una's grip on the wheel was as tight as her jaw.

'Sorry. That was crude of me,' he said. 'You just gave a little helping hand, let's put it that way. First the child, then the mother.'

'I've told you before. The baby was dead when I got to the kitchen. It was Joan's hands on it.'

'Drop me at Melody's,' he said as they passed the church, but Una ignored him, turning down the bridge road at speed.

'For fuck's sake.'

'You don't need any more drink.'

The car bucked over the top of the bridge. Una braked hard and pulled into the grass verge beside the old chapel. With the car stopped, she turned to face him.

'Do you want me up before the guards, would that make you happy? This is serious.'

Davy met her eyes, found himself looking at the black holes in the centre of them, the bit of someone that was supposed to show their true self. Nothing. She was staring back, right into his black holes. It was stupid to think you could know a person. The sound of the river flowing behind them grew in his ears, an unbearable noise.

'A baby's not really a person, is it, Una?'

She shifted her eyes to look out the windscreen. 'Of course it's a person, it has a soul.'

'Did you confess what you did to the priest?'

'I only disposed of it. Protected Joan. Protected you. God will be my judge.'

'You got away with it.'

'You've no idea what it is to live with something like that. I got away with nothing.'

They drove on towards the farm.

'I'll drop you at your house,' said Una, 'you can change, then you'll come down to the farm for your tea.'

A man was walking towards them on the roadside. He had a beige raincoat on, open and blowing back from a pale grey suit. Not the kind of clothes anyone wore around here. The knees of his trousers had mud on them. As they drew closer, Davy recognised the detective from the Dublin police station. He quickly raised a hand to his face. Una looked in the rear-view mirror. Davy turned in his seat. The man stood gazing after them, his coat billowing against the cow parsley that gushed from the hedge.

'Who's that?'

'*I* don't know. Just drop me at the track.'

As he got out of the car, Davy looked back down the road towards town. The man was no longer in sight.

'Come down in about an hour,' said Una.

'I'm not hungry,' said Davy, and started up the track towards his bungalow.

THIRTY

Ali ignored Swan's advice. A bath would fix nothing, and she didn't want to face her aunt. Instead of going to the farm, she walked up to Davy's house. He wasn't there. She sat down on the cement stump that stood like a sentry by the unfinished threshold. The afternoon was mild, but she couldn't stop her limbs from trembling. Down on the road, a car door slammed and soon after, Davy appeared through the trees, walking fast. He was still wearing his dark funeral suit, but it looked looser on him than when she'd seen him at the graveyard, and his tie was gone.

He started to raise a hand in greeting, but then blinked and stood still, looking at her with an expression somewhere between disgust and confusion.

'What have you got there?' he called.

Ali looked down. The doll was lying across her knee. She had forgotten about it.

'It's my doll.'

He closed the distance between them. In the light of the clearing he looked ill, his skin doughy. He stood over her, staring down at the filthy remains of Baby Joy. He brought his hand up to his shoulder and swung it in slow motion towards her face. His fingers delivered a light flick against her cheek.

'You little joker,' he said, but he wasn't smiling.

Ali stood up.

'You've been in the pub, haven't you?'

'Where did you find that aul' yoke?'

'This yoke is the doll I was supposed to get

that Christmas. I found it buried in the cottage on the forestry road.'

Davy started to laugh, low and empty.

'So that's what she did with it. What a retard. So you've been all on your own here?'

'Yea.'

'Only I saw a man on the road, heading for the village — he had city clothes.'

'That's Detective Swan — he's from Dublin.'

Davy took a small bunch of keys from his pocket and bounced them rhythmically in his hand.

'I hope he's not going to take you away from us again?' He hopped past her up on to the doorstep and busied himself with the lock.

'Naw, he's here to talk to Sister Bernadette from my school. She's one of Doctor Nolan's daughters. Well, you probably know that.'

Davy was taking a while to unlock the door.

'Why don't you come in for a coffee,' he said, his back still turned, 'tell me about it, eh?'

'Davy?'

He looked around.

'Who's a retard? When I said I'd found the doll, you said something like *she's a retard*.'

He lifted his shoulders then relaxed them in a long exaggerated sigh.

'Joan. I gave her that doll to help her get over losing the baby that night. Something to hold while she was wailing. We needed the box. I didn't think she'd go and bury it.'

Ali shivered. *We needed the box.* So matter of fact. She did a sum in her head. Davy must have been sixteen when Joan had her baby.

'Do you know about... where the baby ended

up? When we found this doll, I was thinking *where's the real one?'*

'Who's we?'

'Detective Swan and me — he helped dig it up.'

Davy stepped down beside her.

'You're some kid, do you know that? Okay, so…'

Sliding an arm round her shoulder, Davy started to walk her along the rough path towards the farm. The doll hung from her hand, brushing through the grass. Everything was both ordinary and extraordinary, and she felt that she was being carried along on some kind of current, that even though she spoke and moved, she couldn't affect the flow of things. Even Davy seemed strange to her, full of flippant cheer.

'Joan used to stay in that broken cottage with her little brother, just like a pair of tinkers. I don't know what you see in him, by the way, he's closer to livestock than human. He thinks it was me that shafted her. Got her up the pole. An altar boy like me.'

'Do you feel alright, Davy? I don't think I feel right.'

He squeezed her closer to him, but kept walking.

'He'd rather think that than the truth. Better than knowing it was your old man or your uncle or even one of your brothers doing her. That's why she used to stay over in the kitchen — she didn't want to go home. She knew an awful lot for her age, sex stuff. She was very keen to teach it, too.'

The path widened and the trees gave way to farm buildings. Davy released his hold on her, looked about at the barn and outbuildings as if they were new to him, rubbed at his chin.

Ali walked ahead onto the concrete screed of the farmyard, and the view opened up around her — the soft rise of hill, the lines of hedges, and closer in, on her left, the pig sheds. Davy came up to stand beside her.

'Technically speaking, of course, I might have been the father, but I know in my heart it wasn't mine. It was a sickly thing, and its end was sad. I won't have that one associated with me. I won't.'

Gold light slanted across the open fields, but here in the shade of the barn it was cold. Ali tucked the doll inside her cardigan and drew the cloth tight around her. A tractor came into view, crossing the high meadow. Cut grass spewed out behind the reaper blades in quilted lines.

'Looks like everyone's back from the funeral,' she said, her own voice high in her ears. 'Lets go down to the house.'

She took a step forward, but Davy's hand fell on her shoulder, as she half expected it would, holding her in place.

'You asked me a question,' he said, 'at least let me answer.'

Ali turned to look at him. He jumped to one side and landed on a drain cover. It rang from the blow, like a gong.

'Do you know what this is?'

As he said it, her nose opened to the familiar smell. Under the square drain cover was the tank that took all the pig waste. Cement channels ran down from the sheds and under the concrete rectangle they were standing on.

'It's the slurry tank,' said Ali.

'Good girl. Three fathoms deep of shit and piss. The magical thing is you never need to empty it, because the shit eats itself.'

Ali remembered a fear she had when she was

little, when she was helping to brush the slurry down the channels, that she would slip through one of the narrow slits at the end into a bottomless pool of stink. But that had been a groundless fear, the stuff of nightmares, easily dissolved. Nothing like what she felt now, lurking, wide-awake.

'That so?' said Ali. Her hand moved to embrace the curve of the doll's back beneath the thin wool of her cardigan, some animal instinct in her feeling a small presence there. The tractor thrummed somewhere not far away.

Davy drew her close and lowered his voice.

'Una's not a very sentimental person, you know that. It was the middle of Christmas day that you found it. She did what she had to do.' He tapped on the metal with the toe of his scuffed black brogues.

Ali stepped back from the metal hatch, couldn't block out an image of the baby's body sinking slowly into the brown muck, lit by a square of daylight. Una standing above, the grimy box in her hands.

'That's horrible.'

'Women do horrible things, though your Mary O'Shea libbers don't think so. *Oh the poor mistreated women... oh the terrible men that oppress them...* If you hadn't stuck your little nose in, it could have waited. I might have buried it properly on Stephen's Day, when things were quiet.'

'You knew it was under the bed?'

' 'Course I did. I said I'd deal with it. And I would have, but...' he turned from her, 'ach, you were only a child, it wasn't your fault.'

Ali stared at him. He was quieter now — the antic spirit had gone out of him as suddenly as a wind dying. He'd been too young to be involved in something like that, younger than she was now, and she didn't believe that callous tone he was trying to muster. He was still her Davy.

'Let's go down to the house,' she said.

'I don't want to see my sister right now.'

'We could go into town.'

'Too many people.'

The tractor noise was moving towards them, though the machine itself was hidden behind the sheds. The light of the day was fading, shadows gathering like fog in field hollows and the lee of buildings.

'You look tired,' Ali said.

'I'd like to sleep for a thousand years, but I can't even manage an hour. Come back to the bungalow and have a drink with me.'

He held out a hand to her, and after a moment she took it. She had asked and he had told her. That should be worth something. Truth should be worth something.

They walked back through the trees, Davy humming a meandering slow tune. His grip on her hand was reassuring, tight.

THIRTY - ONE

The Nolan home was on a rise of land to the north of the village, half hidden by a lush hedge. It was double-fronted, with wide bay windows, a large brick-arched porch and a thick creeper straddling one corner. They left two police cars blocking the top of the drive-way and the Kinmore guards quickly fanned out in the grounds. Swan, Considine and Fitzmaurice walked round to the front door. An old blue and white vase took centre stage in one of the windows, holding sprays of gladioli. In the deep of the room, a pale face turned to their passing.

After a short wait, it was Sister Bernadette who appeared in the porch, her expression rigid.

'Good afternoon, detective,' she said.

'Good afternoon, Sister. We need to talk to you further, and to your sister Peggy.'

She stood silent as if running through reasons to refuse them. Her eyes moved to take in the Garda that stood by the cars.

'Come in.' She stepped back to allow them into the house. The broad hall beyond the porch was wood pan-elled, with a grandfather clock and a carved oak bench. Discreet good things, handed down. A brass plaque on one door read 'surgery'. Sister Bernadette was attempt-ing to usher them into the room opposite, but Swan hesitated.

'Who else is in the house with you?'

'My father's in his study, working,' she said, indi-cating the door with the brass sign. 'My mother's shopping in Limerick with a neighbour.'

'And your sister?'

'She's having a nap,' said Sister Bernadette. A board creaked above their heads. Swan raised his eyes to the sound.

'Peggy?' Bernadette called.

Bare feet appeared at the top of the stairs, slowly followed by the rest of a young woman. She wore a nightdress and a shawl around her shoulders. Her hair was indeed the colour of a chestnut and curled thickly around her shoulders. She registered no surprise to see them there. Her face was still as wax.

'Peggy, we're going to have a chat with your sister,' said Swan. 'Perhaps my colleague Gina here can keep you company in the meantime?'

Considine was on her way up the stairs when a man with white hair stuck his head out of the surgery door. Garda Fitzmaurice greeted Doctor Nolan in an easygoing way and reassured him that no emergencies were in progress. Swan introduced himself and said he'd be obliged if the doctor could remain in the house for the moment.

Nolan exchanged a furtive glance with his eldest daughter before retreating behind his door.

Sister Bernadette led Swan and Garda Fitzmaurice into the living room and took a seat on the very edge of a chintz-covered armchair, hands demurely clasped over one knee. Swan experienced a surge of impatience in the face of her composure, an urge to shout or throw some delicate ornaments about. Instead, he wandered past her to take in the view from the window, settling his breathing. When he spoke, he addressed the windowpane.

'We've been chasing you round the country, Sister.

Your nuns think you're in Newry.'

'I needed to come home.'

'To check on your sister?' He turned.

She gave him a steady look. 'Yes.'

'I've been to St. Jude's. Your sister stayed there, didn't she?'

A quick nod. 'My sister's not well.'

'How do you mean?'

'I think having a child disturbed her — disturbed the balance of her mind.'

'So you're not going to deny she had a baby or that she stayed in St. Jude's under your care?'

'No.'

'Well, that saves time. Can I ask where her baby is?'

Sister Bernadette looked over at the dried flowers arranged in the empty fire grate. 'You have it.'

'The baby in the shed?'

The nun turned to look at him, her eyes full of rising tears. 'I recognised her the moment I saw her lying in that basket. I delivered her myself. Held her in my arms each day she lived.' She pulled her black sleeve down over the knuckle of her thumb and wiped her cheeks quickly.

'I couldn't tell you at the time, I was worried about Peggy. She disappeared from St. Jude's the day before the child was found. I had to come down here to find her, to talk to her for myself.'

She had deliberately mislead him, had wasted days and days.

'You think your sister killed her baby?'

'We argued about the child. I thought she should keep her, bring her back home, but she wanted her to *just disappear*, that's what she said.'

'Your sister's not married — wouldn't it be tough for her to keep a child and raise it alone?'

'We would have managed. I told her I'd help.'

'But you're up in Dublin.'

'I could have come home.'

More tears appeared and Sister Bernadette swiped at them irritably.

'Your sister refused your help?'

'Maybe I pressured her too much.'

'Did she admit to killing it?'

Bernadette shook her head quickly. 'But I know having a baby can bring on depression. I didn't *think* Peggy could do something like that, but what do I know?' There was bitterness mixed with the grief in her voice.

'And what does Peggy say?' asked Fitzmaurice.

'She says the baby in the shed wasn't hers, that her baby was adopted, that she's been taken abroad. It's a fantasy. I held her dead in my arms, so how can she be in another place and happy? She wasn't just Peggy's, she was *something* to me too... in my head, I call her Grace.'

They sat in silence for a minute while Sister Bernadette struggled to control her breathing.

'Why did you unwrap the coverings from the baby — to hide the blouse was it?'

'I needed to see what was done to her.' She brought a curled fist to her mouth, pressed it hard against her lips. 'I wish I hadn't. I don't know why I hid the blouse; I think I was in a panic in case it was Peggy's. I sent the Hogan girl away for water so I could have some time. Just an excuse — she'd been baptised already in the little chapel at St. Jude's, just the three of us there.' She smiled briefly at the memory.

'We spoke to Sister Dreyfus at St. Jude's,' said

Swan. 'She saw your sister leave with the baby. She saw her being driven off in a car.'

Sister Bernadette looked at him, puzzled.

'Who else did she know in Dublin?' he asked.

'No-one.'

'Did she tell you who the father was?'

'I asked her, but all she would say was that they couldn't be together — yet.' Sister Bernadette took a breath, 'I think he must have been a married man, but she still had hopes for him. The hope was more precious than the child.'

There was a knock at the door, and Considine stuck her head in, asked to see Swan for a moment. They went into the small front porch and kept their voices low.

'I was making small talk, boss, I wasn't trying to do my own interview, but she just started talking about the kid.'

'Okay. What's she saying?'

She says the one found in Dublin wasn't hers. Says that hers was taken to England. She won't say who took it.'

'Do you believe her?'

'It's a bit unlikely, isn't it?'

'Did she talk about being picked up in the car?'

'No — I wanted to hold off till you were there. How's the nun?'

'Chatty. Says she recognised the baby in the shed as her sister's. She thinks her sister snapped and killed it.'

Considine let a grin escape. 'Yes!'

'I'm not so sure,' said Swan, ' She's assuming no one else was involved, but who was driving the car that picked Peggy up from St. Jude's — it wasn't her sister.'

Peggy Nolan sat in the corner of a small sofa in a bright little room off the kitchen, her bare feet tucked under her. The room was painted yellow with pale green woodwork, little mirrors and pictures livening the walls, just the kind of old-fashioned things Elizabeth would like. He remembered the sentimental note he had left for his wife and quickly bundled her from his mind.

Apart from her russet colouring, Peggy was quite different from her sister, made from some heavier element, her face full and sensuous but lacking animation. Moving quietly, Swan took a chair opposite. Considine sat on the sofa beside her, while Fitzmaurice lurked somewhere behind him.

'This is Detective Swan, my boss,' said Considine, 'Can you tell him what you told me?'

Peggy moved her gaze slowly from Considine to Swan.

'My baby is in England, in a house by the sea.' Swan wondered whether the girl was doped. Her dark eyes were hard to read.

'That sounds pleasant. Who took her there?'

She opened her mouth slightly and closed it again, her gaze dropping to the floor.

'Can't say.'

'Was it someone you met in Dublin?'

A slight shake of her head.

'Your sister doesn't think the baby was adopted. She says she recognised her as the one found in the Rosary Garden.'

'That baby was NOT mine.' Although she didn't raise her eyes, an edge of defiance had come into her voice, an anger stirring.

'Look at me, Peggy. We have a way of proving the baby in the garden wasn't yours. You want that, don't you?'

'Yes.'

'All we have to do is take blood from you and from your child's father. That's the way to prove the dead baby's not yours.'

'The only way?' The girl was agitated, slurring her words slightly.

'We'll take care of the arrangements if you just tell us his name.'

'Come on now,' said Garda Fitzmaurice from the doorway. His voice was low, and managed to convey an infinite reasonableness. Peggy looked at him in hope.

'He said we'd have a fresh start. It was him found the good home for it.'

'Of course he did.'

'But now he won't talk to me at all.'

'I could have a word with him,' said Fitzmaurice, 'straighten things out for you.'

'Could you really?'

'No bother.'

Tears tipped suddenly from Peggy's eyes as she got to her feet and shuffled over to put her arms around Garda Fitzmaurice. Swan held his breath and prayed that no one would enter the room to see this.

'Where is he today?' Fitzmaurice asked, smooth as one hand slipping into another.

Peggy shook her head, rubbing her forehead against his uniform jacket.

'Remember that lovely mild evening, Peggy, back in the autumn. When I saw you up in the quarry wood? You were parked in your father's car with someone, weren't you? Davy Brennan, I think it was.'

Peggy had gone very still. Her arms dropped off the Garda's shoulders, and her hands came to cover her face.

'He'll be angry with me. Don't tell him I said.'

'Was it Davy Brennan that took the baby away to be adopted?' asked Swan.

She nodded. 'In England. He gave me a photo of the couple. They have a lot of money, he said, and they're Catholic.'

Swan and Fitzmaurice retreated to the hall. The Garda said he'd seen this Davy in Buleen that morning, but that he'd been up in Dublin for a while.

Dublin. Swan's heart quickened.

'What's he like, this Brennan?'

'Bit of a boyo, but from a respectable family. As you know.'

'What do I know?'

'Sure he's part of the Devane's at Caherbawn. Mrs. Devane's maiden name is Brennan. Like your one on *The Late Late Show,* only she goes by the name of Hogan. He's her uncle.'

Swan's brain raced to absorb this information, throwing up a picture, a memory, from Rathmines Garda station on the very first day of the case. When he walked into the reception area after interviewing Alison Hogan, there had been two people sitting in the chairs. The emotional Deirdre Hogan had shaded her companion into obscurity. But he had been sitting right beside her. Swan tried to conjure him back into memory, but could only see the way his fringe fell forward to hide his features, the dark slouch that he had read as boredom.

He asked Fitzmaurice to phone the farm, to check if Davy Brennan was there.

'Pretend it's nothing important.'

The Garda came back after a short exchange.

'His sister says she hasn't seen him, says he might be away to Kinmore. She was very keen to know why I wanted him, though. I'll put a call out, if ye want.'

'Yes, but no more hanging about — let's just go there. Leave two of the lads here and round up the others. I'll join you in a minute.'

THIRTY - TWO

Davy pushed Ali through the hall of the bungalow and into the kitchen. 'I need a drink. We both need a drink.'

He worked his way along the line of cupboards, opening and shutting doors on empty shelves.

'Is there beer?' said Ali, laying the doll on the dirty counter. The place seemed even more of a wreck than it had been when Davy returned from Dublin. A bucket beside the sink overflowed with rubbish and the cement floor was splashed with brown stains. A queue of bottles stood against the skirting board.

'No beer — I've whiskey somewhere.' He twirled round to face her. 'I haven't told anyone about the slurry pit in — what — more than ten years. It's stupid for you not to know. You're not a child anymore.'

Davy walked over to the small fridge, opened the door and stared into it, even though he had searched it a moment before. 'That's not to say I'm not a little bit annoyed with you.' He addressed the fridge, not her.

'What have I done?'

'You keep bringing these policemen sniffing in your wake.'

'What's that to do with us?'

'What indeed!' Davy slammed the fridge and walked out of the kitchen. Ali followed. From the hallway she watched him do a circuit of the small bathroom, searching.

'I don't want you to be annoyed with me,' she said.

She hoped he would calm down, hoped he wouldn't find any whiskey and that not finding it wouldn't make him angry. She followed him into a bedroom. Davy got down on his hands and knees and started going through his suitcase and the pile of clothes beside it. She needed to ask him something. She wasn't sure she wanted the answer, but the question kept nagging around her head.

'You said that Joan's baby was sickly. She told me it was stillborn.'

Davy sat back, cross-legged on the floor.

'They made that up afterwards, Una and herself. I know what I saw... I saw its little arms waving... I saw it. They treated me like an idiot. Never took a breath, Una says, but I heard it — mewing like a kitten. I was looking through the window at them. When Una laid it on the table it wasn't moving anymore. I don't know what they did to it, or which one of them did it. Una said I didn't see what I thought I saw.'

Ali moved to the mattress on the floor, crawled over it so that she could sit with her back against the wall. She needed to sit very still. Davy was looking at his hands. She remembered him as he was at sixteen, a tall hero. She tried to figure out the likely truth of what he said — whether he could have been mistaken, or spinning a tale. She thought of her mother's story of her grandfather forcing them to kill animals as a mercy.

Minutes passed.

'When I went into the kitchen, Una was tending to Joan. She told me to put it away — so I did — I hid it for her. The next day I saw her coming back down from the pit with the box and she says to me *it's in a better place* with that pious bloody face on her.'

Davy turned to look at Ali, his eyes re-focussing.

'Aaah!' he cried, and she flinched as he lunged in her direction. His hand came from behind a pillow, gripping an almost full bottle of Paddy by the neck. He rolled away and spun the metal top from it with one rub of his palm. He threw back a slug and held out the bottle to her.

'You look like you need it.'

'I don't like it straight.'

'Don't be a fairy.'

She took the bottle and swallowed. It burned inside her mouth and made her lips sting, but as it went down she felt blood stirring within her limbs, like coming back to life. She took another sip and Davy smiled. She wanted to change the subject.

'Hey,' she said, 'aren't these my mother's sheets?'

'Must've taken them by mistake.'

'Mistake?'

'I don't know why you're bothering to go to university — you should just go straight into the cop shop — or the Gestapo — go snooping with the piggy pigs, oink oink.' He grabbed the bottle from her, swallowed deep then wiped his mouth with the back of his hand.

Ali tried again to think of something to talk about, something to make him come back to himself, away from this story. And then she thought of him laughing in the graveyard, the sound of it carrying over Joan's open grave. And how Peggy had stared at him, her eyes burning, and Sister Bernadette beside her, looking too, angry with him for something more than just the laugh.

Ali stood up, wobbled on the mattress.

'Where're you going?'

'I'm going to get a glass — water for the whiskey.'

Ali let the tap run. The night of the marquee dance, she had seen Peggy on the edge of the floor looking out at the dancers with the most miserable expression. And when Ali had taken her place, Davy was two feet away dancing with Valerie, the woman who had broken it off with him for his wandering eye. What was the connection between Davy and Peggy?

She heard him move about the house, then a loud crack of splintering wood. She didn't know what he was up to, but stayed at the sink, moving the glass under the water's flow, filling it and emptying it again and again. What was it that Joan had said to her? She knew nothing. Nothing at all. She did have a sense that if she tried to leave now, Davy would stop her. If she could wait it out, this mood would pass over, or he would pass out.

'You got a lighter?' He was in the doorway.

She wiped her hands on her skirt and took her lighter and cigarette packet out of her pocket and offered them up.

'Get us a glass too — I'm lighting a fire in the front room.'

Ali sat on the sofa, smoking, supping her whiskey and water steadily while Davy assembled a pile of thin wood and newspaper in the rough hole where a fire surround might go one day. He hummed as he touched the flame to the edges of the paper. The wood crisped and spat.

'That's cosy now,' he said, balancing two peat briquettes over the flames. He came to join her on the sofa, filling the tumbler she'd brought for him with whiskey before settling back against the cushions.

'You're very quiet. I'm sorry — but it's better you know. This is what the world is.'

Her tongue in her mouth was clumsy. 'Did something happen between you and Peggy?'

'Aw, Jaysus — that too? Let me make one thing clear — I never fancied her. It was a moment of weakness. You know I'm given to moments of weakness.' Davy put his hand on Ali's knee and give her a rueful smile. She didn't smile back, but glimpsed a foggy image of Davy's face lowering towards hers in darkness. He sighed and removed his hand, picking up the tale.

'It was just once or twice. In the back of her Daddy's Jag, what can I say — the situation appealed to me. Should have just fucked the car instead. She said she was on the pill, said her Daddy got her a supply and I believed her. Next thing she's up the pole, and telling Valerie about it. And I got no say in any of it. That's not fair is it?'

'I don't know.'

'I said she should get rid of it, and do you know what she said to me? She said she would *if* I'd be her boyfriend. She was trying to hijack my life. *My whole life.*'

Davy thumped the arm of the sofa so hard the drink in her glass trembled. She raised the glass to her lips and tipped all the liquid into her mouth.

'I convinced her to get it adopted — had a place set up for her in some residential place out in Connemara. Might have led her on a little bit about my feelings to get the job done, okay, but then Antoinette takes Peggy off to Dublin with her, says she doesn't want her to make any rash decisions…'

Ali thought of the Rosary Garden, of Sister Bernadette standing bereft outside the shed with a dead baby in her arms.

'No,' Ali managed to say, 'no, wait…'

'Like I've no rights, like I'm some fuckin' plank of wood. You women think it's all down to you. I was just trying to get my say. It was half mine.'

Ali tried to get to her feet, but Davy grabbed her hand and pulled, holding her down next to him and pointing a finger in her face.

'You listen — I'll tell you how it was supposed to go and then I'll tell you how *you* messed it up.'

'I feel sick.'

'I don't care.'

Davy looked around for the whiskey bottle, but he couldn't reach it and keep hold of her at the same time. 'Bugger. Anyway, Peggy goes to Dublin to have the baby, and I follow after. The nun's trying to persuade her to keep it, to come back to Buleen and live openly with her little bastard in my own town. I'd never be rid of her.'

'What did you do?'

'I sorted something out. It was perfect. I told her I had a family in England, rich people desperate for a baby, who would give it the life of a princess. We do a deal. I persuade Peggy to give me the baby one night in Dublin, and tell her I'm going to take it over on the ferry.'

'Did you?'

'Of course I didn't. I would have been stopped at the first post. It was just a tale. No, I had a better plan. I figured I could drive as far as Portlaoise and back without your mother missing her car. Drop the baby near the hospital in the dark. I even had a wee bed set up in the back of the car, a Dunne's Stores towel to wrap it in. They'd be searching the midlands for the mother. Nothing to connect it to her or me.'

'It's still alive?'

'It would be if you hadn't arrived at the door with your little blondie friend.'

'Huh?'

'Your house. That night. The thing was screaming — a noise that would strip the skin off you. I popped back to Deirdre's, figured I could get some milk and whiskey down it. Just dope it, like. I knew no-one was in, but still it won't stop crying. I was in the laundry room with it when I hear the key in the door and you two giggling in the hall. You made me panic.'

His voice was accusing, but he wouldn't meet her eye. Ali remembered coming in with Fitz that night, just because Fitz wanted to meet Davy, wanted to meet any man she could, and him coming out of the laundry room all flustered, and her thinking it was shyness.

'What have you done, Davy?'

'I've done no worse than millions of women, than my own sister did. What difference is there between a foetus and a just born baby that knows nothing or no one — days that's all it is.'

'There *is* a difference,' said Ali. His hand grabbed the back of her neck and tightened.

'Don't give me crap. You don't know enough to keep your knickers on either. I had to leave it somewhere, so I thought I'd put it in that little garden you talk about so much. A nice present for Sister Bernadette and her meddling. And there you were, under a tree, getting your titties out for some boy.'

All the air disappeared from her body. He had been there, the figure walking on the path down to the Rosary Garden. He had seen her with Ronan. This wasn't made up.

Davy let go of her, turned away. When he spoke, his voice was barely there.

'I just needed it to shut up.'

'Davy, it wasn't an 'it'.

He wrapped his arms around his head as

if warding her off.

Ali leapt for the hallway, grabbing at the jamb to pivot herself towards the front door. She fumbled with the snib while he called her name from the living room, a forlorn wail that almost made her waver, but the door was opening now and she could see the dusky sky and the path through the trees beckoning her out of there.

Ali stepped out into air, forgetting the ground would be so far. Her body pitched forward, flying down towards the cement stump that suddenly filled her vision.

THIRTY - THREE

Swan knocked on Doctor Nolan's study door. Outside, in the dwindling light, his small team readied themselves for the short trip to Caherbawn,

'Come in!'

It was more of a library than a consulting room, though an examination bench covered in nasty fawn vinyl lurked against one wall. The sight of it reminded him of Ali, and what she had been subjected to on his orders. He soothed his guilt with the thought that the girl and the mother hadn't been quite honest with him — they had never mentioned an uncle being with them in Dublin.

Doctor Nolan was sitting at an old fashioned writing desk, a fat reference tome open before him, a brass lamp casting a civilised light. He slid off some wire rimmed reading glasses as Swan approached. There was a ring of falseness to the pose, as if he had been waiting to be interrupted.

Swan explained to the doctor that his daughters had offered contradictory statements, Sister Bernadette willing to identify the Rosary baby as her sister's child while Peggy claimed the child had been adopted. Nolan's face betrayed no emotion.

'What's your own view, doctor?'

'I would think that Bernadette would be your more reliable witness. My younger daughter's state of mind is not strong.'

'When did you notice she was pregnant?'

Doctor Nolan hesitated a moment. 'She concealed

it from us. I didn't know till quite late along.'

'I thought the signs would be more obvious to a medic,' said Swan.

The doctor tightened his jaw. 'The girls tend to rely on their mother for those kind of confidences.'

There was no regret for his lost grandchild, nor did he seem inclined to protect Peggy against her sister's implied accusation.

'We'll need to take a statement from you and your wife tomorrow at the station.'

'Can't it be done here?'

'I'll see — perhaps if you can help me with another matter.'

Nolan nodded.

'Twelve years ago at Christmas time, another baby was found, at Caherbawn. I believe you were there.'

'Your officer asked me about that previously. Una Devane called me to Caherbawn and I examined the mother.'

'Did the child's body have any marks on it, any signs of violence?'

A hesitation. The doctor shook his head.

'You didn't inform the guards.'

'The child never lived, didn't attain independent existence, as such. Some people's lives are hard enough. I don't see that there's any benefit in making a song and dance.'

'What happened to the body?'

'I can't recall. It was left with the family. You should see Una Devane about it.'

'Are you sure you actually examined the child?'

Doctor Nolan picked up his glasses as if eager to get on with his reading. 'I don't see the point in all this.'

'The mother of the child that you didn't record was buried this morning, drowned. Did you sign off her death certificate?'

'There was nothing to suggest Joan Dempsey's death was anything other than an accident.'

'Don't you need an autopsy to determine that?'

'I examined the body and spoke to Father Philbin and the police. We did not deem it necessary.'

A big man in a small town, thought Swan. Practised here all his life, knew all the secrets. Decided what was best. Deemed it.

'Well, I'm just going to have to order one myself.'

The doctor paled.

'What about my daughter?'

'She can stay here for the moment, but we will be back, you can be sure.'

As he rose to go, Swan noticed the little wire glasses trembling in the Doctor's grip.

THIRTY - FOUR

Branches moving against a deep blue sky. Twilight and shifting air, everything mobile. She thought she was back in the convent grounds with Ronan, that he was about to kiss her and that this time it would be lovely. A face hovered over her, Ronan's face approaching, blocking out her view of the sky. The face wavered, became Davy's, so close to hers that all the light disappeared and she was floating in blackness.

When she woke again, she was aware of stones under her, and although the air was mild, her head was cold and clammy.

Ali raised a hand to her scalp, felt her hair clumped together, sticky. Now she was properly awake, could recognise the outside of Davy's bungalow. She put a hand to the concrete stump beside her, used it to lever herself to sitting. Her hand left dark prints on the grey. She wanted to be sick.

The house was in blackness; the door stood open. Ali got shakily to her feet and tried to think. If he was still there in the living room he could see her through the dark window, might be looking straight at her now. She knew now that he would hurt her if he felt he had to.

Ali turned and hobbled away, picking up speed as she reached the trees, ears straining for steps behind her. Half way along the path she held on to a sapling and stopped to look behind. She couldn't see him, but the trees and their shadows shifted in the breeze, rustled. He could be very close by.

If she could reach the farmhouse, surely her family would protect her. But Davy was family too, closer to the rest of them than she was. A line of fresh blood dripped down her cheek, and she held a hand to it. She had no choice — she might even be dying. Ali staggered in the direction of the farm. She would not die here.

The barn loomed up behind the trees. Not far to go, she told herself. Her feet hit the concrete of the yard and she could see the light from the kitchen window fall across the patch of grass at the back of the house. On the ground to her left, she registered two squares of darkness where the awful slurry tank was. There should only be one drain cover, but now there seemed to be two, one square darker than the other, and something else, some object beside them.

Keep going, she told herself, but her eyes clung to the squares, halting her feet, wanting to make sense of it.

The slurry tank had been opened. One square was the metal cover, pulled aside, the other was the black void it should be covering. She took a few steps towards them. Except for her own ragged breathing, all remained quiet, nothing moved. From six feet away, she peered at the open hole and what was left beside it. It was hard to make it out in the dim light, and Ali moved closer. Now she could see it wasn't a single object after all, it was double, a pair of black brogues. She knew she'd seen them recently, but her head was so fogged it took another long moment until she could make sense of it and remember where.

She stumbled backwards from the open hole, letting her throat open to unleash a wail. In answer to her scream, a raw light burst from a lamp on the side of the barn, raking across the ground. Another voice joined hers and she turned to see Una running from the house towards her — her face distorted in panic.

But even as she turned towards her aunt, Ali couldn't rid her eyes of what she had glimpsed as the light burst across the yard. A dark shape like a sack, or perhaps a rounded back, lolled in the glossy brown swill of the slurry.

THIRTY - FIVE

The scene that greeted Swan at Caherbawn was like some twisted medieval altarpiece — suffering and gesture stamped in light against the grainy dark.

Four figures were illuminated below harsh white floodlights. Two men, smeared with muck, laboured with wooden poles twice their height. They seemed to be prodding the ground, but the poles kept changing lengths and Swan realised they were probing some kind of hole. At their feet crouched two female figures, one middle aged, kneeling with her arms cast out to either side of her in a kind of supplication, her hair wild and her eyes to heaven, the other on her hands and knees, staring into the hole, a shining trail of blood caking one side of her milky face. Ali. His heart contracted at the sight.

Considine leapt out of the passenger seat before Swan could fully absorb what he was looking at, the two guards from Kinmore following. Ali shouted something as they approached, pointing into the hole in the ground. The two men with the long poles froze where they were. The woman got to her feet and stepped behind the men.

The smell was awful, thick in his nose and throat, intimate and revolting. By the time he reached the group he could feel it soak his clothes and skin. One of the Kinmore Gardaí stepped away to retch, affording Swan a view of the dark pit that all attention was centred on. Two feet below the opening he could see the stewing surface of some vast reservoir